## BLUE HALO SERIES BOOK THREE

# NYSSA KATHRYN

**A past that can't be changed. A future as uncertain as their relationship.**

Willow Cross has been a single mother for most of her young daughter's life, ever since the girl's father—a man Willow thought she'd be with forever—inexplicably disappeared. Now, just as mysteriously, he's back, living in Cradle Mountain, Idaho. Blake has always been her weakness, and while she's no longer willing to risk her heart, Willow relocates so her daughter can build a relationship with the father she barely knows.

She can only pray she doesn't lose part of herself in the process.

Blake Cross's life changed for the better when he learned he was having a daughter. Then, two years later, it changed for the worse when he was kidnapped and separated from his family. Finally free, his priority is his child...and her mother. Blake may no longer own her heart, but he still cares deeply for Willow. He can't change their past, but he can promise a better future.

Or can he? When Willow's life is threatened on more than one occasion, both their futures are a lot less certain, forcing Blake to risk everything to protect the mother of his child—and the woman he never stopped loving.

# ACKNOWLEDGMENTS

Thank you to everyone who helped bring this book to life—Kelli, Marla and Jen, you guys are superstars. Thank you to my ARC team for reading this book before anyone else, giving me your honest and constructive feedback before taking the time leave a review. Thank you to my readers—you are amazing, and you are the reason the next book gets published. And lastly, thank you to my husband, you and Sophia are my world and none of this would be possible without your love and support.

# CHAPTER 1

*B*lake Cross moved silently but quickly, his boots barely making a sound as they crushed the fallen leaves and overgrown grass.

It was dark, almost pitch black as he led his team up the mountain. But the dark didn't affect him. In fact, he welcomed it. Because, just like his team, he had skills that most didn't. Advanced speed and strength. Above-average hearing and quick healing.

And night vision.

It was why the FBI had assigned this mission to them. Because, for most, it would be impossible.

Travel through the treacherous mountain terrain of Jabal Sawda. Gain access to a heavily guarded, impenetrable compound. And eliminate the Saudi Arabian terrorist, Saleh Ahmad. A man on the FBI's Most Wanted list. A man, according to FBI intel, planning terrorist attacks on US soil.

The asshole thought the difficulty in accessing his home would discourage visitors. And it did...for most. But Ahmad hadn't counted on *them*. Survivors of Project Arma, a US military experiment that had turned men into more than they should be.

1

A team the US government now sent in for off-the-books missions that should be impossible to complete.

Blake didn't look back at his team. He could hear them right behind him. Aidan, Flynn, Callum, and Tyler. All listening out for any threats. All armed and ready for action.

Wind whipped his face as he moved while branches quietly cracked beneath his feet.

They'd been dropped eighty miles from the compound. For any other person that was a day's travel, possibly more, considering the dangerous terrain. It had taken them less than a quarter of that time.

The walls surrounding the compound came into view ahead. All five of them slowed before stopping completely. The entrance gate was visible. Two guards, one on each side. Both heavily armed. Even though Blake could see them clearly, right down to the small knives poking out of the bottom of their pants, they wouldn't see Blake or his team. Not with the dark and the distance.

Blake lifted his hand, signaling for Tyler to take his shot. He was the youngest on the team. He was also the best sniper.

Tyler stepped forward, bending to one knee. Two precision shots, hitting each guard between the eyes in rapid succession. The silencer on the gun made the kills inaudible.

Tyler remained on his knee, gun drawn, as the rest of them moved forward. He would be the eyes on the outside while the others raided the compound.

Even though the walls were solid brick, the gate was made of metal bars. Blake reached them first, using his enhanced strength to easily tug the bars apart before slipping through. Then he moved, keeping close to the wall, strategically avoiding the cameras and knowing the last man in would bend the metal bars back into place.

It wasn't just the cameras he was trying to avoid. It was also the chance of motion-detecting lights flicking on, alerting anyone inside the compound to their presence.

At the side of the house, Blake grasped a window, pushing it up, easily breaking the lock. He slipped inside first, listening. When there were no heartbeats or footsteps close by, he signaled to his team. One by one, they slipped inside. Silent. Deadly.

A large rectangular table centered the room, a chandelier hanging from the ceiling. Expensive-looking art hung from the walls and a large lion statue sat in a corner.

The bastard liked expensive shit.

Quietly, the team worked their way across the room, guns drawn. There'd been no blueprints to study before the mission, and there hadn't been time to try to acquire any. Not when a bombing was being planned. So they were going in blind.

Another reason his team had been chosen for this.

Blake reached the doorway, scanning a large foyer. Another fucking chandelier. This one larger. And a huge-ass staircase to the left of the space.

Blake moved left, Aidan behind him, with Flynn and Callum going in the opposite direction. He reached a door. About to wrap his fingers around the handle, he paused.

Two heartbeats. Both on the other side. Both moving closer.

Removing his hand, he lifted the gun.

The second the door opened, Blake pulled the trigger.

Headshot. The guard went down.

He searched for the second man, pausing. Not a man.

The dog growled loudly before barking.

That was all it took.

Footsteps rushed from different corners of the house. The rustling of clothes, the whisper of voices. Sounds that normal men wouldn't be able to hear, but they did. Both a blessing and a curse.

Blake swore under his breath as lights flicked on. At the sight of men at the top of the stairs.

Then the quiet shattered as bullets peppered the air.

Almost in unison, Blake and his men took cover. Blake and Aidan flew into the room that had just been opened, the dog running out. Aidan moved behind a desk, while Blake chose the bookcase.

There was the sound of running. Three men. All headed their way.

Blake made eye contact with Aidan. They waited. Right up until the guards were close to the door. Aidan shot the first guard who stepped into the room, while Blake waited for the second, going for a kill shot between the eyes.

The third guard aimed his weapon, but Blake was right there waiting, throwing an elbow at the guy's arm, breaking the bone and sending the gun to the floor. He stepped forward, snapping the guy's neck.

Moving into the foyer, he scanned the area. Flynn and Callum were fighting a handful of men, seconds from killing them. As Aidan joined their teammates, Blake flew up the stairs. Ahmad would know his compound had been infiltrated by now and he would be executing his escape.

Blake couldn't let that happen.

He opened the first door in the hallway. Nothing. He went to the second, surprising a guy who quickly drew his gun.

Blake shot first, three bullets to the heart.

In the next room, he found another guard, this time shooting him between the eyes.

The fourth door was the master bedroom, he could tell based on the size and the opulence. The sheets were ruffled. He moved closer, touching them. Warm. Someone had been here, and they'd been here very recently.

He moved across the space, entering a large connected bathroom. Nothing. Turning, he was about to leave when light sounds caught his attention.

Pausing, he frowned.

Were they…heartbeats?

Turning, Blake studied the space. Where the hell were they coming from?

A large waterfall shower was positioned to his left, a bathtub in the center of the room, and a vanity to his right. He took another step inside.

The heartbeats grew louder.

*What the fuck?*

Blake moved closer to the shower, then the vanity, opening the doors, and peering inside. He knocked on the walls, looking for something hollow.

Nothing.

When he stopped beside the tub, his gaze shot down.

This was where the sounds were loudest.

Lowering to his haunches, he noticed the beats grew louder still. Blake touched the side of the tub, giving it a little shake.

Shit. The thing moved in his hand. It wasn't attached to the ground.

Drawing his weapon, he shifted back, giving the tub a hard kick.

Bullets flew, screams ripping from the dugout beneath the tub and echoing through the tiled room. A bullet hit his shoulder. He barely reacted, aiming his own weapon and shooting the guard, twice in the neck and once in the head.

Then his eyes turned to the woman. She was holding a child in a death grip, limbs trembling as she attempted to shield the child from his view. The kid looked to be seven, maybe eight.

"Please, don't shoot!" Her words were slow and accented. The tremors in her voice matched those in her limbs.

He recognized them. The FBI had shown the team images of both. Saleh Ahmad's wife and child.

Blake lowered his weapon. He was about to turn when she spoke again.

"Please don't leave! We would like political asylum in your country."

He frowned. He wasn't in a position to offer that. And there was every chance her request was a ploy.

He scanned her body, noticing the bruises that marred her face, her arms. Red, angry fingerprints marked her cheek from where someone had pressed fingers over her mouth, likely the guard to stop her from screaming.

Then his gaze went to the kid. His heart clenched. She wasn't much older than his own daughter.

What if this woman and kid were Willow and Mila? He'd want a soldier to save them.

Cursing under his breath, he reached down, helping them out.

Then he heard it. The roar of an engine from above.

Goddammit. The asshole had a helicopter?

He turned to the woman. "How do I get to the roof?"

She continued to hold her daughter tightly, but her eyes steeled as she moved in front of him, running from the room and into the hall. Blake kept his gun raised, ready and prepared to shoot anyone who got in their way.

She took them to what looked to be a small closet, reaching inside and tugging a rope. Stairs released down.

He moved up them quickly, stepping onto the roof just in time to see the helicopter lift into the air.

Drawing his gun, he shot at the engine. The propeller. His bullets barely made a dent in the aircraft as it lifted, moving away.

*Fuck.* He was too late.

Turning, he saw that the woman and her child stood behind him. Then his team, one by one, joined them on the roof, watching as the helicopter flew away.

# CHAPTER 2

*W*illow Cross's fingers flew across her keyboard. The Ketchum Library was quiet, the only other sounds in the large room coming from the tapping of the three members of her study group, Janet, Rob, and Toby, as they typed along with her.

"Argh, Edmond's class is going to be the death of me."

Willow smiled at Janet's frustrated words, her fingers never stopping. They were each writing their own paper on *Promoting Positive Peer Relationships and Wellbeing Within The Classroom*.

It was sheer luck that she'd found a local group of people also studying the same online course to become teachers. She'd found them when she put out a call for anyone nearby her new hometown of Cradle Mountain, Idaho, through the online university's chat portal.

Toby scoffed. "Maybe if you did less complaining and more working, it wouldn't be so bad."

She looked up just in time to see Janet thump him lightly on the shoulder.

Glancing back down to her screen, Willow paused in her

work. Her gaze scanned the table filled with printed articles. Where was that paper?

Leaning over, she shuffled through the sheets.

"What are you looking for?"

She glanced at Rob, sitting beside her. "The paper that makes the connection between peer group behavior and emotional development."

He lifted a wad of stapled sheets, handing them over. "Ah, a favorite of mine. Here you go."

She smiled, noticing how his gaze lingered on her a moment longer than what might seem friendly.

She swore she'd seen him do the same in their handful of study sessions since they'd met.

But then, it was entirely possible it was all in her head.

He was cute, with his light brown eyes and mid-length brown, pushed-back hair. He stood a little over six feet tall, and was physically fit. But he wasn't Blake. No one was.

And wasn't that just the story of her life?

She was just reading the first paragraph of the paper when her phone vibrated against the table. She looked down and her heart gave a little thump.

The man she was just thinking about. The man she was *always* thinking about.

*Blake: You still out, honey? We're just watching Frozen.*

Even though they were separated, he still used endearments when he texted or spoke to her. And he always updated her on what he was doing with their daughter, Mila, on their days together.

He'd returned from his latest mission a few days ago. All she knew about the job was that it was overseas and it was dangerous. Weren't they all, though?

Her heart clenched. Heck, her heart squeezed like someone had a fist around it every time the man left town. And the pressure never released until he returned. It had always been like that.

Ever since he'd enlisted. He wasn't a Navy SEAL anymore, his time was more his own, but not completely.

The worry never ended, together or not. Especially after the "mission" he hadn't returned from for two years.

She sucked in a breath, giving herself a little shake before lifting the phone.

*Willow: Yep, still at the library. Enjoy watching the movie for the 187th time. She'll probably fall asleep before Olaf comes along.*

Of course, that was entirely dependent on how much sugar he'd let her consume. Mila had a sweet tooth, and Blake loved to spoil her. Not that Willow minded. Mila and Blake had lost two years together. Years that had been stolen from them. They had a lot of making up to do.

Janet bumped her shoulder. "Who's put that look on your face?"

She glanced up to see Janet's dark brown eyes peering at Willow's phone.

What exactly *had* been on her face? Relief that Blake had returned safely from the latest mission? Regret that he'd missed a chunk of his daughter's life? Or maybe just lovesick longing...

She smiled at her friend. "Blake has Mila right now. They're watching *Frozen*. It's her favorite." Favorite was probably an understatement. The kid was utterly obsessed.

The group knew she had a four-year-old daughter, and that she wasn't with her daughter's father anymore. Every time she had a study session, Mila stayed with Blake.

"Oh my gosh, your daughter has good taste. *Frozen* is *my* favorite, and I'm a thirty-year-old woman. And that kid of yours..." Janet's eyes closed as she smiled. "I've got to meet her, because in the pictures you've shown me, she looks adorable. Honestly, I could just squeeze her. I love kids."

Willow's heart warmed. It always did when Mila was involved. "Thank you. I mean, I think she's pretty adorable, but then, I'm her mother. And I've watched that movie so many times

I could probably recite the entire thing word for word in my sleep."

It was a joke. But not really. And those songs…gah, it was like the show made them as addictive and stick-in-your-head as possible.

Her phone vibrated against the table again.

*Blake: I'm counting on it. Have a nice night. Don't leave too late. xox*

Her cheeks heated at the kisses and hug at the end. When she looked up, it was to Janet's knowing smile. "You tell me you're not together anymore, but your face says otherwise."

Oh, she could certainly share her life with the man again. So easily.

But as quickly as the thought entered her mind, so too did memories from before he'd been taken. Of the two years after Mila had been born. The absences. The loneliness. The darkness.

She forced a smile to her lips. "We're just good friends who are able to co-parent well."

Another message came through on her phone, drawing her gaze again. She couldn't stop the smile that touched her lips if she tried. It wasn't a text this time. Instead, Blake had sent a photo of him and Mila, wrapped in a blanket on the couch, bowl of popcorn between them.

Why did the man have to be so gorgeous? With his deep gray eyes that lightened and darkened with his mood, his short brown hair and ridiculous muscles that corded every inch of his body. And Mila, well, she was utterly adorable with her light brown ponytail and big brown eyes.

She felt heat against her side as Janet leaned closer. Then there was a short gasp. "Is that him? Holy wow, woman, he's *hot!*"

Willow could have sworn she heard a little huff from Rob beside her. Then he was leaning over her other shoulder.

Blake *was* hot. Always had been. Even when he was a fifteen-year-old boy who'd moved in across the street from her.

Janet moved closer to the screen. "Wait, he looks familiar."

Rob definitely huffed this time as he sat back in his seat, muttering something under his breath that Willow didn't quite catch.

Janet grabbed Willow's arm, clenching tightly. "Oh my God... is he...he's one of those men who were all over the news months ago! He had those drugs given to him that altered his DNA."

Willow swallowed, clicking out of the image and locking her phone. "Um, yeah. He is."

A heavy silence descended over the table, three sets of eyes shooting hot beams into her, causing her to squirm in her seat.

An article had been written and published about Blake and his team. It had exploded on the internet, and media people from all over the country had come to Cradle Mountain, hounding the men for details. Heck, they'd even hounded Willow for information. For more stories.

Thank God the attention had died down. It had been a scary time.

Janet sat back, mouth open, disbelief and shock washing over her features.

"But he wasn't what he is now when you became pregnant with your daughter?" It was Toby who asked. The man was quiet compared to the others, so his question surprised her.

"No, we had Mila before he was...taken." Not that it was any of their business.

"You're joking, right?"

The anger in Rob's voice surprised Willow, causing her brows to tug together. "Excuse me?"

"You moved to Cradle Mountain to be closer to one of *them*?"

*Them?* She opened her mouth to ask exactly what he was getting at but quickly snapped it shut. She'd realized at the start of the media craze that there were people out there who didn't like that Blake and his friends existed. She just hadn't expected any of her study partners to be among the close-minded.

Closing her laptop, she shoved it into her bag. "You know what, I've just about finished my paper. I'm going to head home." She was actually only halfway through, but no part of her wanted to stay. Not when they were looking at her like the father of her child landed on Earth in a spaceship and was here to wipe out the planet. Like there was something infinitely wrong with him.

A part of her hoped someone would speak up. Tell Rob that he'd overreacted and was being ridiculous. To reassure her that everything was fine.

So it only made it worse when no one did. No one said so much as a word when she pushed to her feet or threw the strap of the laptop bag over her shoulder.

Shaking her head, she left the library, stepping into the dark Idaho night. A night that had gone from great to terrible in about two seconds flat.

Grabbing her keys from her pocket, she'd just opened her car door when a hand touched her shoulder.

She turned, finding a slightly out-of-breath Janet behind her. "I'm sorry! We all are. We were just…shocked. And worried about you and Mila. What happened to those guys was…I mean, they're not normal men anymore. I just want to make sure you're safe."

Her back straightened, anger expanding in her chest. "Safe? Mila and I are safer with Blake than we are with anyone else." The man would walk through fire to protect them. "Blake and his team are still just like you and me, only stronger and faster," Willow continued. "And they didn't choose what was done to them. They were taken by force. Kidnapped and held hostage in a compound for *two years*. Drugged. Trained. They deserve your *sympathy*, not your judgment and incorrect assumptions."

Hell, even now they dedicated their lives to protecting people, both through the missions they completed and their work at Blue Halo Security. They were *protectors*.

When all Janet did was wring her hands, Willow sighed, turning toward her car. "I need to go."

"Willow…"

She ignored the woman, pulling her door closed and starting the engine. She didn't spare a backward glance as she left the parking lot.

Well, there went the new study group she'd been so excited about. She shouldn't be disappointed to lose them. They'd only met a month ago. She'd gotten through the first three years of her degree alone just fine, she'd manage the last year on her own as well.

She gritted her teeth and pressed her foot harder to the accelerator, trying to force the group's words out of her head.

Her and Blake's relationship may not have been the best before he was taken, but he was still a good man.

Memories came back of their time together. Their relationship had been so good before Mila was born. She'd assumed they would be together for the long haul. It wasn't Mila's fault the dynamics of their relationship had changed. Life happened. Blake had become a SEAL, and Willow…

She'd lost herself.

She swallowed hard. He wanted her back. She knew he did. And every time he asked her for another chance, her heart yearned to say yes.

Not just her heart. Every single limb and organ craved him.

Groaning, she pushed down the longing. The deep need to feel his lips against hers. His hands grazing her skin. The need to have *him*.

On paper, he was still her husband. Mostly because she hadn't been able to bring herself to file for divorce.

God, she was a mess. Unable to divorce him. Unable to return to him.

She needed to just grow some courage and do it. Because she couldn't go back. Mila was older now. If things regressed back to how they were when she was a baby…no. It wasn't fair to her daughter.

Willow lifted a hand and massaged her temples. Blasted headaches. She was a damn magnet for them. And when she wasn't careful, they almost always turned into migraines.

Luckily, she knew the signs well, having suffered from them since she was a kid. It started as tightness in the front of her temple. If she didn't rest, the pain expanded behind her eyes. The back of her skull. Until a full-blown migraine wiped her out for hours, sometimes days.

She was still massaging her head when a small bang sounded from the engine. She gasped as the car began to slow.

*What the heck?*

Pulling the car over to the side of the dark road, Willow watched in dismay as smoke billowed from beneath the hood.

Crap. This was just what her night needed. Pulling her phone from her bag, she called Bert, the Cradle Mountain mechanic. Also, the only mechanic in town.

The phone rang. Then it rang some more. It got to about five rings when she knew the guy wasn't going to answer.

Not. Good.

She pressed the button to open the hood, then climbed out of the car and walked around to the front. The second she lifted the hood, she took two big steps back, more smoke billowing into the night air.

As much as she'd like to say that this was a surprise, it really wasn't. The car was old. How long had she had it now? Who the heck knew. Definitely since before Mila was born. And it hadn't been new back then.

Nibbling her lip, she sighed and lifted her phone, knowing who she needed to call.

Unlike Bert, Blake answered on the first ring.

"Everything okay?"

The familiar sliver of awareness rushed through her system when she heard the man's deep, gravelly voice.

"Not exactly. My car broke down. There's a bit of smoke

coming from beneath the hood." *A lot of smoke.* "I don't know if there's a car service in Cradle Mountain that comes out at night? Or if one of the guys on your team could give me a lift home and I'll call Bert tomorrow?"

There were seven other guys who ran Blue Halo Security with Blake. They'd all been taken by Project Arma together. The men were now like brothers.

"Send me a pin of your location."

She almost sighed with relief. Of course the guy knew what to do. He always did.

Quickly, Willow fiddled with her phone, sending the pin before putting it back to her ear. "Done."

"Good. Are you in your car?"

"No." As the word left her mouth, a big gust of wind blew across her face, sending goose bumps pebbling over her skin. Christ, even in late August, Idaho was chilly at night.

"Get in your car and lock the doors. Help won't be long."

She nodded, even though he couldn't see her. "Okay."

"And, honey, don't open the doors for anyone you don't know."

# CHAPTER 3

*B*lake pulled his car over behind Willow's, his jaw ticking at the sight of smoke still blowing from the engine. He'd known the thing was old and didn't have many miles left in it. He should have upgraded it the second he'd returned to her.

He shot a look into his back seat. Mila was fast asleep. She'd nodded off the second he started driving. Her lids had already been drooping during the movie. Luckily, he'd already put her in pajamas before leaving his place, so she was ready to be popped into bed.

Stepping out of the car, he walked over to Willow's window. As soon as she spotted him, her eyes widened. Then she opened the door, climbing out.

"What are you doing here? Where's—"

"She's in the car, honey. Grab your stuff. I'll take you home."

Her eyes swung over to his car, a light frown touching her brows. She almost looked like she wanted to say something, but then seemed to reconsider it, reaching back into the car and grabbing her laptop bag before swinging the door closed.

Immediately, Blake slid the bag from her fingers, grazing her skin as he did. The spark of awareness that shot through his system was one he was intimately familiar with. One that he'd felt with each and every touch since he was a teenager. The woman's body spoke to his. Always had. Always would.

Placing a hand on the middle of her back, he opened the passenger-side door, helping her slide in before walking around the car.

He pulled onto the road as Willow's head shot around. He heard her soft sigh as she watched their daughter sleep.

When he spoke, he did so quietly, not wanting to wake Mila. "I'll call Bert in the morning to tow your car to his shop." He'd also start looking into new cars for her, but he'd broach that topic later.

"I can do that."

He lifted a shoulder. "I was already going to call him about my car. You'll be busy with tutoring tomorrow. I don't mind." He changed the subject quickly, not wanting to debate it. "How was study group?"

A moment of silence passed. Then another. He shot a quick look beside him, noticing the deep crease in the lines beside her eyes, the way her lips pinched just a bit too tightly.

His hand itched to reach out and take hers. To touch her in any way. He didn't.

"It was fine." Her breath hitched on the last word, heartbeat altering in its pattern just slightly.

She was lying.

His brows tugged together. "What happened?"

She gave a small laugh, even though there wasn't much humor there. "I hate how you do that. It's not fair that you can tell when I'm not being honest."

"Willow…"

She gave a small huff. "It's nothing. Don't worry about it. And you really didn't need to pick me up. I'm sure one of the other guys could have done it. It might be hard to transfer Mila back to her bed at your place."

"I'm not taking her to my place. When I drop you off, I'll take her to her room."

He felt her eyes on him. "But it's your night."

He lifted a shoulder. "It's Tuesday night, and she's due back with you tomorrow. May as well just pop her into her bed."

Blake had Mila on Sunday, Monday, and Tuesday nights, and Willow had her the rest of the week. It was working well enough. But it was also killing him. He didn't want to be a part-time father. And he certainly didn't want this distance between him and Willow. She was his wife. She belonged with him.

"Okay. Thank you." Willow didn't like being a part-time mom, either. There was some relief in her tone. Relief that Mila would be with her tonight. "Do you have any…ah, trips coming up?"

The muscles in his arms tightened. He knew she hated him going away. Knew it had been a large part of the problem when they'd been together. He hadn't been there for her when she'd needed him most.

"No. None planned at the moment."

But he'd be returning to Saudi Arabia very soon. Everyone was working overtime searching for Ahmad. And his wife was being very forthcoming with possible locations for the man. He was furious at the fact that the asshole was still out there, planning God knows what.

"Mila will be happy," she said softly.

He shot a quick look over at her. "Just Mila?"

Her head turned, and she looked out the window, but before she did, he caught the quirking of her lips.

Yeah, she missed him. She just didn't like to admit it out loud.

When they reached her place, Blake carefully carried Mila to her bedroom. Even though he'd only moved them in earlier this year, Willow had done an amazing job of making the house look like a home. *Feel* like a home.

Willow peeled back the sheets of Mila's bed and Blake lay her down. He pressed a kiss to her head before standing. Willow did the same before they headed out to the kitchen.

She moved straight to the kettle, filling it with water at the tap. "Can I make you a coffee or tea?"

Blake sat on a stool at the small island, watching her graceful movements. "Tea would be great."

He wasn't a huge fan of the stuff, and Willow knew it, but anything that meant more time with her was something he grabbed on to with both hands. His time away from Willow had taught him to never take a second with loved ones for granted. Something he should have learned a lot earlier.

There was silence as she puttered around the space. Blake didn't mind silence. In fact, he welcomed it. Silence with Willow had always been comfortable. Peaceful, even.

When the teas were ready, she turned and handed him a mug. As he took it, he intentionally grazed his fingers against hers.

There was a quick intake of breath. A slight widening of her eyes. Then she whipped her hand back like she'd been burned.

There'd once been a time she would have leaned into him. Touched his chest. Smiled against his lips.

His chest constricted at the memory.

She cleared her throat, breaking the spell. "How far did you get into *Frozen*?"

He lifted his mug. "We made it to Anna meeting Olaf. Just. Didn't quite find Elsa though."

Willow chuckled. The sound was as familiar to him as the rest of her. God, but he lived for that sound. "That's okay. Olaf is the star of the show."

He was to Mila.

Blake was about to lift his mug when he saw the small frown crease her forehead. It was a frown he recognized. "You have a headache." It wasn't a question.

"Only a small one. I should probably go to bed."

It was only eight-thirty. "You need to stop working so hard." Not only was she studying to become a teacher, she did online tutoring for kids overseas.

She rolled her pretty green eyes. Those eyes were the other thing that had haunted his dreams while he'd been away. "I'm okay. Final year of juggling tutoring and study."

He leaned forward, quieting his voice. "You could lean on me. Let me support you while you study."

~

WILLOW'S GAZE lowered to her mug. Blake had said those same words before. On more than one occasion. The idea of leaning on the man, letting him take care of her, was so damn tempting.

But it was equally terrifying.

"I appreciate the offer." She took a small sip of her tea, barely tasting it.

A flash of frustration lit his gray eyes. "But you don't *want* to lean on me, just in case it means something more."

In case? There was no in case. The second she let him look after her, the second she let him close in any way—other than being Mila's father—she'd remember how much she liked it. Missed it. And bit by bit, he'd break down the walls she'd erected around her heart.

She gave a short nod.

A muscle ticked in his jaw, then he sighed. "Okay, honey."

Even though he acquiesced, she heard what he didn't say. *Okay...for now.* He wasn't giving up. She knew that as well as she knew *him*. Because that's just who he was. He didn't give up until he got exactly what he wanted.

His eyes were intense as they watched her, skirting over every little part of her face, like he saw everything. It was too much.

Dipping her head, she took a big sip of her tea, barely registering how it burned her tongue and throat. Turning, she plonked the mug in the sink, knowing she wouldn't be touching the rest. "I think I should be getting to bed now."

She moved around the other side of the island and toward the front door. She was just reaching for the knob when strong, warm fingers wrapped around her wrist, turning her gently.

She hadn't heard him coming, but then, he'd always moved silently, even when they were kids. Silent and graceful. Like a tiger before attacking its prey.

"Willow—"

"Please don't."

There was a small pause. Instead of letting go, he stepped closer, thumb stroking the inside of her wrist. "You can't run from this forever." His words were gentle whispers to her soul. Whispers that she'd heard before in her own mind.

Another swipe across her wrist. She swallowed. "This?"

His next step forward had his chest pressed to her front, heating her. Dwarfing her. His musky, familiar scent intoxicating. "Us. Our connection. What we have. What we've *always* had."

His other hand went to her hip, fingers skirting up and beneath her top, touching the flesh of her waist.

Her eyes tried to shutter, but she kept them open with sheer grit. How often had she dreamed about the man touching her again? Kissing her? Holding her like he was keeping her delicate fragments together?

Her gaze remained firmly on his chest; she was too much of a coward to meet his eyes. "We tried, Blake. We didn't work. Not after becoming parents. I don't want Mila to see us together if we're not forever. And I don't want her to see us in a bad place. She needs stability."

His humorless chuckle finally had her eyes lifting. She immediately regretted it. Thunderous and dark, his gaze had her breath catching. "Baby, there is *nothing* more forever than you and me."

Then, before she realized what he was doing, his head

lowered, his mouth capturing hers.

For a moment she stood completely still. Blood rushed through her body, piercing the heart she'd long ago caged off.

His lips brushed and swiped, tempting. It wasn't until that thumb on her waist grazed her skin again that the last remnants of her restraint snapped, and she leaned into him, sweeping her hands around his neck, humming deep inside her throat.

Blake growled, lifting her in his arms and pressing her against the wall beside the door.

Her core heated against his hard stomach, a low gasp separating her lips. Blake took advantage, pressing his tongue inside her mouth. Tasting her.

This was it. Everything she'd been missing. Craving. The connection her heart would never forget. Heat flared through her abdomen, tingling across her skin. Her fingers tugged and slid through his hair, her pebbled nipples grazing his chest.

His lips tore from hers to trail down her cheek and then her neck. "Kissing you is like fire and ice fusing inside me."

She felt it. All of it. The icy prickles of yearning, the burning of passionate flames. It was the melding of want and desire. Even during their darkest days, the ones where she'd felt not just disconnected from Blake, but from the entire world, this inexplicable physical connection had still existed. Like nothing and no one could break it.

His hand rose, closing over a breast. Holding her. Thumb flicking her tight nipple. Her head flew back, a quiet, strangled cry escaping from between her teeth.

Air touched her breast when her shirt and bra were pushed up. Then his head lowered and her taut nipple was sucked between his lips, pressed against his tongue.

God, the man destroyed her. He knew, he'd *always* known, exactly what to do to drive her crazy. To push her right to the edge.

She ground her hips against him, pressing her chest farther

into his mouth, greedy for more. He was awakening something deep inside her. Something she'd shut down long ago.

Her nipple popped out of his mouth, causing her soft cry to pierce the air. His hand returned to her tender flesh as his mouth trailed up her throat. "We belong together, Willow."

She paused, turning his words over in her muddy head. He'd said that before. So many times. And she'd believed it for so long…until she hadn't.

The bubble of desire popped and her hands went to his chest, pushing. "Put me down, Blake."

He froze, his head lifting off her neck slowly as he studied her. Searching.

What was he looking for? Doubt? Longing?

She clenched her jaw, refusing to let emotion seep in.

"This isn't about Mila," he said softly. "You're scared."

Her breath caught. He was right. So damn right it made her chest ache. But still, she had to ask. "Scared of what?"

He tugged her bra back into place, then her top, covering her breast. A hand went to her cheek, cupping her tenderly. "Of having me again, only to lose me. I'm not sure if you're scared of losing me emotionally or physically. Maybe both."

A little part of her chest cracked. He was right again. They'd lost each other emotionally long before they'd lost each other physically. The two years before he'd been taken had been so dang hard.

And then he'd just…disappeared.

He lowered her to her feet gently. Then slowly, he dipped his head, his breath brushing against her ear. "For as long as I breathe, I will consider you mine. We can be better. We *will* be better. You just need more time to trust that."

Her breath didn't just catch that time, it stopped in her chest completely, denying her air.

His lips pressed to her cheek. "Lock the door after me, honey."

Then he was gone, disappearing into the dark night.

# CHAPTER 4

*T*he ground began to move beneath Willow. No, not ground. Mattress. It was bouncing and shaking, robbing her of the last remnants of her dream. The dream of Blake. Of his hands against her skin. His mouth moving against her lips.

"Mama! Wake…up!"

Argh. Okay, the little sleep thief officially cut her dream short.

Groaning, Willow rolled over onto her stomach. Maybe if she covered her head with a—

The pillow was snatched from her fingers, a small weight dropping onto her back, pressing her into the mattress.

"Mama, come on, we need to get ready for school!"

Another groan, but this one fused with a laugh. "Okay, okay, I'm getting up. Just give me a minute." *Or ten.*

A little face pressed against her cheek, hot breath touching her skin. What was it about the breath of your own child always being so intoxicating? Like a hit of oxytocin.

"Mama, every time you say a minute, you take sooooo much longer than that."

The kid was onto her. A long sigh released from her chest as she rolled onto her back. Wrapping her arms around Mila, she kept rolling, pressing the kid into the mattress. Then she tickled her little stomach.

Mila cackled below her, face scrunching with pure joy.

A similar joy shot into Willow's chest at hearing her daughter's laugh. This kid...she made all the hard worth it.

"Mama, stop! I need to get dressed for school. It's still my first week."

Willow pulled her hands back, sighing. "Okay, I guess I'll allow it, seeing as you're a big school kid now."

Mila pushed up to stand on the mattress. "Yep. And next week I'm gonna be a big five-year-old."

Good Lord, Willow didn't need reminding. How was her baby already in school? Hadn't she been a toddler just yesterday?

Mila dropped down again, this time placing her hands on Willow's cheeks. "Don't be sad, Mama. I'll always be your baby."

Christ, she was only four, but the kid saw way more than she should. And right now, she was going to make her cry. "Good. Because I love you."

"I love you, too." Mila leaned over, kissing Willow's cheek. It had her entire chest filling with love.

A second later, her daughter jumped to the floor. "Now, get up!"

Okay, the tiny tyrant was back.

"How come I'm not at Daddy's house?"

Willow was surprised the question had taken so long. She'd expected those to be the first words out of Mila's mouth.

She climbed out of bed. "I had some car problems last night and Daddy picked me up. He carried you to your bed."

Her brows pulled together. "Is Gigi okay?"

Willow smiled. Mila had named their car Gigi so long ago that she couldn't even remember where it had come from. "No, baby, not yet."

She paused. Wait, if she didn't have a car, how would she get

Mila to school? Crap. She'd been so distracted with all that was Blake, that little detail had slipped her mind.

"I'll call Daddy and see if he can take you to school today." Even though the very idea had both heat and icy shards running through her veins after what they'd shared last night. Pushing it down, she slipped her fingers through Mila's. "Now, let's get dressed quickly so we have time to make pancakes before we go."

Mila's excited squeal bounced off the walls.

Once they'd showered and dressed, they stepped into the kitchen. Willow was just about to lift her phone to call Blake when the doorbell rang. Mila's feet were moving across the living room to the door before Willow had a chance to look up.

"Mama, it's Daddy!"

Of course it was. Unlike her, he realized Mila needed a ride, so here he was. Because all he'd been since he'd returned to her and Mila was perfect.

She drew in a long, deep breath, steeling herself before moving toward the door. Blake had a key, but he never used it. Another perfect thing. He gave her the privacy he knew she needed right now.

She'd barely gotten the door open before Mila flung herself into his arms. His ridiculously muscled arms that looked like they belonged on the Terminator.

"How's your morning been, munchkin?"

Mila pressed her head into his neck, and her voice muffled. "I had to jump on Mama to get her out of bed."

*Oh, jeez.*

Blake chuckled, his gaze sliding up to hers. "She sometimes needs some help to get out of bed, doesn't she?"

His gray eyes darkened, and her heart gave a little thump. Memories bombarded her of how Blake used to wake her. With light touches. Kisses. Sometimes he'd even—

She spun around before she could finish the thought, walking back to the kitchen. Or running. Whatever you wanted to call it. "Would you like some pancakes?" she asked over her shoulder.

Opening the fridge, she grabbed the milk and eggs, taking a moment longer than needed to cool her hot cheeks. When she closed the door, Blake was at the island, Mila by his feet.

"I didn't say good morning to you." Before she realized what he was doing, he stepped forward and leaned into her space, pressing a kiss to her cheek.

The lingering of his lips was something she should be used to by now. She wasn't. Each and every time, a thousand little goose bumps rose across her skin.

"Morning." Christ, did her throat just croak?

A knowing smile touched his lips as he turned to their daughter.

Willow spent the next twenty minutes busying herself making pancakes while listening to Mila and Blake's chatter. They were sitting at the island slicing strawberries and bananas, both looking entirely too perfect together.

"Why does Courtney spend so much time with Jason?" Mila asked as Willow placed the last pancake on the plate.

Willow lifted the platter and almost immediately, Blake was there, leaning across, taking the plate from her fingers and winking at her.

"Because they're dating," he said.

Mila's brows pulled together. "Dating? Like you and that man, Mama?"

Willow froze midway through placing cutlery on the island. She didn't look Blake's way. She didn't dare. But she could feel his eyes on her, questioning.

She swallowed. "We weren't dating, baby. We just went out for dinner one time." She tried to put emphasis on "one" because that's exactly what it was.

The date had been just before Blake was rescued, so two years after he'd gone missing. She'd been lonely, and her accountant had asked her to dinner. Leon had been kind and funny, and his life was put together. So she'd said yes. She hadn't been out to dinner with another person since Blake. That's how sad and lonely her two years without him had been.

The entire evening had been awkward. Which wasn't a surprise. Blake was the only man she'd ever dated. Heck, she'd met the man when she was only thirteen. He was her first and only love. She didn't know how to date or love anyone else.

Mila frowned. "Sandra said you went on a date."

Yeah, well, their former neighbor had an overactive imagination. She'd been Willow's friend. Pretty much her *only* friend, and had looked after Mila on the odd occasion.

"Okay, are we ready to eat?" Because Willow was pretty dang keen to switch the focus.

Once everything was on the island and she finally sat down, she snuck a peek at Blake. The air finally eased out of her lungs. He wasn't looking at her. Not staring holes into her head.

Mila forked a large piece of pancake from her plate. "Mama said I can't get a dog for my birthday this year, but maybe next year when she's finished studying."

Blake nodded, cutting his own pancake. "Sounds fair. Big dog or small dog?"

"Big!" Mila stretched her arms wide, and Willow groaned out loud. Great. This time next year, Willow would be caring for an Irish Wolfhound.

Blake chuckled. "Maybe I can help out."

Maybe? Definitely. And maybe the man could foster the dog at his place each and every night.

"Yeah, I think Mama will need some help. She killed the fish we got for Christmas the other year."

The fork paused midway to Willow's lips. "Hey! That was your fish, kid."

"Mama." Mila gave her a look that made her seem ten years older. One that said *come on now*. "I was three."

Well, the kid had her there.

Blake cleared his throat. She knew that throat clearing. It was the trying-to-hold-his-laugh-in one. "So, who have we invited to this big birthday party?"

Mila frowned, eyes squinting as she thought. The party was going to be at Blake's house. He'd already organized a bouncy castle and a face painter.

"All my friends from my class are coming. And can I invite your friends too, Daddy? And Courtney? And Logan's friend?"

"Grace," Willow said quietly.

"Grace," Mila repeated, nodding.

"Definitely," Blake said. "I think they'd all love to come."

"Do they like *Frozen*? Do you think they'll like my Olaf cake?"

Mila continued to talk about her birthday throughout the rest of breakfast. And Willow spent way too much time watching Blake from beneath her lashes. The way the muscles moved as he lifted his arm. The way his eyes crinkled at the corners when he laughed.

Gah. She needed to stop.

When she was finished eating, Willow rinsed her plate before popping it in the dishwasher.

"I'll get my bag ready, Daddy."

Mila ran from the room. And the second it was just the two of them, Blake's gaze clashed with hers. And she knew, before a single word was spoken, that he was going to bring up the date thing again.

Grabbing the other plates, Willow quickly turned toward the sink, running water over them. Blake's heat pressed into her side as he took the plates from her fingers, placing them in the dishwasher.

"So you dated while I was away?"

She wet her dry lips, scrambling for an answer. "No. I went out with one man for dinner, one time."

"And…?"

She looked up. His face was so blank, she had no idea what he was thinking or feeling. "And what?"

"How was it?"

She turned so that she was facing him. "You're asking how my date was?"

His head tilted to the side. "You just said it wasn't a date."

Ah, hell. "It wasn't." The man was entirely too close, and he smelled too good. He was sucking up her ability to think. "And it wasn't good. Our conversation was stilted. And he took me to a steak house."

Blake's lips quirked. Yeah, he knew. She hated steak. She didn't eat red meat at all. Something she'd told the accountant once in a conversation, but he'd clearly forgotten.

*A mistake Blake would never make.*

"Did you kiss?"

His hand lifted, cupping her cheek, the pad of his thumb grazing over her bottom lip. Almost involuntarily, her lips parted, but no words left her mouth.

"Willow…" he prompted.

Memories from that night rushed back to her. Of Leon walking her to her door. Of his gaze hitting her mouth. And of an overwhelming hollowness filling her chest that he wasn't the man she wanted him to be.

"No." One word. Barely a whisper.

She expected a smile. What she got was fire. Like she'd just admitted that she was still his. Had always been his.

She wet her lips. "I didn't kiss any other man while you were gone."

The glint of his eyes almost turned predatory. Because she'd just confirmed that Blake was still the only man she'd ever kissed. Their first kiss had been when she was fourteen years old. The day he'd ruined her for any other man.

"Good." The word was low, vibrating down her spine to her abdomen.

Tiny footsteps pounded down the hall.

Willow took a large step back, and Blake's hand dropped. She felt the loss immediately. It was so much more than just the loss of touch. It was warmth. It was connection. All of that left with his hand.

"Ready!"

At Mila's excited voice, Willow walked over, giving her a tight hug. "Have a good day at school, darling."

Mila hugged her back. "I will, Mama."

When Willow stood, she felt the heat of Blake's hand on the small of her back, escorting her to the door, then the press of a kiss to her cheek. "Have a good day. I'll sort out the car."

Then he was gone, and Willow was left standing there, watching the two people who owned her heart drive away.

# CHAPTER 5

"*S*he's given us the locations of two other homes her husband owns," said Steve, their FBI liaison, as he shuffled papers. He was on the smart projector screen while they all sat at the Blue Halo conference room table. "As well as the names and locations of two of his brothers, both of whom he's close to."

Blake nodded. Aidan, Flynn, Callum, and Tyler also acknowledged Steve's words.

"And we definitely trust her?" Aidan asked. It was the same question that had been festering in Blake's own head, and no doubt everyone else's.

Steve didn't hesitate. "I trust her. The woman has looked terrified since she arrived. It's a reaction I don't think she could fake. I'll send you a recording of her talking to an FBI agent so you can see for yourself. Her medical report showed a lot of past injuries, as well as present. From everything we've learned, the marriage was forced upon her and wasn't a happy one."

Blake's fists clenched. Even more reason to hate that scumbag Ahmad.

"I think she also has strong fear for her daughter," Steve

continued. "That she may be sold off to someone. Exposed to the same abuse she's endured."

Another shard of hate trickled through Blake.

"Did her husband ever talk to her about his plans?" Callum asked.

Frustration washed over Steve's face. "No. She says her husband didn't let her in on 'the business side' of his life."

If the asshole forced the marriage and was beating her, that wasn't a surprise. He clearly didn't see her as an equal.

"How would you like us to proceed?" Blake asked.

"I'm going to send some of my guys to watch the locations she's given us. If we catch a sighting of him in any of those places, I'll send in your team."

"Done." Flynn reached for the connected laptop. "Keep us informed."

"Will do."

When the call ended, they all leaned back, taking a breath. Failing a mission was never easy. Especially when that failure meant dangerous men had the freedom to plan attacks on American citizens.

"He was found once, he'll be found again," Tyler said with a nod.

"I'm counting on it." Blake tapped the desk before standing. "All right, well, if we're done here, I've got to call Bert, get this car stuff sorted for Willow." He was about to step out when he stopped and turned. "Almost forgot, you're all required at my house this Saturday, ten a.m."

Flynn raised a brow. "What's at ten?"

"My daughter's fifth birthday party. The theme is *Frozen*. Feel free to dress up as a snowman."

Callum frowned. "*Frozen?*"

He almost rolled his eyes. "Yeah, the movie." He'd watched the thing so many times, it was almost unimaginable that someone hadn't.

Flynn looked at Tyler. "You're younger, you should be up with the kid stuff."

Tyler tossed a pen at him. "I'm only two years younger than you, asshole. And I don't make a habit of watching animated shit."

Callum, the biggest man on the team, lifted his large shoulder. "Maybe you should. You could use some wholesome entertainment in your life."

Aidan smirked. "And maybe *you* should dress up. A six-and-a-half-foot snowman would make Mila's day."

He wasn't wrong.

Callum smirked. "Maybe I will."

Blake grinned. "Don't be late."

Leaving the conference room, he walked down the hallway and into his office. They'd only opened the security business a few months ago, but already it was feeling like home. As well as their off-the-books jobs for the FBI, they offered whatever their clients required, whether that was private or corporate protection agents, consultation on personal security, or self-defense education.

He sat behind his desk. Today, he was the unlucky bastard dealing with their admin duties. Their last receptionist hadn't ended so well, so none of them were in a rush to hire a new one.

He was just lifting his cell when the very man he was about to call popped up on his phone.

"Got some good news for me, Bert?"

The mechanic grunted. Blake tensed his jaw to hold in his laugh. The older guy didn't mince his words. Rough around the edges didn't even begin to the describe him. Blake liked that. You got what you saw.

"Depends on what you call good news. Her car belongs in a junkyard. It's a hunk of shit."

Yeah, Blake knew that, and he was kicking himself for not replacing it earlier.

"I have a list a mile long of things that need replacing and fixing. I haven't started on it yet because it'll probably cost more to repair everything than the thing's worth."

Blake ran a hand over his face. "I suspected as much."

"That other car I told you about, the one I have for sale, is ready to go if you want it."

He should probably talk to Willow about it first. But the newer car was expensive, and he knew her funds were low. She'd opt to either wait for a cheaper car or just fix the one she had. And there was no way he wanted her driving it again. Bert was right, it was a hunk of shit. Even if he fixed everything, there was still a chance something else could break. And what if he was away and couldn't help next time? What if Mila was with her?

Blake sighed. "I'll buy the new car from you, Bert."

WILLOW SMILED as she watched Omar read the sentence out loud. She'd been tutoring the kid for over a year now, and the progress he'd made was out of this world. He lived in Egypt and spoke Arabic, but his family wanted him to be fluent in English. He was well on his way, by far the quickest learner she'd had, and so advanced for his ten years.

He looked at her through the screen, the smile on his face wide. "How was that?" He said each word slowly and carefully.

She leaned forward. "Omar, you're doing an amazing job!"

She closed her tutoring book, their hour-long session now at an end.

The ten-year-old beamed back at her, dipping his head. "I have been practicing. And I have also been, ah, watching American TV."

Excellent. That had been one of her recommendations. Not just American TV, but any English-speaking shows. "And what have you been watching?"

"Hm…" His little brow furrowed. He did that a lot when he

was trying to think of a word. Lord, he was a cutie. "Riada..." He shook his head. "Sport."

She nodded. He was good at correcting himself when he slipped up. Another thing to commend him for. The kid was motivated and enthusiastic. "And what sport have you been watching?"

"Everything. Kara al-sala. In English, you say basketball. And kara al-qudam. Football. I have also been watching some movies."

She wasn't a big sports fan. Movies, on the other hand...heck, there was once a time when she'd loved a good romance flick with popcorn.

These days, it was *Frozen* or *CoComelon*.

"My daughter loves her movies and TV shows too." She smiled. "Well, I would ask what my new word is this week, but you just gave me three, riada...sport. Kara al-sala," she said slowly, "basketball. And kara al-qudam. Football."

Those last two were tongue twisters, that was for sure, and she'd need to practice if she wanted to remember them.

She always ended her sessions by asking her students for a word they could teach her in their language. It allowed the student to feel like the teacher for a moment. Plus, she got to learn a heap of new words.

"Thank you, Miss Cross."

"Keep up the good work, Omar. I'll see you next week."

Clicking out of the screen, she leaned back in her seat, stretching.

Sweet Jesus, her neck was tight.

The only downside to her job was having to spend so many hours sitting in front of the computer screen. She tried to take a break between sessions, get outside as often as she could and move, but some days it was impossible.

Standing, she headed to the kitchen, swearing she could hear each and every bone in her body creak and groan. Lifting the kettle, she was filling it with water as her phone buzzed with a message. When she looked at it, she froze.

Janet.

She'd assumed she wouldn't be hearing from her again—or anyone else in her study group. Not with them thinking the father of her child was something other than human.

She was almost tempted to ignore it, but reluctantly clicked into the message.

*Janet: Hey! Are you coming to our study session tomorrow night?*

She frowned. For a moment, words were completely lost on her. Was the woman joking? Of course, she wasn't going. Did they think she'd just forget what they'd said? How they'd acted?

*Willow: No, I'm not, Janet.*

If she was a confrontational person, she would have written more. A lot more. But she wasn't, so she left it at that.

She was just grabbing a tea bag when her phone buzzed again.

*Janet: Okay, I should have prefaced my last message with this—I'm sorry. We all are. We were just shocked. Please come so we can apologize in person.*

Willow paused. If it was herself they'd said hurtful things about, then forgiveness would probably be easier. But it wasn't. It had been about Blake. And it had been so unfair and uncalled for. He hadn't asked to be kidnapped. None of the men had. And to speak about him like he should now be an outcast in society, like people should actively fear and avoid him, was just wrong on so many levels.

*Willow: I appreciate the apology, but I think it's best I don't come to any more study sessions.*

The second the message was sent, it felt...right. Would she miss having people around to bounce ideas off of and motivate her? Yes. Was she disappointed that she'd started to consider the three of them friends and had already lost them? Definitely. But she didn't want to be friends with such narrow-minded people. She couldn't. Even though Blake and her weren't together, he still was, and always would be, the father of her child. He was family. Heck, they were still married.

The day after they'd found out they were pregnant, Blake had given her a ring. And a week after that, they'd eloped, just the two of them. It had been...perfect.

The word whispered in her head. So much of their relationship had been perfect before becoming parents. Maybe that's why she hadn't divorced him. She couldn't be with him right now... maybe not ever...yet the idea of breaking those vows still tore at her chest.

When the phone didn't buzz again, she grabbed a mug from the cupboard, dropping her tea bag in before filling it with boiling water. She was just about to step into the front yard to get some fresh air when the phone rang, Janet's name on the screen.

*Oh jeez.*

For a second time, she considered ignoring the woman, letting the call go to voicemail. Maybe listening to it sometime in the future. Or maybe just deleting it.

Then she gave herself a quick shake. No. Best to deal with it now and get it done.

She waited until she'd stepped outside, under the sun, before answering. "Hi, Janet."

"I'm sorry. Really sorry. We just...we didn't know what to say. *I* didn't know what to say."

Yeah, well...what she'd gone with certainly hadn't been a winner. "He's the father of my child, Janet. And he's a good man. Life has thrown a lot his way. He didn't ask for any of it."

"I know." She took a quick breath. "But I'm a small-town girl, you know? Everything tends to stay the same around here. So when we heard what happened to those guys, and that they were living so close to us, we got scared."

Willow's fingers tightened on the phone. They thought he was dangerous despite not even knowing him? Blake had never, and *would* never, hurt an innocent. He was a protector. Always had been, always would be.

"Scared because we don't know them," she hurried to add. "Scared of the unknown. But we're getting to know *you*, and we'd like to continue to get to know you, and if you say he's a good man, we'll believe you."

"They all are," she said quietly. "Good men."

"Well, it's fortunate we met you then. Please come. Study with us. Tell us about him."

She shook her head, walking around her small yard, enjoying the warmth of the sun on her face. It probably wasn't Janet's fault that she was afraid. The media had reported the facts, emphasizing the physiological changes in the men. What should have been emphasized was that they were heroes. Men who'd dedicated their lives to protecting others. Men who *still* dedicated their lives to protecting others, even after what happened to them.

"Please?"

Willow sighed. Maybe it would be a good idea to spend time with them. Affirm that they had nothing to fear. "Okay."

The sigh was loud across the line. "So you'll come tomorrow night?"

She looked at her empty driveway. "I still can't tomorrow, sorry. My car broke down last night. But even if it hadn't, I'll have Mila tomorrow night."

She'd been planning on asking Blake to take her while she went to the session, but truth be told, she wanted Mila with her. She missed the kid enough on her days with Blake.

"Okay, what if we came to yours?" Janet asked. "What time does she go to bed? We could do an hour or two while she sleeps. We're quiet."

Willow nibbled her bottom lip. Having them around would make writing her essay quicker and easier. The three of them were smart, and whenever she got stuck, they always had the answer or the reference or whatever it was she needed. And some company while she studied at night wasn't terrible.

"I can bring snacks," Janet added.

Willow chuckled. Janet always brought snacks. She was the snack queen. She brought everything from Red Vines to carrot sticks. "Okay. I'll send everyone my address and we can cram in a couple hours."

"Oh, great! It will be so fun. I can't wait."

Willow was just saying goodbye when a truck stopped on the road in front of her house, closely followed by a red Ford sedan, which pulled into her driveway.

Her mouth dropped open. She watched Bert climb out of the Ford. The old man walked up to her, holding out the keys.

"Ah, hi, Bert. What's this?"

"It's your car, love." When she didn't reach for the keys, he pushed his hand out insistently until she took them.

"No, it isn't. My car is a little beat-up Subaru called Gigi." She didn't know why she added that part. Maybe because she was in a shocked state of confusion. "This thing is new and shiny."

And probably out of her price range. Way, way out of it.

"The Subaru is being sold for parts. The parts that I can salvage, that is." He muttered the last words under his breath.

Turning, he walked down to the truck, and Willow hurried to follow. "No, Bert, I can't pay for this. I need *my* car."

He was already climbing into the passenger side. "Blake paid for it."

Then the door closed and they were driving away.

Willow stood like a statue, holding her tea in one hand and phone and keys in the other, mouth hanging wide open.

Blake bought her a car?

# CHAPTER 6

*B*lake's jaw tightened as he watched the recorded interview between the FBI agent and Saleh Ahmad's wife, Akela. She had an interpreter, but even speaking in Arabic, there was no escaping the despair in her voice. The hopelessness as she spoke about her life with her husband.

It was a hopelessness that couldn't be faked.

Now he understood why Steve believed her. Her stories had Blake's fists clenching and the air hissing out of his chest.

She'd been bought like a piece of property at a young age and shown nothing but abuse ever since. She spoke about the lack of freedom. The guards with weapons who stood watch over her day and night, ensuring she didn't escape.

And there was other stuff. Darker stuff that had him wanting to punch his fist through a wall.

Blake's memory went back to the guy who'd been in the dugout with her. If he could go back and kill the guy a second time, he sure as hell would, except he'd make the death more painful and drawn out. Bullets were too kind for a man who helped keep an abused woman hostage with her child.

At the sound of the door to Blue Halo reception opening, he

paused the video. The footsteps were short and light, but they were quick. A woman.

He closed his laptop a second before Willow stepped into his office. Immediately, her scent permeated the air. It was a mix of lilies and citrus. All sweetness.

When his gaze clashed with hers, his muscles tensed. She wasn't happy. Not even a little bit.

She held her hand up, keys dangling from her fingers. "No."

He kept his tone even, his features neutral. He definitely should have called her before he had Bert deliver the car, but, God, he could be a coward sometimes. Only when it came to her though. "You need a new car."

"Is Gigi unfixable?"

He frowned. "Gigi?"

"My car, Blake."

His lips twitched. "Mila came up with that, didn't she?"

"*Blake.*"

Sighing, he rose from his seat. "Bert said that fixing…Gigi," yep, sounded just as strange attaching the name to the car out loud as it had in his head, "would cost more to fix than the thing was worth. I made a call."

Immediately, her eyes narrowed.

*Shit. Wrong thing to say, Blake.*

"You made a call? You didn't care to get in contact with *me*, the car owner? See what I thought about this *call*?"

Yeah, he'd definitely screwed up. Slowly, Blake walked around the desk, closing the door to his office. His team would still be able to hear, but at least a closed door gave him the illusion of privacy. "You need a safe car. For Mila."

*And for you.*

The words were right there on the tip of his tongue, but they never reached air.

"I don't know how much you paid, but I do know it's too

much for me. I'll buy a cheaper car from him." She held the keys out once again.

He took a small step closer. "Take the car, Willow." Again, probably not the best approach, but the woman was too goddamn stubborn. Well, he could be stubborn, too.

"No."

"Why not?"

"You know why."

Another step forward. "Remind me."

She swallowed, still holding out the keys like they offended her. "Because we're not together, and if my car needs fixing or replacing, then that's my responsibility and I'll take care of it. I should have insisted that I would deal with Bert." Her voice lowered. "I appreciate you trying to help, but I don't need you looking after me when I can look after myself."

"Willow, you're still my wife, and I will *always* look after you." Day or night. Together or separated. There was no getting around that one.

A flicker of emotion. It shot across her face before she was able to conceal it.

She still loved him. He didn't need her words to know that. He felt it as strong today as when they'd said, "I do".

This time it was Willow who stepped forward, pressing the keys against his chest, heat from her hand pummeling through the material of his shirt. "Please, take the keys."

"No. This is all Bert had, and you need a car."

A flurry of emotions crossed her features this time. Frustration. Anger. Indecision. The anger won out. But then, anger had always been her comfort zone when everything got too heavy. Only, it had taken him a long while—too long—to realize the anger was a shield for something else. A mask to stop him from seeing what was really going on.

His hand wrapped around hers, but instead of taking the keys, he closed her fist around the metal. Then both his hands covered hers. Spirals of awareness traveled up his arms and through his limbs.

"I don't want to fight you on this."

Her gaze flickered between his eyes. "Then take the keys."

He should have seen that one coming. "No."

Her green eyes had always reminded him of a forest. Right now, that forest was dark and stormy. "Fine. I'll pay you back in installments."

She pulled her hand out of his, stepping away from him. She tried to open the door, but before she could, he pressed his hand against the wood, above her head, keeping it closed.

"Willow, please." He wasn't just talking about the car now, and she knew it. His voice lowered. "It can be different this time. You're better now, but even if you weren't, I'm *also* better. Different. Let me take care of you." If he could go back and do things differently, see the signs that he'd missed, he would. He'd do it in an instant.

A moment of silence ticked by. He stepped closer. God, being around her, breathing her in, was like coming home.

"I can't, Blake." Her head dipped just a bit, voice clogged with emotion. "I'm not yours anymore."

He almost wanted to laugh at the absurdity in that statement. "Honey, you've always been mine—and I've always been yours."

There was a short stuttering of her breath. A pounding of her heart. He lowered his head, hovering his lips near her neck. He felt the shiver that racked her spine. She knew his words were true. She just wasn't ready to admit it.

"I need to go." Her voice was anything but steady.

He pressed a soft kiss to her neck. His lips tingled, fire dancing between them. Then he stepped back.

Willow took off like she was being chased.

He moved back to his chair, dropping into it before leaning his head back and shuttering his eyes.

The next footsteps that neared his door were heavier. He opened his eyes to see Aidan.

The man raised a brow. "Want to talk about it?"

Did he? Who the hell knew? "It's hard. So damn hard. Having her here, within arm's reach, but not having her..."

Torture. That was the only way to describe it.

Aidan dropped into the seat on the other side of the desk. "You've never really talked about what your relationship was like before you left."

Because the very thought had his heart wrenching in his chest. Even in the compound, he'd talked about being worried for Willow and Mila, how much he loved them, but he hadn't talked about what their relationship was really like in those final two years.

"Willow and I have loved each other for a long time." The second his fifteen-year-old self had seen the green-eyed thirteen-year-old across the street, he'd known. "Things were great. But they changed once Mila was born."

He scrubbed a hand over his face. It was hard to comprehend that some of the best years of his life, the years of meeting and loving his child, were also some of the hardest. Willow's hardest.

"Changed how?"

He ran a hand through his hair. He almost hated himself for not being the person she'd needed him to be. "I'd just become a SEAL before she was born. The missions were long, and I was away a lot." He shook his head. "I could see Willow struggling. I could see her becoming a shell of the woman she once was. But I didn't do enough about it."

He didn't do *anything*, dammit. He just kept telling himself it was normal for things to change temporarily. That their relationship would go back to the way it was eventually. They just needed time.

He was wrong. So wrong.

"Postpartum depression?"

Blake frowned. "How did you know?" Hell, *he'd* barely known about postpartum depression. And he certainly hadn't known Willow was suffering from it. Not until he'd gotten back and Willow had explained the sickness. How she'd sought therapy the second he'd gone missing, since she was all Mila had at that point, and the therapist had diagnosed her.

Aidan lifted a shoulder. "It's a hell of a lot more common than people think."

"I didn't know."

His brows tugged together. "She's okay now?"

"She got help from a therapist. Took medication." *Thank God.* "Doesn't change the fact I wasn't there for her when she needed me most."

"You can't change the past. But you can be there for her now." His friend leaned forward. "I know what it feels like to lose a woman you love. The difference is, yours is here, within arm's reach. Be there for her."

For a moment, Blake paused, pulled out of his own misery and tugged into Aidan's. The man had been dating someone before he was taken by Project Arma. When he got out, he learned that she was married. That her wedding had occurred less than a year after they'd been taken.

If that had been Willow...

His chest constricted at the thought. It would have torn him in two.

"Have you gone to see Cassie?" He was pretty sure he knew the answer, but he hoped he was wrong.

"No. I can't. Knowing she's married is already gut-wrenching. Seeing it...I'm not strong enough."

Blake wouldn't be either. That was the thing about him and his team. They were soldiers; so dangerous, they could kill with a single hit. But they loved hard. All of them.

"What does she need from you?" Aidan asked.

The man didn't want to talk about himself anymore. But then, he rarely did.

"I'm not sure. She's putting up a wall. She says it's to protect Mila. She doesn't want our daughter to see us together if we aren't going to last, or see our relationship turn into something ugly. But I think it's more than that." He tapped his fingers on the desk, letting everything Willow had ever said wash over him. "I wasn't there for her when she needed me most. I put my work before her. As a SEAL, that's common. And she'd never cared about my military commitment before, but after Mila was born, she needed more from me. I think she's scared to trust me again. To trust *us*."

Aidan lifted a shoulder. "You're different now. After Project Arma, we all are. She just needs some time to see that."

He nodded. He knew that. Had told her the same, in fact. He just had to hope he could survive the time apart until she decided to return to him.

# CHAPTER 7

*W*illow reached across the table, grabbing another handful of popcorn. Janet had brought the bag of kernels and Willow had cooked them in butter and salt. Not the healthiest, but exactly what her tired, overworked brain needed.

Janet leaned back from her computer, rubbing her eyes. "I'm not sure my eyes can take any more screen time. I think I'll go blind."

The woman sat on the floor of Willow's living room, laptop on the oak coffee table, while Willow and Rob had the couch, and Toby sat in an armchair.

"It's like you took the words right out of my mouth, hence my brain break," Willow said, popping a piece of popcorn into her mouth, reveling in the saltiness.

The evening had been surprisingly pleasant. Everyone had apologized for the way they'd reacted to Blake, then they'd all just whipped out their laptops and started studying.

Rob shook his head. "I can't believe this is our final academic year."

"Tell me about it." Janet groaned. "I feel like I've been studying to become a teacher my entire life. Once we're done, we need to party and we need to party hard."

Willow scoffed. "Yeah, right. Pretty sure my partying days are behind me." Had been behind her since the strip turned pink.

"Were you with Blake when you started studying?"

Willow's brows rose at Toby's random question. She'd kind of been expecting someone to bring Blake up eventually, but not him.

"Ah, yeah, we were together. I started studying before I got pregnant. I took some time off after she was born, and the rest of the degree has been done part-time."

So, for her, it felt like she'd been studying for years, because she really had.

"How come you're not together anymore?" Janet asked. Then she quickly shook her head. "Sorry, I shouldn't have...It's none of my business."

She gave the other woman a small smile. "It's complicated."

Blake probably wouldn't agree. She was sure he thought it was really quite simple. That they should still be together. That they belonged together.

"But you don't see yourselves getting back together?" Rob asked.

"No." She quickly stuffed some more popcorn into her mouth, giving herself a moment before continuing. "Over the next year, I'll probably be too busy to date anyone anyway. What with finishing the degree and dealing with job applications."

That probably wasn't true. She wasn't willing to move Mila away from Blake, so there were only so many schools she could apply for. Not that she minded. Something would come up at some point, and she had her tutoring job, which she loved, until a school position became available.

Working with kids in any capacity was her passion. Not just to teach the fundamentals of subjects like Math and English, but to teach life skills, give tips on how to build relationships.

She wanted to have an impact.

Janet frowned. "Girl, you sound like it's all work and no play. We need to make time to enjoy ourselves. It's our last year before becoming serious teachers. We need to at least make time for a bar stop or two."

Willow chuckled. "I guess a couple of bar stops wouldn't hurt."

As the three of them started to talk about their favorite bars, Willow lifted the bowls and plates off the coffee table, taking them to the kitchen. Most were empty because, as per usual, they'd all snacked like crazy over the last couple hours. Heck, it was basically sentence-snack, sentence-snack, or at least it felt that way.

Willow rinsed the dishes before placing them into the washer.

Janet came up behind her, handing her another plate. "Thank you for having us over tonight."

She gave the woman a small smile, taking the bowl and rinsing it. "You're welcome. It was nice to have the company while studying."

"Oh, good." Janet wet her lips, casting a quick glance over her shoulder before stepping closer. "Hey, I was meaning to talk to you about something."

Willow almost groaned. *Please don't let it be about Blake, or what he's gone through, or anything on the topic at all.*

The dread must have shown on her face, because Janet quickly touched her arm. "Oh, it's nothing bad, and it's not about Blake. I really am sorry about what happened the other night."

A small puff of air blew out of her chest.

"I, um, actually wanted to invite you to visit the church we all attend."

Willow's brows rose. "Church?"

"Yeah. It's actually how the three of us met and formed our study group. There are tons of younger people there, and we do lots of social events, so it would be a great way for you to meet new people in the area. We're also strong social justice advocates. We love to get out into the community and help where we can, as well as educate others on spirituality."

Willow listened, unsure what to say. She wasn't against church, she'd just never been very religious.

Janet squeezed her arm. "Think about it. Our church is called Divine Purity."

Before Willow could respond, a door opened down the hall and then Mila stepped into the room, rubbing her eyes.

Willow moved straight over to her and lifted her into her arms. "Baby, are you okay? Did we wake you?"

She yawned. "I'm thirsty."

Willow turned, but Janet had already pulled a glass from the cupboard and filled it with water. "Here you go, honey."

"Thank you."

Janet's smile grew. "Well, you're just a little cutie-pie, aren't you?"

Mila sipped the water before leaning her head against Willow's neck. "Mama says that, too."

Another yawn.

Willow took the glass and placed it on the island. "Thanks, Janet. I'm just going to put her back to bed." She walked down the hall and stepped into Mila's room, tucking her into bed.

"Can you stay with me while I fall asleep, Mama?"

"Of course, baby." Mila didn't even need to ask. Willow had been lying with her daughter while she fell asleep her entire life. It was her favorite part of the day.

She lay there, stroking her hair, for a full five minutes. That was all the time it took for her daughter's breaths to even out.

Beautiful. Everything about the kid. The peaceful look on her face was otherworldly.

God, she loved her so much.

Mila hadn't always been a great sleeper. Willow's therapist had said that her lack of sleep had contributed to the PPD. At her worst, Mila woke hourly. She'd been a colicky baby, never quite settled.

The sleep deprivation was something she didn't think anyone could have prepared her for. It made nights so hard. Even when Blake was there, she hadn't wanted to wake him. In her head, she'd rationalized that he needed the sleep more than her. Thinking back on it now, she wished she'd asked him for more help.

One thing was for sure, she would never be taking sleep for granted again.

Pressing a light kiss to Mila's head, she sighed, moving back into the living room. The group was packed up, everyone lifting the last of their things.

Janet straightened. "Oh, my goodness, Willow. Your daughter is so beautiful." She sighed. "Kids are just...they're little angels, aren't they?"

"Thank you. I'm definitely smitten by her."

Janet chuckled, pulling her bag strap over her shoulder and moving to the door with the others.

Toby paused on the porch. "Thanks for having us over, Willow."

"No problem."

Janet gave her a quick hug. "Yes, thank you."

"I should be thanking you guys for coming here," she said. She wouldn't have completed half of what she'd gotten done on her own.

She gave them a wave from the porch as they headed to their cars. Willow was just turning back toward the door when quick footsteps sounded on the path again.

Rob dashed up the steps. "Sorry, I think I left my phone on the couch."

He ducked back inside, returning a second later with phone in hand. Instead of walking straight back to his car, he stopped in front of her, pushing his phone into a pocket.

Then he took a step closer.

Willow almost frowned, tempted to step back. She only just stopped herself.

"Hey, I just wanted to make sure there are no hard feelings about the other night."

She wouldn't forget his words, but she was hoping the more time she spent with him, with all of them, the more she could convince everyone how wrong they were. "It's all good, Rob."

He nodded, eyes flicking to the street, then back to her. "I also wanted to tell you that you can call me anytime. For help with studying. For company. Dinner. Anything. I'm sure being a single parent on the days you have Mila isn't easy. My own mother was a single parent, and she did a hell of a job at it, but I know she struggled."

Oh, well…that was sweet. She opened her mouth to respond, but before she could utter a word, he was speaking again.

"I also wanted to say that I'm not sorry you and Blake aren't together." He took another small step forward, diminishing the already miniscule space between them, hand going to her arm.

Her skin prickled from the touch…but not in a good way.

She was a second from pulling back when a car pulled to a stop in front of the house. They both looked up to see Blake climbing out of his vehicle and moving toward them. *Storming* toward them. And the look on his face…it could have stopped the dead.

Stony, dark anger.

Oh no. He'd always been crazy jealous when it came to other guys. The smallest touch was all it took to set him off.

"Blake—"

He squeezed into the tiny space between them, shuffling Rob backward. "Take your hand off her."

Rob's fingers were forced from her arm. She swallowed at the silence that followed, trying to wet her suddenly dry throat.

Rob's features hardened, his eyes narrowing.

"Rob was just saying good night," Willow interjected quietly.

"Didn't look like it." Low, angry words from Blake.

The lines beside Rob's eyes deepened. When he looked at her, his features softened, but only a fraction. "Good night, Willow."

She waited in thick silence until Rob drove away, then Blake turned, and she let the anger take root inside her. "What the hell was that?"

"I thought you said there were four of you studying here?"

Her brows rose. "What?"

"Was it just the two of you all night?"

"No. Janet and Toby were here too. They were all leaving together but Rob left his phone inside." Not that she needed to explain herself to him.

Blake scoffed before muttering something that sounded a lot like "bullshit" under his breath.

Her fists went to her hips. "What are you even doing here?"

"I was driving home from Tucker's. I always drive past your place on my way home. I only stop when I see assholes about to kiss you."

She shook her head, turning back toward the house. "He wasn't about to kiss me."

Even as she said the words, she heard the flicker of uncertainty laced around them. If she was honest with herself, she wasn't entirely sure *what* he'd been about to do. Kiss her? Just ask her out?

Blake's fingers curled around her arm, spinning her around. He grabbed her in almost the exact same place Rob had, but where Rob's touch had left her feeling uneasy, Blake's sent shots of awareness straight to her belly.

"I don't like other men touching you."

She knew that. In her senior year, he'd picked her up from school one day and just about knocked a guy out for placing an arm around her waist. And that was just one of many examples.

She tried to snatch her arm away, but Blake's hold didn't give.

Not even a little. It was like a band of steel holding her in place. But even though he held her securely, his touch was somehow gentle.

"You don't get to choose who touches me."

Something flashed through his eyes. A warning.

His hand released her, only to ease up to her shoulder, leaving a trail of fire before finally resting on her cheek. His head lowered, his breath brushing her cheek. "The next man who touches you, gets a broken jaw."

# CHAPTER 8

*W*illow rubbed a hand across her forehead. God, she was tired, and it was only eight thirty. The exhaustion was causing a light throb at the back of her eyes. She was almost done though. She could practically hear her bed calling for her from the other room. And boy, did she need sleep before Mila's party tomorrow.

She spun the cake around on the turntable, a smile stretching her lips. She'd been working on it all day. Well, just about all day. While Mila had been at school, she'd baked the cake, and when Mila went to bed she'd started decorating. So just about every second she hadn't been working, sleeping, or caring for her kid, she'd been on cake duty.

So worth it.

Olaf stared back at her, his smile as wide as his face. She'd made him out of white fondant, adding some food coloring for the orange carrot nose and black eyes and buttons.

"Yeah, you would be smiling," she said quietly to the edible figurine. "You haven't been on the go all day."

She filled the piping bag with wet white icing. The final touch.

She just needed to pipe it around the curved edge of the cake, making sure it dripped down the sides, and she'd be done.

She'd baked Mila's birthday cakes every year since the kid was born. It had become somewhat of a tradition. And each year, she got better. No one had ever taught her how to bake or decorate a cake. Certainly not her mother. No, that woman barely taught her anything. In fact, her entire family had always been incredibly absent in her life. It was something she and Blake had in common. Something that had bound them closer together.

It was also why, when Mila had been born, they'd received no help. None. No one had popped over in the afternoon to give her a chance to shower or prep dinner or breathe. No one had shown her how to feed or diaper her baby. It had all been on her and Blake. But mostly her.

Another leading cause of PPD, according to her therapist.

Blake had definitely witnessed her struggle. Not all of it. She'd hidden what she could. But that last night before his final mission when she'd asked for his help…

She swallowed, pressing the piping bag to the edge of the cake and squeezing as she rotated the turntable.

She'd needed him, and he hadn't been there for her. And right or wrong, she was scared to lean on him again. To need him, only to have him choose work over her—again. Everyone she'd ever cared about had shown her that relying on others was a risk that wasn't worth taking. At the end of the day, the only person you could really rely on was yourself.

Once she'd done a full circle of the cake, she placed the piping bag on the island and inspected her work.

Finished. And it was beautiful.

Her heart gave a little kick as she pictured Mila's reaction when she saw it. The kid was going to lose her mind.

Walking over to the fridge, she opened the door, shuffling a few things around to make room. Leaving the door open, she walked back to grab the cake. Carefully, Willow lifted it, walking slowly to the fridge.

She'd just about made it when she stepped on something hard. A sharp edge stabbed into her foot, causing her to lean back and lose her balance.

A small screech left her lips as she started to tumble. She tried to save the cake, she really did, but the thing slid from the plate, toppling right into her neck and chest as she hit the floor.

She barely felt the throb of her backside when it collided with the tiles, or the stretch of the muscles in her legs. Her entire focus remained on the icing that was now smeared all over her top. On the formerly round cake, which now resembled more of a wonky semi-circle.

For an entire minute, Willow sat there, breathing through her shock. Her frustration. Her exhaustion.

When tears pricked the back of her eyes, she scrunched them shut.

*It's just a cake, Willow. You can make another.*

Yeah, a cake that she'd spent hours making. A cake her daughter was beyond excited about seeing tomorrow. A cake she had nowhere near the required energy or time to recreate tonight.

Her head hurt just thinking about it.

When her phone rang in her back pocket, she eased the squashed cake to the floor, grabbed for the phone, not even checking who it was. "Hello?"

There was a small pause. Then Blake's deep, rumbly voice. "What's wrong?"

If she'd had the energy, she would have laughed. Of *course*, he heard she wasn't okay. "Nothing." Definitely not something she should be on the verge of tears about. "What is it?"

"You're lying, honey."

Closing her eyes, she breathed through the ridiculous devastation. "It's nothing. I just slipped and fell."

A small pause. "Are you okay?"

No. She was ready for a twelve-hour sleep but instead, was about to start a brand-new cake. "I'm okay. The cake, on the other hand, is not." She studied it. The thing had smushed so heavily against her chest, she already knew it was beyond fixing. She'd have to start again.

The idea had the pain in her head compounding.

Blake's tone softened. "Mila's birthday cake?"

"Yep. I'd just finished it…but now I'll be making another."

She sent a look of longing in the direction of her bedroom. Lord, how she craved to roll herself beneath the sheets. The thing was, if she did that, she knew that Mila would understand. The kid was amazing. It was Willow who wanted the cake to be done. Who wanted to see the joy on her daughter's face on her fifth birthday.

Sighing, she pushed up to her feet, grabbing a towel from the counter and scrubbing at the icing. "I'm gonna go and get started on it." And maybe drown her sorrows in a bottle of wine.

For the first time, she looked down to see what she'd stepped on. A small Olaf figurine. Oh, the irony.

"Are you sure you're okay?"

*No.* "I'm okay. I'll see you tomorrow."

BLAKE STOPPED at Willow's door, pulling out his phone and sending her a quick text.

*Blake: Come to the door, honey.*

He heard the faint sound of an egg cracking. Of the shell being tossed into the trash. Then the movement stopped, following by the light pitter-patter of her heartbeat as it sped up. He almost chuckled, just imagining her standing there, eyeing her phone, then the door.

*Blake: Please. x*

Another beat passed before her footsteps drew closer. Slow, light steps. Hesitant.

When the door pulled open, Willow stood on the other side. And even though it wasn't the polished, put-together Willow he was used to, his breath still caught. His knees still felt weak.

The only woman able to weaken him.

Strands of brown hair fell into her face and against her neck. Streaks of icing slashed across her chest, and stains marred her top.

"What are you doing here?" Her chest rose and fell, slightly quicker than it should.

"I was wondering if I could stay over on your couch? Wake up here for Mila's birthday." That wasn't the only reason he was here. But that was his soft ticket inside.

Willow's green eyes softened. Her gaze skittering over to the couch before returning to him. She stepped back. "Sure."

Blake entered, immediately bombarded by her sweet scent that he loved so much. This time, it was mixed with cake and icing. He stopped in front of her. Unable to help himself, he leaned in, brushing his lips across her cheek, tasting the sugar on her skin. When he straightened, his gaze caught on the dark circles under her eyes.

Like his hand had a mind of its own, it rose, his fingers grazing the darkened skin.

There was a slight hitch in her breathing. The softest heating of her eyes.

When his hand dropped, it felt like a kick to the gut. Any separation felt like a kick in the gut, no matter how small.

He was just closing the door when a car drove past. He paused, noticing the way it slowed just slightly before speeding up again.

Frowning, he was about to step outside when a light hand touched his shoulder.

"Blake, I'm going to get back to the cake."

He kept his eyes on the road for another beat before closing the door and moving over to the couch to drop his bag.

When he looked up, Willow was already in the kitchen, lifting a whisk and plunging it into a bowl.

He stepped up beside her, taking the whisk from her fingers. "I'll do it, darlin'." Her susceptibility to migraines was always at the forefront of his mind. Even while he'd been imprisoned by Project Arma, worry that she'd work herself too hard and suffer migraines was always there.

When she didn't fight him, his worry increased.

Moving across the island, she picked up something. "Olaf mostly survived." She held up the tiny, slightly disfigured snowman. His orange nose was a bit squashed and his eyes wonky. "I can quickly fix him, so at least I don't need to make him again. The little snowflakes and snowballs, on the other hand…"

"You get started on those, and I'll continue the cake."

Again, no argument, just a nod. Man, she really was tired. The woman knew he didn't bake. Not well, at least.

"What was the theme of Mila's cake last year?" he asked softly.

A small smile touched her lips. "CoComelon. She was obsessed with the show. I made a big JJ fondant figurine and she kept it in the fridge for a solid six months." Willow chuckled. "We couldn't even get in the car without playing songs from the show. I swear I sang the songs in my sleep."

Blake smiled, the expression a bit raw. Because he hadn't been there to help with the cake. Or watch the shows or sing the songs.

She flattened some fondant before reaching across the island for a knife. When her skin grazed his arm, there was a slight widening of her eyes before she snatched her arm back.

*I feel it too, baby.*

He didn't need to say the words out loud. She knew. Since they were teenagers, they'd always been so affected by each other,

61

they could barely think straight. Barely breathe. Some days he swore the woman made him drunk for her.

He watched as she carefully sliced the fondant into even squares.

"Will you tell me about some of the things I missed?" he asked quietly.

Two years. That was a long time in a child's life. The milestones. The memories. The laughter and tears. All of it missed.

Willow wet her lips. "We started swimming lessons just before her third birthday. At first, she hated them. The teacher made her walk across this wobbly board and dunk her head under the surface." Willow shook her head. "Each week I saw her confidence grow though, until eventually she was asking, *begging*, for me to take her to lessons, even on days we had none."

"Reminds me of her mother," Blake said. "Cautious until she realizes she has nothing to fear."

For a moment, she paused. He probably shouldn't have said that. He'd already been pushing the woman. But it was true. And what he wouldn't do for her to just…trust. Trust in him. In them. That they could be better than they were before.

He lifted the bowl of wet ingredients and tipped it into the dry that Willow had already prepared, before whisking them together. "What else?"

"I took the training wheels off her bike. I was so nervous that she'd fall and hurt herself. But she was amazing. It was as if all she had to do was watch the other kids do it, and she was a pro. I remember thinking she got those gross motor skills from her father."

He chuckled softly.

"And the day she started preschool…" Willow shook her head, and he almost swore he saw a glint of tears in her eyes. "It was so hard. Not for her. She was fine. When I hugged her at the classroom door, I didn't want to let go. It felt like I was losing my baby. Whereas she was wriggling so hard to get out of my arms."

Didn't surprise him. The kid was still a social butterfly. Who she got that from, he had no idea.

He took his eyes off the mixture he was beating to look at Willow. When their eyes clashed, he saw the undeniable hint of unshed tears.

Her voice lowered. "She missed you. So much. No matter how much time passed, it never got easier."

His gut clenched, his heart feeling like it was being torn in two. He'd missed her too. Both of them. So damn much. Some days, the pain had crippled him.

His next words were tentative. "Just her?"

A sharp inhale. A quickening of her pulse. "No. Not just her."

Honesty. He liked it.

She looked down, quickly returning to slicing the fondant. He followed her gaze—just as the knife slipped.

He moved quickly, yanking her fingers out of the way before the sharp edge sliced into her.

Willow gasped. "That was…You're so fast now."

Yeah, he was different in a lot of ways. "I told you. I'm not the same man I was before I was taken." Nowhere close, physically or emotionally.

"You're not."

His thumb grazed the skin of her wrist. Her heartbeat fluttered beneath his touch. "You're tired. You should go to sleep. I can pop the cake in and take it out when it's done. Then tomorrow morning, I can play with Mila while you quickly decorate it before the party." The cake needed to cool before it could be decorated anyway. He didn't know much about cakes, but he knew that.

Longing washed across her features. "Are you sure?"

So exhausted. "Go."

"Thank you." Her words were soft.

Man, he wanted to kiss her. To tug her into his arms and carry her to bed. But Willow needed to know she could trust him first. To be there for her. To support her. To carry her when she was weak.

He gave her wrist a gentle squeeze before releasing it. Then he watched her leave the room.

Once she was gone, he got started on coating the cake pan in butter. Luckily, the printed recipe sat on the island, so he knew how long it needed in the oven. Probably the only reason she'd left him out here.

Once it was in, he moved down the hall to Mila's room, pushing open the door and watching his daughter sleep.

Her little chest rose and fell in long, deep breaths. Beautiful. So beautiful.

Two years of missed memories. Two years of missed firsts.

Never again. Never would he let anyone take him away from his family. And anyone who tried would wish they hadn't.

# CHAPTER 9

$\mathcal{W}$illow watched as people milled around Blake's backyard. Kids from school, parents, Blake's team...the lawn was packed.

Luckily, it wasn't too cool. The sun just poked through the clouds, taking the edge off the Idaho chill. She watched as the kids jumped in the bouncing castle. As they waited eagerly to have their faces painted. All of them were dressed as characters from *Frozen*. Especially Elsa. There were lots of her.

The yard buzzed with guests talking. Laughing. And then there was Blake. He was playing a game with some of the kids where they'd jump onto his back, and he'd fall flat on his stomach like he was in pain. The kids loved it.

Her heart gave a little kick.

Man, he was good with them. Not a surprise though, he was good at a lot of things.

A little voice whispered in her head that maybe it was time to let go of the fear of history repeating itself. To trust.

Her breath shortened at the memory of his hand on her wrist last night. At the way the pad of his thumb had stroked her pulse, touching her heartbeat.

Sucking in a deep breath, she rubbed her temple. The headache from last night had still been there when she woke. And now, in her first moment of stillness for the day, she was feeling it.

She needed to slow down. Rest.

Her gaze swept across to Mila, who was jumping in the castle with Courtney. They were holding hands, both with huge smiles on their faces, and Courtney was tugging her much higher than she would have gotten on her own.

"Hi!"

Willow jumped. Man, she'd been so deep in her own thoughts she hadn't even noticed Grace come up beside her.

Grace's brows lifted. "I'm sorry, I didn't mean to sneak up on you."

Willow almost laughed at the woman's words. Could you sneak up on someone in broad daylight at a busy kids' party? "You don't need to apologize, I was distracted." Ha. That was putting it lightly.

Grace smiled. The woman was fairly new to Cradle Mountain, only having arrived a couple months after Willow. She was dating Logan and had opened her own business, McKenna Counseling. Willow really enjoyed her company. Any time she'd caught up with either her or Courtney—who owned and ran The Grind —she'd always been made to feel comfortable.

Grace nodded toward the crowd. "This party's great. You've done an excellent job organizing everything."

She'd do anything for her kid. Even stay up all night and recreate a cake that had taken her hours to make the first time. Not that she'd had to, thanks to Blake.

"Thank you, but as much as I'd like to take the credit, Blake did a lot." The jumping castle. The face painter. The preparation of his yard with chairs and tables. It had all been him. "He made it a lot easier than previous years. Truth be told, I'm so used to doing everything myself that having someone else shoulder half the workload almost feels like a holiday."

Grace's brows pulled together. "It must have been hard doing everything on your own."

"It was." She nibbled her bottom lip. "Blake was away a lot before he went missing, but I always knew he was coming back. I craved his return." It had been the only thing that kept her sane some days, knowing he'd be back. She still couldn't believe she hadn't realized what was going on in her mind sooner. "So when he disappeared...it wasn't good. I sought help as soon as I could, knowing that I needed to be okay for Mila."

Another twitch of Grace's brows. "Grieving his loss while taking care of Mila must have been difficult."

The hardest thing she'd ever had to do in her entire life. She'd never known pain like that before. It made everything else seem inferior.

Willow's gaze tracked her daughter again. "Without seeking help, I would have broken. Mila needed me to be strong."

Therapy and medication had helped, but the pain of Blake being gone had never disappeared. The hole in her stomach, the hollowness, had just become a part of her. A part that she'd learned to ignore by keeping herself busy.

"How are you doing now?"

Willow smiled as Mila fell onto her back in the castle. The smile on her face was like medicine in itself. She looked back to Grace. "I'm okay now. When Mila got her father back, it was like a gift we'd both always wished and prayed for, but feared we'd never receive. Now I just pray that those two are never separated again."

Grace looked like she wanted to say something. She opened her mouth, then seemed to reconsider it, closing her lips and smiling instead.

When Willow looked away, her gaze caught on Blake. He

wasn't playing with the kids anymore. He was standing across the yard, his eyes dark as they looked her way.

She swallowed, remembering the moment he'd returned to her. There had been tears. And joy. But a part of her, a large part, had also felt fear. Fear of ending up back where she'd been when he'd left. That dark place that she thought she'd never tear herself out of.

When she told him that she couldn't be with him, that she needed her own space, she'd seen the utter disbelief. The deep hurt. And maybe a little bit of challenge. Because there had never been a Willow and Blake *without* them being together.

She wrenched her gaze away, looking back to Grace. "What about you? Enjoying Cradle Mountain?"

The woman's features smoothed. "I love it here. It's funny how life works out. I was never planning to stay. Cradle Mountain was supposed to be a pit stop before I moved elsewhere. But here I am, making it my home."

Willow nodded. Blake had hinted at something dark in Grace's past, which had caught up with her in Cradle Mountain. He hadn't given any details, and she hadn't asked, knowing it wasn't her business. "Fate has a way of throwing our plans out the window."

She chuckled. "That it does. Hey, I wanted to mention that Courtney and I are having a girls' night this Wednesday. It will probably just be drinks at home, so really low-key. Would you like to join us?"

Willow's brows rose. "Really?"

"Yeah. Only if you want to and have time. I know you're really busy, but Courtney and I would both love to get to know you a bit better."

Her lips tugged up. She'd never had many friends. It was just one of the reasons she hadn't hesitated to follow Blake to Cradle Mountain. Working, studying, and being the sole caregiver for Mila left her little time. "I'd love that."

Grace's eyes lit up. "Great!"

Suddenly, Mila catapulted herself into Willow's legs. When she looked down, all she saw was white. The kid was dressed as Olaf but was looking more like a cloud from this angle.

Laughing, she bent down to pick her up. "Hey, baby, are you having fun?"

Mila's orange-painted nose wrinkled.

Willow frowned, pushing some hair back into place that had escaped her headband. "What's wrong?"

"I fell out of the jumping castle and hurt my knee."

Willow followed her gaze, spotting the specks of blood.

"Oh, no. We can't have a grazed knee on a birthday, can we? Should we ask Daddy if he has some Band-Aids?"

Her eyes lit up. "*Frozen* Band-Aids?"

Ah, yes. *Frozen* Band-Aids. She was pretty sure Blake wouldn't have any, but luckily, she kept an emergency stash in the car. It had been the first addition to the new car.

She pressed a kiss to her daughter's head. "Sure, baby. You play with your friends and I'll go get them."

Setting Mila back onto her feet, she went into the house, grabbing her car keys before heading out front. She'd parked in the driveway, whereas everyone else had parked on the street. Opening the passenger-side door, she grabbed the small first-aid kit from her glove box. She'd quickly come to realize it was mandatory in Mom life. Even something as innocent as a park play could end in tears.

Rummaging around, it took less than a few seconds to find the box of *Frozen* Band-Aids. Next would be finding an Olaf one. Opening the box, she grabbed a couple out and held them up to the sun. It was at about the fifth Band-Aid when she spotted him.

"Gotcha, Olaf."

Willow was just closing the car door when something across the street caught her eye. Frowning, she took a small step forward.

Strange. No one seemed to be there. But *something* had definitely moved.

She was just taking a second step forward when a hand touched her shoulder.

Turning, she saw Flynn behind her. "Hey, Flynn. What are you doing out here?"

A frown creased his brow as he shot a quick look over her head toward the street. "Just saw you come out here and wanted to know if you needed help with anything. Everything okay?"

She nodded. "Yes, everything's fine. I'm just grabbing a Band-Aid for the birthday girl. Although for a moment, I thought I saw someone," she waved her hand, "somewhere. But I guess I'm just tired."

And to be honest, her head was aching more by the minute, both due to the lack of sleep and the way she'd been go-go-go all day.

Flynn glanced back across the street. His expression had her pausing. It was the same one that Blake often wore. Intense. Hard. Eyes of steel.

~

BLAKE SIPPED HIS DRINK. It was yellow and sweet and tingled on his tongue. It was terrible.

But the drink wasn't what had his stomach in knots. It was Willow's words.

*"I always knew he was coming back. I craved his return."*

The familiar pang of regret clenched at his chest. He'd seen her anxiety each time he left. Felt her desperate need to have him stay. And he hadn't done a goddamn thing about it. Nothing. She'd had to deal with her postpartum depression on her own. Then he'd disappeared, and she'd had to grieve his loss and care for their daughter while shouldering every responsibility for her household and small family.

His insides knotted tighter, a sick churning in his gut.

He watched as Mila ran up to Willow, and she swung their daughter into her arms.

"You look pained."

Blake heard Logan, but he didn't look his way. His eyes remained on the two people who always commanded his attention. "I am. How do I get her to trust that I'm not going anywhere? That I'll be there for her in the dark days as well as the good ones?"

"I'm not an expert on the topic," Logan said quietly. "But don't they say time is the cure for most things? It might take a while, but eventually she'll learn to trust."

Logan was right. Willow's trust had been fractured, and he needed to rebuild it. Needed to help *her* rebuild it.

His eyes tracked her all the way into the house before she disappeared.

"Don't give up."

Blake tugged his gaze away, giving Logan's shoulder a squeeze before heading toward the house. He placed the sugary crap he'd been drinking in the trash before stepping inside. When he didn't see Willow in the house, he headed out the front. She was standing by her car with Flynn.

"Glad you're okay," Flynn said, his gaze skittered across the road. Scanning.

Blake followed his line of sight, seeing nothing out of place. When his friend left, Blake approached Willow. Just like always, the soft pitter-patter of her heart sped up a fraction.

"Everything all right?"

She nodded. "Yeah, Mila just needs an Olaf Band-Aid."

He chuckled. Of course. He needed to get some of those. Giving a small nod, he was about to turn when Willow's hand touched his arm.

Her gaze darted between his eyes. "Before you go, I wanted to say thank you for coming over last night. For helping this morning. For everything you do for Mila and me."

"We're a team, Willow. You don't need to thank me for doing my share of the parenting duties."

When she stepped closer, he froze. The woman *never* initiated affection. Not anymore. So when her fingers touched his neck, tugging his head down, and her lips pressed to his cheek, his chest rumbled with fire.

Her kiss burned him. Stripped him. Destroyed him.

When she pulled away, she smiled, then brushed past him and back into the house.

Yet again, Blake made that same promise to himself that he'd been making for months. To get her back...not part-time, not as a co-parent. But as completely *his*.

# CHAPTER 10

*W*illow finally sat, the soft couch sinking beneath her thighs. She wasn't sitting for long. Almost immediately, it wasn't enough. She lowered to her side, eyes shuttering as she attempted to block out the light, which was threatening to jackhammer into her skull.

She hadn't stopped. Not for the entire day. Cake and presents and pancakes in the morning, followed by party setup. Then the party itself. And after that came the clean-up. And not just the cleaning at Blake's house. The second she'd stepped inside her own home, she'd unpacked the leftover food and presents, and then it had been time for Mila's dinner and bath.

She scrunched her eyes tighter.

She kept telling herself she'd take a break soon. That there was just one more thing to do. But there'd always been another thing after that.

Now she was paying the price.

The throbbing felt like a big pendulum hitting the back of her eyes. Pressing. Cracking.

Frowning, she tried to focus on the sounds from the hallway. Mila was shuffling around in her bedroom, putting on her paja-

73

mas. The night had turned into "just make it to Mila's bedtime", but suddenly, she wasn't sure she would. Hell, even rising to her feet felt like too much.

She was so foolish. She should have rested earlier.

Nausea pressed at her stomach.

Where was her phone? She needed to call someone to make sure Mila got to bed and was okay overnight.

Light footsteps sounded down the hall. They were barely a whisper, yet they beat at her skull. The nausea crawled up her throat.

"Mama, are you okay?" Little fingers touched her cheek. "Are you sick?"

The concern in her daughter's voice had Willow forcing her eyes open. Pain thrashed at her skull, but she kept them open with sheer will. There had been only two other full-blown migraine incidents in the last two years. Luckily, Willow had been close with her neighbor, so she'd sent Mila next door.

Now, she didn't even know her neighbor's first name.

"I am sick, baby. Can you get my phone?"

Mila's brows pulled together as she scanned the room, determination taking over her face. When she walked away, Willow's eyes shuttered again. She knew she should keep them open, but it was just so dang hard. And now that they were shut, would she have the strength to open them again?

Mila's soft footsteps grew close, but this time, instead of pounding at her head, they sounded far away. Like she was in a tunnel and Mila was at the other end.

Fear stabbed at her chest. Fear that she wouldn't be able to call for help. That Mila would be on her own tonight.

Willow tried to peel her eyes open. She really did. But the light against her lids was too bright.

When a voice sounded, she frowned. Even that small movement hurt. It wasn't Mila's voice, it was a man's. Then Mila spoke.

She tried to tug their words closer. Fit them together and make sense of them. But the migraine demanded too much of her attention. A second later the voices stopped, the couch dipped, and a ball of warmth pressed into her stomach.

Mila. She would recognize her daughter anywhere.

She breathed a sigh of relief, having her daughter here and close. Finally, she gave her body permission to relax. White-hot pain still jolted her head, but the combination of silence, stillness, and having Mila against her made it so she could almost forget.

Willow was just lulling to sleep when the sound of the door opening echoed through the room like the returning of a jackhammer. She frowned as Mila left her arms. Soft whispers floated through the room. Through the pain and the fog, she recognized Blake's voice.

She breathed out the last bit of anxiety.

Blake was here. He'd take care of Mila. He'd make sure everything was okay.

Minutes passed. Maybe five, maybe ten. She was just falling asleep again, her mind darkening, when arms wrapped around her back and knees, lifting her, waking the monster behind her eyes.

A small whimper slipped from her lips. Then the chest below her cheek vibrated as quiet words were spoken.

"I'm sorry, honey. You'll be in bed in a second."

She let his warm, familiar voice soothe her.

His strong heartbeat pounded against her ear, but surprisingly, it didn't add to the agony. No. It snaked its way into her chest, almost becoming a part of her.

Her back hit the soft mattress gently. She whimpered again, but this time it wasn't from pain. It was loss. Loss of his heart beating against her cheek. His strong arms, like bands of steel, holding her close.

Hands were at her waist, carefully peeling off her jeans. Then her socks. A blanket covered her, seconds before something was at her lips.

"Open for me, honey."

Her lips separated. At this moment, she would do anything the man asked. He was her thin connection to reality. To safety.

A pill touched her tongue, then a straw. She swallowed before closing her lips again.

When a hand touched her head, she sighed. It was so nice to have him here. But it was also scary. So scary. Because she knew that his presence could break down some of the hard casing around her heart, and she would begin to trust him again.

"God, I love you."

A small frown touched her brows. Had she dreamed those words, or had Blake actually spoken them?

Something else touched her forehead. Something light but warm. A kiss. Then it was gone.

A second later, he was leaving. She didn't hear his silent footsteps, but she felt the loss of his presence.

"Blake…" The single word had her head splintering. Still, she forced more words out. "Stay with me."

A whispered plea from her heart. For a second, she wondered if he'd heard. Wondered if those last three words had even left her lips.

There was no response. No noise at all. Maybe he'd already left the room.

Just as she was about to drift off, rustling noises sounded, then the bed dipped behind her. Heat pressed against her back. Heat and hard, rigid muscles. And the soothing heartbeat returned.

~

Blake's arms tightened around Willow's waist. It was early morning, and he'd held her all night. She'd woken twice, sick both times.

He knew she'd sleep for a while longer. Migraines always wiped her out for a long time.

God, he hated them.

A short moan escaped her lips, and his muscles tensed. Seeing her in pain was worse than experiencing his own. If he could take it away and put it upon himself, he would. Every day of the week.

When Mila had called last night, her small, worried voice had almost caused his lungs to seize. Wasn't this the nightmare that had plagued his mind while he'd been away from them?

He was here now, though. With his family.

The only good thing about this moment was holding her. When she'd asked him to stay, it was like she'd given him permission to breathe.

He pressed a soft kiss to her neck as he untangled his arms and rose from the bed. The sun was just poking through the curtains, which meant Mila would be up soon.

Like his thoughts had conjured her, soft, muffled movement sounded from down the hall. Smiling to himself, Blake threw on his jeans and a shirt before heading out of the room. He was just pulling the bedroom door closed when Mila stepped out of her own room.

She walked up to him, her little feet moving slowly as she tried to be quiet. When she reached him, he crouched down to his haunches.

"Sleep okay, baby?"

She gave a small nod, worried eyes darting to the closed door. "Is Mama okay?"

His heart clenched. Lifting a hand, he smoothed some of her hair from her face behind her ear. Her hair had always reminded him of Willow's in the morning. Long, untamed locks of brown waves.

"She's going to be okay. She just needs some rest." He was still kicking himself for not seeing the signs yesterday. For not forcing her to stop. To take a break and rest. "I've asked Courtney and Jason to take you to the park today, but before that, should we make some pancakes for breakfast?"

Her brown eyes lightened. "With chocolate chips and sprinkles?"

He chuckled. Rising, he took her hand. "Is there any other way to eat pancakes? Mama does keep chocolate chips and sprinkles, doesn't she?"

"Yep. She tries to hide them, but I know where they are."

Of course she did.

The second they entered the kitchen, Mila released his hand and ran over to grab a step stool before placing it in front of a cabinet. Then, reaching behind a stack of containers, she grabbed two smaller ones, holding chocolate chips and sprinkles.

Oh jeez. He needed to be careful around this little detective.

Shaking his head, he opened the fridge door. "You grab the rest of the dry ingredients, I'll get the wet."

The two of them made pancakes a lot. It had become somewhat of a tradition, and they'd developed a good system. And if it wasn't pancakes, it was waffles.

They were just combining the wet and dry ingredients when Blake frowned, realizing Mila was very quiet. Which was definitely not the usual. Not for this kid.

"It only happened two times when you were gone."

Blake looked up, brows tugging together at Mila's words.

"Migraines."

The news sent a dagger to his chest. "Tell me about them, baby."

She stirred the mixture. "Both times she told me to run next door to Sandra. Sandra looked after me while Mama rested. They were friends and she looked after me sometimes."

He gave a small nod, wanting her to think he was okay when

he really wasn't. He should have been there. He should have been the one taking care of his daughter. Making sure Willow was okay.

He swallowed the anger, forcing it down until another time. He met his daughter's gaze, both of them already having paused in what they were doing. "You did a good job calling me last night. Just like we practiced. And I promise you, I'll try to be here next time. And if I can't because I'm away for work, one of the guys will."

Mila nibbled her bottom lip. "So you won't disappear again?"

His heart fucking tore in two at hearing those words. They'd told her he'd been away fighting the bad guys. That he hadn't had a choice in the matter. Both of which were true.

He stepped closer, taking her little face in his hands. "No. I'm never disappearing on you or your mom again."

He would destroy anyone who threatened that promise. Tear down any wall that tried to separate him and his family. Without thought. Without hesitation.

He tugged her into his arms, holding her close.

"I know I told you already, but I missed you," she said quietly.

Another tear at his heart. His arms tightened. "I missed you too, baby."

So fucking much it still hurt.

# CHAPTER 11

*a* tear trickled down Willow's cheek. She would have thought she'd be done crying by now. That she'd cried so many tears for Hawk she'd be plain out.

Maybe that wasn't possible. Maybe a person didn't have a maximum number of tears inside them. Maybe the saddest people on Earth could just spend their days crying, tears trickling down their cheeks, faces never dry.

Her mother's words came back to her. "He's just a bird, Willow. I don't know what you're getting so upset about."

Another tear fell. He wasn't just a bird. She was only thirteen and even she knew that. He was her friend. Her companion. The only one who'd listened to her when she rambled on about her day. When she needed someone to talk to about the million little things that had gone wrong.

Her mother wouldn't understand that because her mother didn't care.

She'd actually started to realize that her mother cared about very little in this world. She certainly didn't care about her father...but then, he didn't seem to care about her, either, so that was probably fair. They were just two people living in the same house, committed to a loveless marriage, barely ever interacting with each other.

Was that normal? She'd always believed it was, but she was starting to think otherwise. The parents of kids at school didn't seem like that. She'd even seen Dora's parents holding hands the other day.

She scrubbed away another tear, eyes never leaving the small mound of dirt she'd shoveled on top of Hawk. The hole had taken her all morning to dig, and yet, it felt too shallow. How deep were you supposed to dig before you buried something? Her granddad had been buried really deep. She still remembered looking into that dark hole, fearing standing so close.

She blew out a long breath, wishing the tears would stop.

Her gaze skirted up the tall pine tree. She'd wanted to bury Hawk in her backyard, but Mother had said no. She didn't want the yard dug up, because there was no way Mrs. Foster could have anything less than perfect.

It was okay though. The park at the end of the street was probably better. Right under the tree where she'd found him. She still remembered that day. He'd hurt his wing and had been laying on the ground, his soft cries all but breaking Willow's heart.

She knew what it felt like to be sad and have no one care. She'd lived and breathed that loneliness more times than she cared to remember.

It had taken a lot of convincing to make her mother take him to the vet. Then even more for her to allow Willow to keep him until he was better. After that, she was supposed to set him free.

Three months later and she still hadn't been able to. A voice at the back of her mind told her that she should. That the bird was a free animal and needed to be out in the air and the trees. But in a quiet house, where all she'd ever wanted was someone to talk to, she'd always managed to put it off. Every morning, she'd told herself just one more day.

Until this morning...

Her throat constricted at the memory of finding Hawk on the bottom of the cage, unmoving.

*Why did you die, Hawk? Did the suffocating quiet kill you like it's killing me?*

*Footsteps sounded behind her, but she didn't turn. She was past caring about people seeing her cry in public.*

*The footsteps slowed as they drew closer.*

*Suddenly, someone dropped down beside her. Now she* did *turn. And when she saw who it was, she sucked in a quick breath. The boy from across the street. He'd only moved there a week ago. She'd watched him from her window, wondering what his name was. How old he was. He went to her school, and she knew he was older. But that was all she knew.*

*He looked sixteen, maybe seventeen? And he was tall, with broad shoulders. Big.*

*She almost didn't breathe as his unwavering gaze hit hers.*

"Are you okay?"

*A slight tremor coursed down her spine at his voice. It was deep. Deeper than the voices of the boys in her grade. And there was a rough edge to it that made her tummy feel funny.*

"Hawk died." *She whispered the words, his eyes holding her in a trance.*

*He switched his gaze to the mound of dirt, and she almost wanted to beg him to return it to her. Then he did.* "Who's Hawk?"

"A bird." A friend. My only friend.

*She continued to watch his eyes. They were the most beautiful shade of gray she'd ever seen. They reminded her of the clouds before a storm. And she'd always loved storms. The pitter-patter of rain on the roof. Watching the wind and the cold from her warm room.*

"Why are you by yourself?"

*What an unusual question. No one had ever asked her that before. How many times had she been upset and by herself in this very park? Angry at something her mother had said. Hurt by her father's absence. So many time's she'd lost count.*

*People had seen her, thrown sympathetic looks her way, but no one ever stopped. And certainly no one asked her why she was alone.*

"My mom's getting ready for drinks with her friends. And Dad's..." She didn't actually know what he was doing. Disappearing for large chunks of time was just what he did. She was so used to it now that she never questioned it. "He's busy."

The boy leaned back, getting comfortable beside her. Which made her even more confused. She'd expected him to ask his questions and leave.

"My parents are like that," he said quietly.

He wasn't watching her anymore. Instead, he was looking at the tree, the gray in his eyes darkening.

"They didn't even ask me if I wanted to move here," he continued, his voice roughening. "They just made the decision and a month later, here we are. Like I'm luggage. Like what I want doesn't matter."

Stormy. Just like the sky.

"I can't wait to enlist," he muttered.

She nibbled her bottom lip, not sure what to say. She'd never been a huge conversationalist. She'd always wondered if maybe that was why her parents didn't talk to her very often. So she settled on the only words she could think of. "I'm sorry."

He turned those beautiful eyes back to her, and she almost lost her breath again. "Why are you sorry?"

"Because having absentee parents sucks." She tried to look away but couldn't. It was like he was holding her hostage.

His gaze flickered between her eyes. "Some people shouldn't have kids."

Willow swallowed. "I'm not going to have kids."

Why had she gone and said that? Sure, it was true. She'd known for a long time that she wouldn't have children, because she was scared that she'd turn into her own mother. That neglect was genetic. That her child would feel just like her. Unloved.

For the first time, a smile stretched his lips. It was a small one, but it was enough to have something warm and fuzzy trilling through her veins. That smile almost had her forgetting the reason she was here. The sorrow that had been drowning her.

"I don't believe you."

She frowned. "You don't know me."

He lifted a shoulder. "Maybe not. But I'm good at reading people. You're making that decision based on fear, and decisions based on fear are never right and rarely hold."

He sounded too old to be sixteen or seventeen. Maybe he was an adult masquerading as a teenager. "How old are you?"

The smile widened, his eyes crinkling. "Why? Do I sound wise?"

"Yes." There was no point in lying.

"I'm fifteen." Fifteen. Only two years older than her. "My name's Blake."

Blake. She let it roll around her head, wash over her limbs. She liked that name. It sounded rough and masculine, but at the same time...soft?

"I'm Willow," she said quietly.

"Willow." Another tremor rocked her spine, this time at the way her name sounded on his lips. Intimate. She realized she wanted to hear him say it again. But also knew she wouldn't ask.

When a beat of silence passed, he looked again at the little bird grave, hands locked around his knees.

"You don't have to sit with me, you know." She liked him sitting with her. It was a bit strange how much. And she realized for the first time that her eyes had finally stopped watering. But she didn't want him to feel like he had to.

"I know." He didn't look her way. "But I don't want you to be alone while you're upset. No one should be alone when they're sad."

More words that no one had ever said to her before. Words that made her confused, but that she wouldn't dare question, in case they were never spoken again.

# CHAPTER 12

*W*illow groaned quietly in her throat. Her mouth felt dry, but there was no jackhammering pain in her skull. No nausea in her belly.

She had vague recollections of waking. Sometimes it was because the nausea had crawled up her throat and caused her to be sick. Other times it was because her mouth had felt like sandpaper, so dry she could barely breathe.

There was one constant through every awakening, though. Blake. He'd been there with a bucket or water or medicine, each and every time.

Slowly, she peeled her eyes open, sliding her gaze around the small bedroom. Thin rays of light seeped through the curtains. Afternoon light.

How long had she slept? Sleeping twelve to twenty-four hours wasn't unusual after a migraine.

Rolling onto her back, she half expected pain in her skull to jolt to life again. Or for the back of her eyes to throb. She felt neither.

Willow sighed. Finally, she'd come out the other side.

She tried to listen for any sounds. Sounds of Mila or Blake or TV or dishes. The house was silent.

Pushing down the blanket, she sat up slowly, noticing she wasn't even dizzy. Good.

She looked down. She was wearing a different top, but the same bra and panties. Her jeans and socks had been removed. Swinging around, she touched her feet to the ground and stood.

Immediately, she realized her mistake. She may not have felt dizzy, but she was weak.

Her knees buckled and her butt hit the ground with a thud. *Crap.*

She was grumbling beneath her breath when Blake was suddenly by her side, appearing from seemingly nowhere.

He bent to his haunches, cursing softly. "Are you okay?"

She looked up, and her words stalled. The man was shirtless. He'd been muscular before Project Arma, but now he was even bigger. Muscles covered every inch of his body.

"Yes." Man, her voice was raspy. Like she hadn't talked for days. "I'm okay. I was just going to the bathroom."

A growl rocked his chest. Then he was lifting her, his perfectly smooth and muscled chest sliding against her side. "You should have called for me."

Well, if she'd known he was there...

Actually, no, that was a lie. She probably still would have toughed it out on her own. "Where's Mila?"

"She's spending the day with Courtney and Jason. They're going to drop her off before dinner."

She frowned as Blake lowered her to her feet. His hands stuck to her waist like glue. Clearly, he didn't trust her legs, which was fair. *She* barely trusted her legs. "What's the time?"

"About four in the afternoon."

Wow, almost twenty-four hours. The migraine had really wiped her out.

One of his hands lifted, gently stroking the side of her face. She almost leaned into it, craving his touch like a starved woman.

"You should have rested more."

She knew he wasn't talking about now. Blake was referring to yesterday when she'd woken with a headache and then pushed herself all day. He was right. She'd ignored the signs her body had thrown her way, which was a dangerous thing to do. "I know."

For a beat, there was silence, his eyes boring into her own. Then his voice lowered. "Talk to me next time. Trust me to help you, Willow."

She gave a small nod, not confident in her voice. She shot a look to the toilet, then back at him. "I, uh, need to go."

His fingers hovered near her waist, like he expected her to tumble to the ground. When she remained steady, he slowly left the room, pulling the door closed after him.

She took a step toward the toilet, legs almost caving again before she righted herself. Yeah, Blake had every reason to be concerned.

She used the toilet quickly before washing her hands and brushing her teeth. When she finally looked up—something she'd been trying to avoid because she knew she'd look a mess—a small shriek escaped her lips.

So much worse than she'd thought.

Again, Blake was by her side in an instant. "What is it? Is it your head again?"

In a way... "Blake, I look like roadkill!"

Literally. Her hair was everywhere, and her face was pasty white. It looked like someone had hit her with their car and she'd tumbled down a weed hill.

His eyes softened, a spark of amusement lighting them. "You look beautiful."

No. She really didn't. She shot a pointed look toward the door. "You need to go and I need to shower."

"If you think I'm leaving you alone in a shower after waking from a migraine, you're delusional, honey. You just fell out of bed."

She gritted her teeth. He was right, but she needed to wash. She could already feel the dried sweat on her skin, and it made her want to scrub her skin clean. "Fine. I'll have a bath."

One of his brows rose—and she already knew what was coming next. "You think I'm gonna let you drown yourself instead?"

She rolled her eyes. "I won't drown."

"Willow, I distinctly remember you sitting on the couch after a twenty-four-hour migraine. I turned my back for a second, *one second*, and you immediately toppled straight off, hitting your head on the coffee table." His finger grazed the small scar on her forehead from that incident.

In her defense, though, she'd thought she was fine. The wave of dizziness had come out of nowhere. Next thing she knew, blood was pouring from her skull, and Blake was going nuts.

Right on cue, her legs began to tire, and she shifted to the edge of the tub, perching herself there. Willow sighed. "Blake, I need to bathe. I feel disgusting."

"Okay. I'll sit on the edge to make sure you're okay."

Ah…that was a big fat no. "I am not getting in that tub naked while you sit to the side, fully clothed." *Absolutely not.*

Blake seemed to consider her words for a moment before nodding. "That's fair enough."

Reaching over, he turned on the tap. She started to relax.

Then his hands went to the buckle of his jeans.

She gave a little squeak, covering her eyes moments before the sound of his zipper lowering filled the air. "Blake!"

His deep chuckle settled into her bones, heating her blood. "Honey, you've seen it all before."

She knew that. There was a time in her life when she felt more familiar with his body than her own. But that was years ago.

The sound of material sliding to the floor had her belly sizzling. Then his lips were by her ear, his whispered words humming through her chest. "My briefs are staying on. But you're welcome to go either way."

Then came the sound of water sloshing in the tub, of Blake lowering himself.

"Blake…"

"Willow, it's just a bath. We've had hundreds of them together before."

When she finally uncovered her eyes, it was to see him sitting in the tub, briefs still on as he'd promised, legs apart.

She swallowed. He was right. How many times had they bathed just like that? Her sitting between his legs, his heat surrounding her…

The very memories were etched into her brain, never to be forgotten.

She shot a glance to the door, considering walking right on out. But her skin really did feel dirty, even a bit sticky, and God, did the clean, warm water call to her.

Sucking in a quick breath of courage, she quickly tugged her top over her head before climbing into the tub. Blake's large hands went to her hips, helping and guiding her. She braved a look back, almost gasping at the way his pupils dilated. At the way his features darkened with a ferocity that nearly stole her breath.

She dragged her eyes away, and the warm water lapped around her torso. But it wasn't just the water that had her body heating. It was the feel of his long, muscled thighs that bracketed her own.

"Relax." His warm breath danced across her cheek, fluttering all the way down to her belly.

One by one, she made an effort to relax her muscles. Then, almost on its own, her body leaned back into his hard stomach and chest. Just like before, she fit against him perfectly. Like they were designed to fit together, two pieces of a puzzle.

Willow cleared her throat, trying to distract her body from its treacherous desire. "I was impressed Mila knew how to call you."

"We've been practicing." His voice caused a light vibration across her back. She felt Blake reach for something behind them. A second later, his hands ran up and down her arms in slow strokes, scented body wash slicking over her skin. "I ask her to recite my number before bed. It's a little game of ours. When she makes a mistake, I tickle her. I swear she does it on purpose sometimes."

Smart. So damn smart. Willow had taught her daughter how to call nine-one-one. But she hadn't thought about teaching her how to call anyone else. "Thank you, Blake. For keeping our daughter safe."

His hands momentarily paused. "I told you, you don't need to thank me when it comes to Mila. We're a team."

Team. The word floated through her head and into her heart. A heart that had been alone in the parenting game for so long.

Slowly, his hands shifted to her ribs and stomach. Her breath caught, skin tingling. His hands didn't move straight away. They paused. Hesitating. Waiting for her to stop him.

She bit her lip. She should tell him no. She could rub the soap on her own body. But the feel of his hands on her stomach, the promise of them gliding across her skin...she was too weak to pull away.

Slowly, his hands started to glide over her deprived skin in slow circles.

Sucking in a quick breath, she closed her eyes. Biting her bottom lip to stop a moan from purring out of her chest.

His lips brushed her ear. "Bend your left knee for me, honey."

His words barely made sense in her muddled head. But eventually, she did as he asked. His large hands wrapped around her thigh, gliding up and down as they washed her.

Her breasts felt heavy. Skin over-sensitized. She didn't know how long his hands slid over her thigh, but each time they traveled upward, a thunderous need built inside her.

His mouth went to her ear again. "Other leg."

She lowered the first, almost whimpering when his hands dropped. The second the other knee was up, his hands circled her, gliding up and down.

Her core throbbed with need. Her breaths shortened with every stroke.

Blake would know what he was doing to her. There was no way he couldn't. He could hear her every heartbeat now. But she couldn't be angry. After all, she'd known that stepping into the tub was dangerous. That *Blake* was dangerous. The second she'd taken off her top, she'd consented to this. And she'd done it because she was starved for the man who still set her blood soaring.

"Blake…" His name was almost a whimper from her lips.

His head pushed hers to the side, lips pressing to her neck as his hands traveled up. "Do you want me to stop?"

He knew she didn't. But he wanted the word.

"No." A whisper. A desperate plea.

His hands slid to her back, slipping between their bodies and releasing her bra. Her breasts sprang free. She heard the light thud of material hitting the tiles outside of the tub, but she barely noticed.

He reached for more soap, then his hands returned to her ribs, rising slowly before covering her breasts. Her next breath hissed between her lips when his thumbs grazed over her hard nipples. Once. Twice.

On the third graze, she groaned deep in her chest.

"You're so beautiful." His lips nibbled her neck, his thumbs torturing her peaks. "Two years without you was agony. I craved you every day. Dreamed about the day I would see you again. Touch you."

"Me too." All of it. Every word he said, she felt. "Every day."

The days had been long and torturous. Not knowing where he was. Whether he was dead or alive.

As the pads of his thumbs continued to graze back and forth, her limbs began to tremble in his hold. "What do you need, baby?" His voice was still smooth.

She tried to speak, but her words stuck in her throat.

Instead, she reached up, grabbing one of his hands and guiding it down to the thin material that covered her core. She pressed it underneath.

His big hand covered her completely.

The first soft swipe of his finger against her clit had her body jolting, her flesh heating. Then he did it again. And again.

His mouth was still nibbling her neck, his thumb still grazing and flicking her nipple.

She was on fire. Every inch of her. Breaths heaving in and out of her chest. Toes curled. He whispered soft words against her neck. Words that barely made sense in her feverish brain. "Beautiful" and "never enough" pierced her mind.

The pressure built. She was close. So close, her muscles bunched and pleasure throbbed low in her belly.

The hand at her nipple lifted and pressed her chin until her head turned. Then he was kissing her. Devouring her lips like he was consumed by her. His tongue worked hers as his fingers circled and grazed her clit. It was too much.

A finger went to her entrance, thumb taking over to strum her clit. Then, slowly, he pressed inside of her.

He swallowed her sharp intake of breath as her hands latched onto his thighs. He slid his finger out before pushing back inside her again. Every penetration pushed her closer to the edge, right until her world exploded, white-hot waves crashing behind her eyes. She vibrated and trembled in his arms, and all the while, Blake continued to work her right until she collapsed against him.

His finger slowly slipped out of her body, hands going back to her arms as another kiss pressed to her neck. Her breaths were loud in the quiet room.

When she felt his hardness against her back, she reached for him, but he was quick to halt her. "No, baby. That was just for you."

She turned her head, looking at him. Her heart rolled and thudded in her chest.

Love. It was there in his gaze, and it was intense.

Suddenly, she questioned everything. Her fear. Her hesitation. She'd missed him for two whole years. Was it better to protect herself by pushing him away so they didn't fall into a shadow of a relationship again? Or should she take a chance? Risk her heart and soul for a man who made her feel alive?

# CHAPTER 13

*W*illow leaned forward, warming her hands on the fire. The orange and yellow flames colored the dark night sky.

They sat in Jason's backyard. Not that Jason was here. The second he'd started the fire, Courtney had banished him inside the house.

Reaching down, Willow lifted her cocktail and took a sip, almost cringing at the sweetness. She shouldn't drink too much more. Hell, she probably shouldn't drink any. Sugary drinks had always upset her stomach.

"My God, woman, you make a good cocktail," Courtney said a bit too loudly to Grace. How many had Courtney had? Three? Four?

Grace chuckled. "Well, there was once a time when I did it each and every night."

Willow lifted the glass to her lips again, heat coiling her belly. It was probably a normal level of sweetness, actually; she was just sensitive. Or maybe it had just been too long since she'd had a drink. "You worked in a bar, Grace?"

There was a subtle change in her features. It only lasted a

second and almost had Willow wondering if she'd actually seen it. "I did."

Willow didn't miss the way Grace's fingers pressed a bit harder against the glass she'd been cradling all night.

"Well, I, for one, am glad you became a therapist. You're a magic worker." Courtney turned to Willow. "A month ago, I couldn't step inside an elevator without turning into a mess. I was terrified...of an *elevator*! Grace healed me with her therapist superpowers."

Grace shook her head. "No, *you* healed you. You sought help, and you did the work."

"It's true," Willow said, taking another small sip. The drink became less sweet with each one. "You only get better if you want to get better. I would know. I lived through postpartum depression for almost two years. It took Blake disappearing for me to finally recognize something was wrong and ask for help."

She hadn't been planning to tell the women that, but it also wasn't a secret. Not enough people spoke about the illness. They should. Maybe if it was more widely discussed, she would have known what was going on sooner.

Grace's eyes softened. "That must have been so hard."

She nodded. "I didn't even know it was PPD until I saw a therapist. I just thought being a mom was supposed to be hard. That losing yourself was part and parcel of motherhood." She swung her glass in a little circle, watching the liquid swirl around. "But it was more than that. I was going through the motions while never actually feeling...okay. And the anxiety..." She shook her head. "It was bad."

"Was Blake there for you?" Courtney asked quietly.

"He was away a lot for work." The flames flickered behind her drink. "I remember being so angry with him. Like I needed him to do better. To be a better support for me in this new role I'd found myself in. Looking back, I feel like that was selfish of me. He'd worked so hard to become a SEAL."

"Maybe you were just trying to survive," Courtney said.

"That's exactly what it was. I spent a lot of time trying to hide the depths of my struggle. I felt like I should be doing okay. Everyone else I'd known who had a baby seemed to be okay."

That had been her mindset at the time. But she'd started to wonder how many others put on the smile in public? Made the world think they were okay when really, they were drowning?

"Did you ever ask him for more help?" Grace asked.

Willow sucked in a sharp breath at the memory of *that* night. The only night she'd spoken up about it to Blake. How many times had she let that conversation haunt her?

"The night that he left for his final mission…the one he didn't return from…I finally admitted to him that I was really struggling. It was the first time I'd ever vocalized those words, or even really admitted them to myself. Deep down, I think we both knew, but neither of us wanted to face it. Like if we said it out loud, it would make it real. That night, I told him I needed more from him. I needed him to be more present."

A tremor cascaded down her spine at the memory. She hated thinking about that night. Hated that those were her final words to him before he'd been taken. Kidnapped from his hotel room just before he was supposed to be sent out on a mission.

Courtney frowned. "What did he say?"

"Nothing." She continued swirling the drink, still watching it without actually seeing. "For a moment, he looked like he was going to say something, but then he just…didn't. He lifted his bag, kissed me on the forehead, and walked out the door. And I just stood there feeling…empty."

Empty was the only way she could explain it. Because admitting those words out loud to Blake, after two years of silently battling the illness she didn't even know she had, had been huge. And for a moment, she'd thought he would somehow help her. Save her.

When he left, she hadn't known what to do.

Courtney's gasp was loud, whereas Grace was silent in her sympathy.

Willow wet her lips. "He's been amazing since coming back. And I know he wants us to give the relationship another go. I tell him that I don't want to because of Mila. And that I'm scared he'll disappear again. But really, I think I'm just scared that we'll end up where we were before. Not me falling into a depression again. But me needing more than he can give."

There was a moment of silence. It was heavy. Then Grace nodded. "That fear is very valid."

"Do you still love him?" Courtney asked quietly.

"So much that my heart hurts." It was a pain she feared would cripple her some days.

The other women gave each other knowing looks.

Willow almost laughed. "You guys think I should give us another try."

"I think that fear can be our greatest protector," Grace said. "But it can also rob us of a lot of beautiful things that could be."

Courtney shrugged. "So yeah, we think Blake can do better now, and you should totally do the guy."

This time, Willow *did* laugh.

"But if he ever walks away from your pain or your cry for help again, you call us in," she continued. "And we'll call Jason and Logan in."

They all laughed again.

Maybe they were right. Maybe she'd spent too long trying to protect herself since his return, and in doing so, she'd cheated herself of happiness.

Screw it. Willow took a big gulp of her cocktail before lifting her phone.

"AND AS THE plane left the station, the smooth takeoff made her eyes feel heavy. She drifted off to sleep." Blake closed the book.

Mila's little hands tugged his wrist. "Again, Daddy!"

"We've read it twice, baby girl. Aren't you tired?"

"No." The second the word left her lips, her mouth stretched into a yawn. At least she was a cute little liar. "I like this book. Mama read it to me on the plane when we flew to Lockhart. It was the first time she didn't look so sad."

Blake tried not to tense up. "Sad?"

Mila's eyes started to shutter. "She had sad eyes for a long time. Sometimes her mouth would be sad too."

He stroked his daughter's hair, her words tugging at his heart.

"Mama talked about our new house on the plane. She said it was a new start. She wasn't so sad in the new house."

His jaw clenched. Before Blake had been taken, the three of them lived near his base in Virginia Beach, Virginia. He'd returned to find Willow and Mila in Lockhart, Texas. He'd always wondered about the move, knowing it hadn't been for work or study.

"I don't think Mama knows that I saw how sad she was. I think she tried to hide it." Yet again, Blake was reminded of how damn smart and perceptive the kid was. She saw so much more than she should at her young age. "Do you think she'll ever get sad like that again?"

Not if he could help it. "No, baby. I don't. But if she does, I'll be here to take care of everyone." Both physically and emotionally. It was a silent promise he never planned to break.

Mila snuggled further into the pillow. "I love you, Daddy."

Every protective instinct hummed to life. He stroked his daughter's hair. "I love you too." He pressed a kiss to her forehead, but he didn't stand. Not yet. He sat there for a long while, just watching the peace wash over her face. Listening to the soft breaths moving in and out of her chest. The light thuds of her heart.

He traced every inch of her face with his eyes, casting every little line and ridge to memory. His gaze paused on the small scar on her chin, and his stomach cramped at the knowledge that he had no idea where it came from. He didn't have that story. That memory.

When he finally rose, he moved to the door slowly, pulling it almost closed before switching off the light.

He'd just stepped into the hall when a text came through.

*Willow: Did you get Mila down okay?*

He smiled. But then, he always did that when her name popped up. He headed to the kitchen and pulled out a glass before filling it with water. Then he responded.

*Blake: After a hundred and one books, little miss is deep asleep.*

Three dots popped up to show that she was typing before they quickly disappeared. He frowned. *What were you about to write, Willow?*

She was having drinks with Courtney and Grace at Jason's place. He had no idea if "drinks" meant just a couple, or more than that. He didn't care either way. The woman deserved a night off. Hell, she deserved many nights off. So if she wanted to have a few cocktails, he hoped she did exactly that.

He was just sipping the water when the next message came through.

*Willow: Do you ever wonder what would have happened with us if you hadn't been taken?*

One big thump of his heart in his chest. *Yes.* His glass hit the bench so he could respond.

*Blake: Every damn day.*

Would he have smartened up and been the man she needed him to be? Would he have thought about her words during that last mission and realized they were a cry for help?

Those questions plagued him. Haunted him.

When she didn't respond, he sent the next text.

*Blake: One thing I know for certain, my love for you would have been just as strong as it is now, regardless of whether we'd been together or not.*

Even if he hadn't smartened up. Even if she'd walked out on him, his love for her would have been guaranteed. It always had been.

The one constant in his life.

There was so much more he could say. That he was sorry. That he'd *never* stop loving her. That if he could live that time again, there was so much he'd do differently.

*Willow: I'm sorry I made you feel guilty for doing your job. I was just trying to keep my head above water.*

Her words were like a physical blow to his gut. *Trying to keep my head above water.* She'd been drowning, and he'd been oblivious.

*Blake: Come over tonight, honey.*

He wanted to see the woman. Touch her. Hold her. They'd lost so much time. Too much. He'd been back for almost a year, and he'd tried to show her in every way possible that he could do better than he had in the past.

He was done waiting. It was time they learned to trust the new versions of themselves.

# CHAPTER 14

Willow took a deep breath as Logan pulled up outside Blake's home. She hadn't responded to his last text. Mostly because she hadn't been entirely sure what she was going to do. Not until Grace has asked her where she wanted to be dropped off...as if she'd known.

Grace and Logan started unbuckling their seat belts, but Willow was already halfway out of the car. "It's okay, you don't need to come in."

Grace looked back. "Are you sure?"

"Yes."

She needed the short walk to the front door to work out what she was going to say. To get her jumbled thoughts into some kind of order. "Thank you for the ride."

Closing the door, she headed up the path. An intoxicating mix of fear and longing and excitement rushed through her like wildfire.

The walk was entirely too short, because when she reached the door, she still had no idea what she was going to say. Heck, she had no idea what she was doing at all. She'd come here based on...what? A desperate yearning? A plea from her heart?

Taking a breath, she lifted her hand to knock, but before her fist touched the wood, it opened. And there he was, all six feet four of him. Looking tall and fierce and so achingly hers.

His gaze bore into her own, tangling with her soul.

She was vaguely aware of the sound of an engine as Logan and Grace drove away. She barely noticed it. In her mind, it was just her and him. He'd always had a way of driving away everything else.

For a second, she didn't move.

This was one of those moments. The ones that defined your direction. That could change everything with a single word. A single touch.

That wasn't to say that this moment hadn't been inevitable since the day he'd returned. Because it had. He'd stamped himself onto her heart a long time ago. A stamp that could never be erased.

"Willow."

His voice...so familiar that her heart physically hurt. Longing stole her breath.

She was done fighting it.

Stepping forward, Willow flung her arms around his neck and kissed him.

Strong arms swept around her waist, lifting her against his body. The door closed, the lock clicking. Then her back was pressed against the wood.

When the man touched her, kissed her, it was like the missing parts of her soul returned.

The unwavering invasion of Blake's tongue in her mouth had her groaning deep in her throat. She kissed him like she was desperate. Like she didn't dare stop in case her lips never found their way back to him.

Her eyes never cracked open. Not as the air moved around her, not as his hand roamed her body.

When the air stilled, his hand moved to her clothes, and

together they worked to remove her jacket, her top, her bra. Each piece of clothing hit the carpet with quiet thuds, including his shirt.

When her bare breasts pressed to his chest, his low, guttural growl splintered the quiet. Then his head dipped, his lips wrapping around her pebbled nipple, sipping, sucking.

For a moment, her body stilled, fire burning through her veins, desire and yearning stealing her breath. She bit her bottom lip hard to keep from shouting. To stop a feverish cry from tearing through the house.

With his free hand, Blake found her other nipple. His fingers closed around it, plucking.

Her back arched, pressure building in her lower abdomen. Her breaths were now whooshing in and out of her chest hard and fast.

"God, I've missed these." His words were rasped against her nipple, the brush of his breath causing a tremor to run down her spine.

Her back hit the mattress. Blake hovered over her, his hand and mouth returning to her breasts, playing. Torturing.

Willow writhed and groaned, her body unable to remain still.

After endless minutes, he shifted up, mouth returning to hers.

With desperate fingers, she reached between them, unclasping his jeans before reaching inside his briefs. He went completely still above her, muscles tensing and expanding. Then her fingers closed around his length.

She'd almost forgotten how thick he was. How long.

Blake's head dipped, the veins in his neck bulging like he was in physical pain.

She moved her hand gently. Touching and stroking, re-familiarizing herself with him. Slowly, her movements became surer, fingers tightening, hand shifting from the base of his length, all the way up, rolling her thumb over his tip.

Molten lava pooled in her belly as Blake's shortened breaths rippled over her face. She'd always loved touching him. Bringing such a big, powerful man to his knees.

She'd barely begun exploring when suddenly, his hand came around her wrist, pulling her hand away. There was a feverish, wild look in his eyes.

"You need to stop."

She wanted to object. To tug her hand away and return to him. But then his head lowered, nipping at her neck, her breast. He grazed every inch of her body with his mouth until he reached the buckle of her jeans. A second later, the last remnants of material that covered her were pushed down her legs, leaving her bare and exposed.

She sucked in a quick breath when his mouth hovered over the apex between her legs. His arms encircled her thighs, widening her. Cool air brushed against her clit, causing a tremor to rock her spine.

Her breath stopped in her chest, anticipation tingling over her skin.

Then his head dipped, his mouth locking around her clit and suckling.

White-hot desire ripped through her like a flame fueled by alcohol. The air thickened until she could barely breathe. Or maybe that was her chest seizing.

The power of what he did to her was so intense, it had her legs attempting to snap together, her back arching off the bed. Blake kept her still, holding her in place.

His tongue swiped and swirled around her clit, pushing her higher.

Oh, Lord. She remembered this. The endless nights of torture. The way he knew exactly what to do to push her right to the edge of that cliff.

Her inner walls began to tighten, her muscles tensing.

"Blake..." Her voice almost sounded foreign to her. It was too raw. Too desperate.

One more swirl, and then his head lifted. Slowly, he shifted back up her body until he hovered over her again. He didn't kiss her; instead, his intense gray eyes watched her, claimed her, held her captive. Watched her so closely that she felt stripped of every shield she'd ever put up.

"If we do this…that's it. You're mine again, Willow." He grazed the side of her face with his fingers, his stormy eyes never losing her. "I can't get you back, only to lose you a second time."

Her breathing went shallow, small bumps exploding over her skin. "I've always been yours, Blake."

And he'd always been hers. Two souls meant to find each other. Never to forget.

Something primal flashed over his features. His lips took hers again, hard and unyielding. When he started to pull away, her fingers tightened on his arms.

"I need to get—"

"I'm on the pill."

Had been since Mila. And she'd never been more grateful than at this very moment. She wanted to feel him inside her. All of him. Without any barriers. They'd had barriers for long enough.

His eyes darkened. He leaned to the side, tugging off his jeans and briefs. Then he returned to her, nestling between her thighs, his hardness right there at her entrance.

For a moment, it was all she could do to keep her breaths moving. How long had it been since she'd felt him inside her? Since she'd felt like he was a *part* of her?

So long that her entire body ached with need.

His hand went to her cheek again, his gaze holding her captive. Then, slowly, he pressed inside. The delicious stretch of her walls around him had her lungs seizing.

When he was completely inside her, they were chest to chest.

This was it. The place where she was most at peace. Where she'd always been most at peace.

"I thought about you every day," he whispered. "From the

moment we met, it's always been you."

Her heart kicked, another part of her soul realigning with his, reminding her who it belonged to. "It's the same for me. All of it."

BLAKE'S MUSCLES were so damn tense he thought they'd snap. It took every scrap of self-restraint he possessed to keep himself where he was.

Being inside her again, inside the woman who had built a home within his heart so many years ago and lived there ever since, was both heaven and hell.

Slowly, he raised his hips, then drove back in. Willow's brows tugged together, her eyes shuttering, head tipping back.

*Mine.*

He did it again. This time, Willow's fingers dug into his arms.

Fuck, but she was beautiful. Beautiful and sexy and all he'd ever wanted or needed.

He thrust again and again, knowing that for as long as he lived, he would never tire of this woman.

"Faster." Her word was a quiet whisper, only just touching his ears.

His breath hitched, his thrusts picking up pace. She was hot and tight around him, encasing him so firmly it bordered on pain. Her hard nipples pressed into his chest, her soft whimpers the same sounds that had haunted his dreams while he'd been away from her. Sounds that his heart had memorized, clung to, craving to hear again.

His hips moved faster still, her nails clawing down his shoulders, over his chest.

"Blake…"

Fuck, but his name on her lips drove him crazy. No one else had ever said it like that. She was his one and only. She owned every part of him.

Another thread of restraint snapped. He thrust harder. Faster. The crease between her brows deepened as the moans from her chest grew louder, drifting through the quiet.

Goddammit, he was close, only holding on by a single thread.

He dipped his head to her neck, nibbling and sucking on her heated, salty skin.

Her feet pressed into his backside, urging him deeper.

Sliding a hand between their bodies, he touched her clit, feeling the intense jolt course through her limbs. He swiped his thumb. Once. Twice. Then he moved in a hard circular motion, knowing what it would do.

Suddenly, her back bowed, lips separating. He claimed those lips, swallowing the cry that broke from her chest. He kept pumping, but at the feel of her inner walls pulsing around him, his body tensed and rippled, a deep growl releasing from his throat as the world exploded.

His breaths were deep as he slowed, then eventually stilled. Silence descended on the room, her heavy breaths the only things breaking the quiet.

When he finally lifted his head, his heart squeezed, because for the first time in a long time, she looked at him without hesitation. Without uncertainty or restraint. And in her eyes, he saw everything he'd been waiting for. Love. Desire. A peace so honest he could almost believe the last few years hadn't come to pass.

Finally, he said the words that had been silenced, tangled in his heart and soul for too long. "I love you, Willow."

The emotion in her eyes deepened, covered by the slightest sheen of wetness. "I love you, too, Blake. I don't know how *not* to love you."

His breath trembled from his chest. This was what he'd been waiting for. For his heart to feel whole again. The wrongs in the world to right.

Leaning down, he pressed his lips to hers, peace rolling over them both.

# CHAPTER 15

*B*lake stroked Willow's back. She lay half on top of him, her head resting on his chest. The sun was only just poking through the blinds, but he'd been up for a while. Listening to the steady beat of her heart. Feeling the soft rise and fall of her chest.

How long had he craved to wake up like this, tortured by the possibility that it might never happen again?

Every day for nearly three long years.

She was his. She'd said the words herself.

*I've always been yours, Blake.*

He'd known it. But hearing the words out loud, having her give herself to him so freely, hit differently.

He hadn't been good enough to her last time. Yes, his work had demanded a lot of him. Yes, he'd had little control over his own time. But he'd had three years to reflect on the fact that he hadn't even tried to get time off. And even when he had been there, he wasn't always available for her emotionally. Not at the end.

There was a light shift in Willow's breathing. A small grazing of her fingers on his chest.

His stroking of her back stilled, and his chest tightened.

The only time he ever let fear touch him was when it came to his family. And right now, he could feel it creeping up his spine, tingling over his skin. Fear that she'd wake, and the new day would shatter the promises of last night.

He knew the exact moment she realized he lay beneath her. There was a tightening of her muscles. Her breaths stopped brushing against his chest. When she raised her head, a myriad of emotions washed through her expressive eyes, and he caught every one of them.

Uncertainty. Recollection. Surprise. And then...contentment?

"Morning." She almost sounded shy.

His lips stretched into a wide smile. "Morning, honey."

Her cheeks tinged pink, and she dipped her head back to his chest, resting her cheek against him once again.

Hiding?

She swallowed loudly. "Is Mila—"

"Asleep? Yeah, I'll let you know if I hear her get up."

Her body melted against him. She started drawing small circles on his abdomen. His stomach muscles tried to tense, but he forced them to relax.

She used to do that often. During their lazy mornings lying in bed, her fingers would roam across his stomach. Explore his skin with soft grazes. And just like every other time, it had his skin burning.

"How are you feeling?" he asked gruffly.

"Good."

Even though she couldn't see him, he lifted a brow. "Just good?"

Her soft chuckle filtered through the room. "Okay, better than good."

At the small sound of a phone vibrating, she turned away from him, climbing to her feet and grabbing her purse from the floor. She took something from inside, popping it into her mouth.

"The pill," she said as she slid back into bed, resting her head against his shoulder.

He remembered her going on the pill shortly after Mila was born. She hadn't been on it before getting pregnant, and they hadn't been too careful, either. Often, they'd been too desperate for each other to wait.

That's why Mila had been a shock, but at the same time, she hadn't.

A part of him was surprised Willow had been taking the pill while he was gone. But then another part of him wasn't. Not after what had happened to her hormones after giving birth. It probably just added that extra feeling of security.

Her hand returned to his stomach, drawing more circles. "Will you tell me what it was like in the Project Arma compound?"

His jaw ticked, a huge part of him rebelling against the request. He didn't like to think about his time there away from his family, much less talk about it.

He shifted his hand, fingers spanning her hip. "We weren't beaten or abused. They used threats against our loved ones to keep us in line." He swallowed the bile that rose in his throat at the memory of the threats against Willow and Mila. "We were fed well. The house was huge and the property sat on extensive land. If it wasn't for the electrical fencing keeping us in, I'm sure most people could forget they were hostages."

"But you didn't." It wasn't a question.

"To me, it was a hell worse than any prison. Because I didn't get to see you or Mila for over two years. I didn't get to hear your voices. I was told you were both safe, but all I had was their word. And even if you were safe from them, I didn't know if you were okay."

He felt the slight tensing of her muscles. "I sought help the second you were declared missing," she said quietly. "I wanted to lock myself away in a dark room, roll into a ball and let the depression swallow me whole. But I knew I couldn't. I knew that Mila needed me more than ever."

God, the woman was strong. But then, she'd had to be.

"You did good, baby. I will forever be grateful that you were able to give our daughter the love and support she needed when I couldn't."

Her fingers were now tracing the ridges of muscle on his stomach, leaving a trail of awareness in their wake. "I missed you."

His chest burned at her words. Mila had said the same ones last night. "You have no idea. I missed so much about you, Willow."

"Really? Hm, what did you miss? The way I'd scold you for leaving your dirty cups on the coffee table?"

She was joking, but he didn't laugh. "I missed the way your eyes pinch in the corners when you smile. The way we used to stay up all night whispering to each other about anything and everything. And yeah, I even missed the way you used to get on my ass for leaving my shit everywhere."

She laughed. And his heart clenched. Again, he couldn't even crack a smile.

"And your laugh…Christ, I missed it so much. I heard it in my sleep every goddamn night. It both kept me sane and drove me crazy."

Her hand paused, her breathing pattern shifting.

"I know there wasn't much laughter in those last couple years," he continued. "But I swear I will work to make you laugh and smile every day for the rest of our lives."

She sat up a bit, palms pressed to his chest. "Please don't apologize. I think I was so deep in the thick of…everything, that I didn't see what I should have."

He frowned. "What's that?"

"That you were struggling, too. You were struggling with the demands of work and home. Struggling with the new role you were thrust into." She inhaled deeply. "You may not have been clinically depressed, but no one can prepare you for parenthood. And having no support made it so much harder for us."

He stroked the side of her face. "I still should have been stronger for you. I *will* be stronger in the future." He'd hold the entire goddamn house on his shoulders if she needed him to. "And I hate that you had no one else."

Both of them had absentee parents who never gave a shit. She was an only child. He had a brother who he'd never been close to. A brother who'd left home at eighteen without a backward glance.

Her eyes darted between his, her voice lowering. "I'm sorry it took me so long to get here. I kept telling myself that it was easier for us to remain apart. That we were just a moment in time."

His gut clenched.

"I thought that if I let you back in, I was leaving myself vulnerable for us to fail. And for that to destroy a huge part of me again."

His hand tightened on her cheek. "We're so much more than a moment." They were a collection of every moment rolled together. A continuation of forever. "And we won't be failing."

"I know." She opened her mouth to say something else, but suddenly the color left her face.

Blake frowned. Was it a headache? A migraine? She hadn't been in pain a moment ago. "What's wrong?"

Suddenly, she was on her feet, running to the connected bathroom.

Blake threw the sheet off and trailed closely behind her, cursing under his breath when Willow dropped to her knees, throwing up in the toilet.

He lowered to his haunches behind her, lifting her hair off her back to keep it out of the way.

When she was done, she leaned back, eyes shuttering closed.

Blake rose to grab a wet cloth before quickly dropping down again. "The alcohol?"

The woman had always been sensitive to the stuff, especially sweet drinks. He still remembered when they'd gone to a bar together for the first time. A few short hours later, she'd been sick.

She nodded. "I knew I shouldn't have drunk whatever it was Grace made. It tasted like a cup of sugar."

He pushed some hair off her cheek. "Are you okay?"

"Yes. Thank you."

A second later, something sounded from down the hall. Mila was awake.

~

"E."

Willow held Mila's small hand tightly as they walked down the street. They were playing a game of Name, Place, Animal, and Thing—Mila's favorite—while walking from school to The Grind. It would have been a lot faster to drive, but after spending an entire day at her computer, Willow craved the fresh air and exercise.

Mila's brows tugged together. "E...Elsa." Willow almost laughed. Should have seen that one coming. "England. Elephant and...egg."

"Good job, baby."

Mila beamed. "Your turn. I choose...B."

"Hm. Blake." Mila giggled. "Barcelona, bear, and blackberry."

"Those were good ones, Mama."

Ah, she could always count on her daughter for a little ego boost.

"Are we gonna move in with Daddy now?"

Mila's sudden random question had Willow's eyes widening. "Ah, not at the moment."

Willow barely had time to throw on a T-shirt before Mila had run into the room earlier that morning. The kid hadn't stopped talking about the fact that Mom had slept at Daddy's house, in Daddy's *room*.

Usually, if anyone slept anywhere, it was Blake at Willow's place, on the couch with a pillow and blanket.

Mila had gone on about it all morning, right up until school drop-off.

"Will you sleep at Daddy's again?"

Hadn't she answered that question? "I'm not sure."

To be honest, she had no idea about anything. All she knew was that she'd decided to stop resisting him. And it felt good. So good.

Everything about last night, everything about waking up with him this morning, just felt so right. It made her wonder why her stubborn ass had resisted the guy for so long.

"I think we should all live in the same house," Mila said firmly.

A small smile touched Willow's lips. Because she liked that idea too. "We'll see what happens, Mila. How was school today?"

She needed a change of subject because otherwise she was just going to get a hundred more questions that she had no answers to.

"It was great! We're learning the letter 'C' this week. Mrs. McCauliff went around the class checking how everyone was holding their pencil as we wrote our letter, and she said my hold was perfect."

Willow chuckled. "Good job."

"I even helped Samuel with his pencil. And we practiced counting with colored counters and we went outside and played a game where we had to get into teams and steal bags from other teams' corners. My team didn't win but we were close."

"There'll always been more games to win."

"That's what Mrs. McCauliff said." Then her little brows furrowed the way they always did when she was thinking really hard.

*Oh, boy, please don't let whatever she says next be about Blake.*

"Before we went back in, I saw a man on the other side of the road. He was just standing by his car watching us."

Willow stopped. Only for a second, then she quickly continued walking again. She was careful to keep her features neutral even though her insides jerked at Mila's words. "Did you tell Mrs. McCauliff?"

"No. Because we went inside and Samuel asked if we could share our popcorn at lunch, so I forgot."

Yet the guy's presence had affected Mila enough to mention it now. "What did he look like?"

"Hm...he had brown hair and was smaller than Daddy. He was across the street, so I couldn't see him too good."

She nodded, making a mental note to pass the information on to Blake. It was probably nothing. A guy standing outside an elementary school would probably be a parent waiting for their kid. Still, she didn't like that Mila was uncomfortable enough to feel the need to tell her.

They'd almost made it to The Grind when a man stepped around the corner from a side street, almost running straight into them. It took Willow a second to recognize him.

"Rob! What are you doing in town?"

The second the question left her lips, she felt silly. Her entire study group lived in Ketchum, for Christ's sake, a town that was literally a few minutes' drive away. They probably came here all the time.

"Just grabbing a meal with some friends." He smiled down at Mila. "Hey there! My name's Rob."

Mila straightened. "I'm Mila. How do you know Mama?"

He chuckled softly. "We're both studying to become teachers, so sometimes we study together. I was at your house the other night when you woke up, but you didn't see me. I was in the living room."

Mila nodded, seeming way too old for her age. "Do you bring snacks too?"

Willow muffled her laugh. Janet had left some snacks specifically for Mila. The Red Vines in particular were a winner.

"Nah, Janet's the snack queen. But I can bring some next session and ask your mom to pass them on if you like?"

Mila's eyes widened. "Yes, please!"

Even though sugar wasn't necessarily something Willow wanted her daughter to have on a regular basis—because really, who needed a hyped-up five-year-old—she gave Rob an appreciative smile.

"Did you want to pop in and have a drink with us?" Willow offered, nodding toward The Grind. "They do really good coffee."

"And milkshakes," Mila added quickly.

Before Rob could respond, the door to The Grind opened, and Blake stepped out. His gaze immediately zeroed in on Rob, studying the guy.

Rob turned his head, his jaw tensing.

*Oh, Lord.*

Blake stepped up beside her. "Hey, everyone."

Rob's eyes narrowed a fraction. "Hey." He looked back to Willow. "I'll leave you guys to it. I'll see you at the bar on the weekend, Willow."

He gave her a small nod before stepping around them and heading down the street. Willow turned to Blake, temped to say something about the thick tension between the two men, but Mila was already flinging herself into his arms.

He immediately lifted her before tipping her backward, pretending to eat her belly.

Willow's heart softened at the sound of Mila's laugh. At the sight of pure joy on her little face.

Blake tipped her back three times before finally snaking his arm around Willow's waist. "I got off work early. Thought I'd join you guys for a drink."

With Blake's arm holding her, any annoyance she'd been feeling about the tension between the men eased, and she leaned into him. "That sounds lovely."

# CHAPTER 16

*W*illow took a sip from her glass. She was sticking strictly to water tonight because she didn't want to end up with her head in the toilet bowl again.

Janet had chosen a place called Lefty's Bar and Grill in Ketchum for the group to meet. From the outside, it looked like a house, but when you stepped inside, there was no mistaking it was a bar and grill. Not with its large wooden bar and the open kitchen behind. The place had been refurbished well.

Willow lifted a fry from the plate in the center of the table. "This place is awesome."

"Favorite place in Ketchum," Rob said from beside her.

They sat on stools around a tall bar table. Unlike her, Rob, Janet, and Toby had all gone with beer.

Janet grinned. "We come here a lot. Probably too much."

"It's never too much. Not when they have burgers and fries this good," Toby added.

She'd spotted quite a few people with burgers. And yeah, they looked good. In fact, they were making her regret the dinner she'd eaten before coming here.

"I still think you should reconsider that water, girl." Janet gave her glass a pointed look. "This is a celebration."

"What are we celebrating?" They still had months of studying left. Although, she had to admit, she could smell the finish line.

Janet leaned forward. "Uh, how about surviving the first three years? We're in the home stretch."

Well, that was true. "Okay…maybe one beer won't hurt." Beer didn't have the same effect on her as cocktails anyway. She'd just been trying to be cautious.

Hopping off the stool, Willow moved across to the bar. It was only when she got there that she realized Rob had followed.

He held up his empty glass. "All out."

The bartender stepped up to them. She was all smiles. "What can I get for you both?"

Willow smiled back. "I'll have a Guinness."

When she looked beside her to Rob, it was to see his brows raised. "A stout?"

She nodded. "Yes, you have a problem with that?"

He shook his head. "No, ma'am. I just didn't peg you as a stout woman." He turned back to the bartender. "I'll have the same."

"Coming right up." The woman grabbed two glasses.

This time, it was Willow who raised her brows. "I can't be a stout person, but you can?"

"I didn't say you couldn't be, just that you didn't look like one. And I'm definitely *not* a stout man, but figured I'd give it a go if you are. Maybe I'm missing something."

"Hmm. If I don't look like a stout woman, what do I look like?"

"Shiraz. Definitely a Shiraz woman."

"Ha. I don't even remember the last time I had a Shiraz."

The bartender placed their stouts in front of them and looked to Rob. "You can never properly peg a woman. We're too unpredictable. And the second you think you know what to expect, we'll surprise you."

Willow flung back her head and laughed. So true.

Rob nodded, grinning. "I think you may be right."

Willow reached for her card, but Rob shook his head, passing his to the bartender first. "I've got it."

"Thanks." She was tempted to say she'd get the next one out of politeness, but she knew that, for her at least, there would be no next one.

When the bartender moved away to the next customer, Rob lifted his drink. "Here's to the last academic year of our lives."

She'd cheers to that. She clinked her glass to his before taking a small sip.

He cleared his throat. "Janet mentioned she'd invited you to attend our church. Have you put any thought into it? I know everyone would love to have you."

Willow swallowed the cold stout. "Yes, I have. I think I'm going to give it a miss. I really appreciate the invitation, but I'm just not that religious."

There was the slightest tightening of Rob's mouth before his smile returned. "No problem. The invitation stands if you change your mind."

She dipped her head. "Thank you."

He took another sip of his stout, his gaze never leaving her. "You look beautiful tonight, by the way."

Her mouth slipped open a fraction. Beautiful? She was wearing jeans and a tunic. "Um, thanks."

He took a small step closer. "I've been meaning to ask if you'd like to do something with me sometime? Just us. We could grab a bite somewhere. Catch a movie."

She swallowed, trying to word her next sentence carefully. "That's really sweet of you to ask, Rob, and I would have considered it, but I'm kind of seeing someone."

Kind of...definitely. Same thing.

He frowned. "You are?"

She gave a small nod. "It's…new."

In a way. But in another way, it was something that had been going on for so many years, she couldn't remember a time before.

His next smile was tight. "He's a lucky guy then."

When they reached the table, Willow sat quickly, taking a big gulp of her stout.

Janet and Toby were discussing the upcoming ski season and who would be faster down the mountain. Janet turned to her. "Has Mila skied before?"

She shook her head, giving the woman a small smile. "No. I was thinking I might put her into some lessons."

"Good idea. Living around here, that's a must." She tilted her head to the side. "Is she with her dad right now?"

Willow wet her lips. "No, she's at a school friend's house." She debated not saying the next part, mostly for Rob's benefit, but there was no point. They'd all see him the second he stepped inside. Something—right or wrong—she was suddenly regretting. "Blake's actually stopping here after his work meeting."

Three sets of brows lifted. A moment of silence passed. It was Janet who broke it. "Oh. Are you back together?"

Their gazes suddenly felt like beams searing into her. It made her feel uncomfortable and hot. But again, there was no point in hiding the truth. There was also no reason she *should* hide it. "We are."

Like she'd conjured Blake with her words, a strong arm wound around her waist.

"Hi," he whispered into her ear. Even though she felt uncomfortable with the attention from around the table, the knots in her belly eased with his touch.

"Hi."

BLAKE LEANED CLOSE, brushing his lips against Willow's ear. "Your friends don't like me."

They rocked gently to the music on the small dance floor, Willow fitting perfectly in his arms and against his body. He'd joined the group for a beer, but the conversation had been awkward and stilted. Finally, Willow had suggested they dance.

He wasn't complaining. Holding her was exactly what he needed after the long day he'd had.

"Yes, they do."

Her quiet words almost had him chuckling. He was trained to spot a lie, but he was sure even an untrained civilian could hear that one.

He shot a quick look over to the table. They weren't watching him. Not anymore, at least. The way the three of them had looked at him since he'd arrived, the energy they emitted...it wasn't good.

"Is it because Rob likes you?"

She looked up, eyes wide, before shooting a quick glance at the table, then back at him. He saw the answer seconds before she spoke. "He doesn't..."

She trailed off at Blake's raised brow.

"Okay. He may have asked me out."

Jealousy, hot and heavy, heated his insides. It wasn't a surprise. But it still had his arms locking around her waist a bit tighter. "Tonight?"

She gave a small nod.

"What did you say?"

She tilted her head to the side. "What do you think I said?" At his silence, she sighed. "I told him I'm seeing someone else."

Damn straight she was. He lifted a hand to her cheek, grazing the soft skin. "What if the last week had never happened?"

Her fingers smoothed the material over his shoulders in an almost maddening way. "Then he just would have gotten a simple no."

"Is that right?" His voice was gruffer than it had been a moment ago.

"Mm-hmm." Her eyes softened, but at the same time, they studied him. "It's always been you, Blake."

For a moment, the noise around him quieted. The woman's words, her eyes on him, her *everything*, stripped him of the ability to focus on anything but her.

"You're something else, Willow."

The smallest smile touched her lips. It wasn't enough. He wanted the full smile. He wanted every little part of her.

"Something good?"

His head dipped, lips hovering above hers. "Something so damn perfect that no words created by man could do you justice."

Then he kissed her, took her lips with his own and devoured them. Every time he tasted her, it was the same feeling. The accumulation of every best moment in his life combined.

When he came up for air, it was to see her eyes glazed, her features soft.

He tugged her closer, just holding her. Barely swaying.

They remained like that for a while. At one point, he offered to take her back to her friends, but she was quick to say no. He wasn't sure if she said it for his benefit or not, but he let it slide, too weak to share her.

Maybe he shouldn't have come. But when Willow had mentioned she'd organized a sleepover for Mila at a friend's house, then invited him out, he hadn't been able to give up time with her. He'd *never* be able to say no to that.

And today, in particular, he needed to hold her. The team had spent the entire day going over details for their return to Saudi Arabia next week. They didn't know how long they'd be gone, because they still didn't know exactly where Ahmad might be. The FBI hadn't been able to confirm any sightings. But they couldn't continue to wait. So all they had were the locations provided by his wife.

Blake was hoping the trip would be a quick one, but he wasn't holding his breath.

"Are you okay?"

Willow's question dragged him out of his head. When he glanced down, he saw she was looking up at him, a small frown creasing her brows.

"You just tensed up," she said quietly.

He hadn't even realized it. Immediately, he forced his muscles to loosen. "I'm okay."

She looked at him like she didn't quite believe him. "How was work?"

He sighed. The woman was just like her daughter. Saw and knew too much. "We have to go away again. Next week."

Usually, he wouldn't mind, but his trips had been a big point of contention once upon a time. And now that they were back together, he almost didn't want to bring it up.

Willow's features didn't change at all. "Okay. Why are you looking like it's a bad thing?"

"I wasn't sure how you'd take it."

"If we're going to be together, I need to accept that your job involves leaving me and Mila for periods of time to save people. Things are different now. Mila and I will be okay."

Her words eased some of the tension in his chest. "I don't know how long I'll be away."

She lifted a shoulder. "We'll be right here, regardless of whether it's a few days or a few weeks." Then she leaned up on her toes. "I'll miss you, though."

He dipped his head, kissing the woman like it was both their first and last kiss. When they separated, she whispered against his lips, "If this is my last weekend with you for a while, let's get out of here."

The woman didn't need to tell him twice. He took her hand.

"I just need to use the bathroom," she said quietly.

They moved across the room. Blake waited in the hall as she

stepped inside the ladies' room. As he waited, Janet passed him, giving him a tight smile before pushing into the bathroom.

Immediately, he heard their voices from inside.

"Hey, we're just heading out," Willow said.

"Okay."

There was a small pause, followed by Willow's sigh. "Janet. I thought we were past this."

"I'm just…worried about you. He's—"

"Janet, *stop*."

"You shouldn't be with him! Heck, *Mila* shouldn't even be around the guy! We all think so."

Blake straightened, ice whipping down his spine.

"You have no idea what you're talking about." Willow's voice was low and clipped, anger lacing her words. "I need to go."

When she stepped out, her lips pressed together in what he was sure was an attempt at a smile. She took his hand, tugging him toward the exit. It wasn't until they stepped outside that she looked up at him almost nervously. "I'm sorry."

"Why are you apologizing?"

She lifted a shoulder. "Because I should have known better."

"You should have known better about what?"

"Never mind."

She tried to walk away, but Blake grabbed her wrist, pulling her gently back to him. "Willow…"

"That night when my car broke down, they said…similar stuff." A pained expression crossed Willow's face. "They apologized, and I thought if I kept hanging out with them, I could help them realize how wrong they were…*are*. I should have cut ties completely."

He slipped his arms around her. "It's not your fault. There will always be people in the world who don't like what I've become."

Anger marred her features. "I hate that. You and your team are heroes, Blake."

He lowered his head, his temple touching hers. "The only opinions I care about are yours and Mila's."

A small smile returned to her lips. A real one this time "Well, I think you're amazing, and that Mila and I are very lucky to have you."

"That's all I need to know."

illow smiled as Omar read the final sentence. The kid's progress was out of this world. He was basically fluent, and they'd only been working together for a couple of years.

Omar glanced up, looking proud of himself. "How did I do this time?"

"Amazing, Omar. Absolutely amazing. You must be practicing so much."

He nodded. "I am very, ah..." There was a pause.

"Motivated?" she suggested.

He dipped his head. "Yes. Very motivated."

"Well, I can tell." She pushed the textbook to the side of the desk. "Okay, time for you to teach me your word of the day before we sign off."

The smile wiped from his face, brows tugging together. She almost chuckled. Her students always loved this part. Omar, in particular, took it very seriously. "I have put a lot of thought into a word. I have still been watching a lot of American sport. But my new favorite is *albisbul*."

"*Albisbul*. Hm, I'm going to go out on a limb and say that it means baseball?"

He gave an excited nod. "Yes, very good! I like watching how far they hit the ball." His eyes were wide, becoming more animated as he spoke. "And how fast they can throw it."

"Which team is your favorite?"

"The Red Sox. They are very good."

Her smile deepened. She wasn't a huge baseball girl—heck, she probably wouldn't even be able to pick a Red Sox uniform out of a lineup—but she loved that *he* loved it.

"A favorite in this country. Many people would commend your choice." She leaned forward. "I'll send through your reading tasks for the week in a day or so. Maybe I'll try to include some baseball in your homework."

His nod was vigorous. "Yes, please."

She chuckled. "Keep it up, Omar, you're doing a great job."

"Thank you, Miss Cross."

Once they both clicked out of the video, Willow leaned back in her seat, stretching. God, her neck felt sore.

It wasn't the only place she felt sore…

Her cheeks heated. It was Friday, almost a week since she'd gone to the bar in Ketchum…another week of Blake. Of him staying at her place, and vice versa. Of late nights together.

She sucked in a deep, shuddering breath as she pushed to her feet and moved to the kitchen. She was happy. The kind of happy she hadn't felt in a very long time.

Surprisingly, other than that first day, Mila hadn't asked many questions. It was almost like she'd expected this to happen.

Willow wouldn't be surprised. The kid was five going on thirty.

Filling the kettle, she put it on the stove before grabbing a mug and tea bag. The only thing that had dampened her joy over the last week was her conversation with Janet at the bar.

Her jaw clenched at the memory, fingers tightening around the edge of the counter.

*Mila shouldn't even be around the guy. We all think so.*

For a moment, her eyes closed, fury and guilt ripping through her body at the fact that Blake had heard.

What the heck was wrong with the woman? What was wrong with *all* of them? Blake was both a victim and a hero, yet they spoke about him as if he was some sort of mass terrorist or abomination. The woman didn't even know Blake. None of them did. The fact that she would dare say something like that when Willow had known the man her entire life was absurd.

He deserved so much more than that. And Mila...she was the luckiest kid in the world to have Blake as a dad. No one could ever, or would ever, convince her otherwise.

Releasing the counter, she poured the boiling water into her cup. She wasn't surprised that no one from her study group had tried to contact her since. To be honest, she was glad, because she would have told them exactly what she thought of them in no uncertain terms.

When her phone beeped with a message, she pulled it from her pocket, her heart giving a little flutter when she saw it was Blake.

*Blake: Hey, beautiful, are you able to grab Mila from school today? I've gotten caught up in a meeting.*

The man had been stressed all week. He'd tried to hide it, but in the little moments when he thought no one was watching, she saw. There was the slight tightening of his eyes. The tic of his jaw.

Something had gone wrong during their last mission. That's what the mission he was leaving for tomorrow was about—correcting whatever had happened.

She quickly typed out her response.

*Willow: Of course. I have one more tutoring session for the day but will have plenty of time to grab her after. I'll take her to The Grind so if you finish early, you can meet us there. If not, we'll see you tonight at my place later.*

*Blake: I love you. Xox*

Her abdomen dipped at his words. They got her every time.

*Willow: I love you too. Xxx*

Pushing the phone back into her pocket, she wrapped her fingers around the warm mug. She'd only taken one step into the living room when she heard something from elsewhere in the house.

Mila's bedroom, maybe? The sound had been light, barely touching her ears.

Frowning, she moved down the hall. Maybe Mila had left one of her battery-operated toys on. She loved the things, whereas Willow hated them.

Stepping inside the small bedroom, she was checking the floor for toys when her feet stopped. A chill crept over her limbs and dread crawled along her spine.

The window was open. *Wide* open.

Willow hadn't done that. And Mila wasn't able to unlock it. She took a couple of slow steps closer, studying the lock. Her breath caught.

Broken.

Spinning around, ready to run—her feet stilled, heart catapulting into her throat.

A man stood in the doorway. A tall man wearing a white bag of some kind over his head, the eyes cut out. His shoulders were broad, eyes dark, and he wore a baggy sweatshirt and jeans.

She took a step back. The man took a step forward.

A strong scent permeated the air. Some sort of chemical?

Her gaze flicked to the cloth in his hand, every muscle in her body tightening.

Oh, God, what was on it? What did he intend to do with it?

But she already knew the answer.

Suddenly, he lunged forward.

Willow reacted on instinct, throwing the contents of the mug at him, aiming for his face.

The guy turned his head to the side just before the hot liquid hit, crying out as it covered the bag covering the side of his face and neck.

Willow tried to dodge past him, but strong arms wrapped around her middle.

The mug slipped from her fingers, shattering on the floor. Immediately, she grabbed the arm around her middle with both hands, dropping her weight, just like Blake had once taught her.

The attacker stumbled, and she took advantage of the moment, elbowing him and twisting out of the hold.

Again she tried to run, but this time, the guy shoved her hard from behind, propelling her into the wall. Her face collided with the solid surface seconds before she dropped to the ground.

A splintering pain pounded through her head.

As she tried to push up, a heavy weight suddenly pressed on her back, pushing her to the floor. The cloth covered her mouth.

Her eyes watered, the skin around her mouth stinging, burning. Willow held her breath as she writhed beneath him, refusing to inhale the chemical. Something to the side caught her eye. A shard of broken porcelain.

Stretching out her hand, she closed desperate fingers around the jagged piece of mug. The sharp edge cut into her flesh, but she ignored the sting, flinging her hand back over her shoulder and thrusting it toward her attacker.

Another loud cry pierced the room. The cloth dropped from her face.

Pulling the shard back, she saw crimson coating both the piece of mug and her hand. She had no idea where she'd stabbed the guy. She didn't care.

The man was already half off her. She dug deep, using every ounce of strength she had to push him the rest of the way off.

Struggling to her feet, she realized fog clouded her vision, blurring everything in front of her.

She fought it with everything she had. Grabbing the wall, she used it to keep herself upright, leaning heavily as she moved out of the room.

Her breaths were shallow as she stumbled her way down the hall. When footsteps sounded behind her, she all but threw herself into her bedroom, just clicking the lock before the knob twisted from the other side.

She fell backward, the thud to her backside hardly registering.

"I-I'm calling B-Blake. He's...fast. He'll be here within...minutes."

Her words started to jumble, her brain not working. Her tongue was almost numb.

It took her three goes to get her phone from her pocket as her fingers refused to work.

In the back of her mind, she knew that she'd inhaled whatever had been on that cloth. It would have been impossible not to. She also knew she didn't have long. Her limbs were shutting down, her vision blurring more by the second.

She tried pressing keys on her phone, she really did, but getting her eyes to focus was impossible. Even worse, her fingers felt so heavy that the phone was slipping from her hand.

Darkness hedged her vision. She grit her teeth, holding the blackness off by sheer will and determination.

She forced her voice to work. "Blake, y-you need to...come to...my house." She cried the words as loud as she could, praying the man bought the lie. "Two minutes. You'll be here in...two minutes..."

The last word had barely left her lips when her lids shuttered, too heavy to keep open. She heard movement from the hallway but couldn't be certain the man was leaving her home.

She prayed he was. It was her final thought before the world darkened around her.

# CHAPTER 18

"*I* think that's it, boys. We're ready to go."

Blake leaned back in his seat, nodding at Aidan.

He scanned the blueprints scattered across the Blue Halo conference room table one last time. Blueprints created based on the information Ahmad's wife had provided. Blueprints they'd spent the last week analyzing.

The locations were just like the previous place they'd raided. High fences, heavily guarded, almost impenetrable.

Steve had allowed them to talk to Akela a couple of times over the course of the previous week. She'd spoken to them via Skype, and each time, she looked stronger.

Her need for safety, for both herself and her daughter, was so desperate, it filled Blake with dark rage to consider what her husband must have put her through to instill that kind of fear.

Ahmad was a dead man. There was no two ways about it.

"Get lots of rest tonight, everyone," Tyler said, tapping the doorway before leaving.

Blake almost laughed. It was as if those words were directed at him, even though he knew they really weren't. He'd been getting very little rest the last several days. He had three years of lost moments with his woman to make up for. Three years of stolen kisses. Of holding her while she slept. Listening to her deep breaths.

He shot a look at his watch, beyond ready to see both her and Mila. Their daughter's school day had ended twenty minutes ago, so they should be at The Grind by now.

Perfect.

"How are things with you and Willow going?" Flynn asked.

He smiled. "Unbelievable. I feel like I can finally breathe easy, knowing I have my family back."

Aidan smiled.

Flynn chuckled. "Damn, that's awesome, man. I need to find myself a woman who makes me feel like that."

"You won't regret it." It was like a hit of every feel-good hormone there was, every damn day.

He was just standing when his cell rang. He frowned when he noticed it was Mila's school. "Hello?"

"Hi, is this Blake Cross, Mila Cross's father?"

"Speaking."

"This is Helen Smolder, from the office at your daughter's school. We've got Mila here in the office and were wondering when someone will be picking her up?"

A trickle of unease twisted in his gut. He noticed Aidan and Flynn pause by the door, eyes on him.

"Her mother hasn't been by?" He'd texted her less than an hour ago, and she confirmed that she'd be there.

"No, Mr. Cross, she hasn't. We tried calling her, but it went through to voicemail."

This time it wasn't just unease twisting his gut—it was stone-cold dread. Willow would never leave Mila unattended. Not in a million years.

His gaze shot across the room. "Flynn Talbot, a family friend, will be there in a couple minutes to pick her up. Keep her inside with you until he gets there."

Blake hung up before the woman could respond. Flynn gave a single nod before moving quickly out of the room. Blake was moving too, running down the hall, Aidan close behind.

The fear was now sitting in his stomach like a rock, causing nausea to crawl up his throat. Where was she? What had happened between their last text and now that would stop her from picking up their daughter and answering her phone?

He moved down the stairs quickly, sprinting to his car and throwing himself behind the wheel. Aidan dropped into the passenger seat, the door barely closing before Blake was racing down the road, not paying a lick of attention to the speed limit.

Aidan called Willow's phone twice while they drove. Both times it rang until they heard her recorded message. More dread sliced through Blake's veins, icing his blood.

He'd always thought of Willow's house as being close to Blue Halo, but right now, the five-minute drive felt ten times as long. Too damn far.

Outside her place, he slammed his foot on the brake and threw the car into park before running up the drive.

Fresh terror tore at him at the sight of the open front door.

Inside, he saw the blood. Large drops of it between the master bedroom and Mila's room.

He took a moment to pause, listening for any heartbeats.

He heard a steady thump from Willow's room. He ran to her door and turned the knob, breaking the lock easily.

Inside, his body seized, ears buzzing, and blood draining from his face.

Willow. So damn still, lying on her side with blood covering her left shoulder.

He dropped to his knees, hands going to her shoulder, searching for a wound. There was none. "It's not her blood." His words were more to himself than Aidan.

He turned her over gently, jaw ticking at the dark bruise on her forehead. At the redness around her mouth and nose. He lifted her into his arms, moving out to the car, and sliding into the back seat. Aidan jumped behind the wheel and started driving.

"Chloroform," Aidan said, his voice barely concealing his rage. A rage Blake shared. So black and thick, it threatened to consume him.

He pushed some hair from her face, being careful to avoid the bruising.

It was definitely chloroform. Someone had put the stuff over her mouth. And when he worked out who, he was going to murder the fucker.

BLAKE HELD Willow's hand as she remained still in the bed. The doctor had checked her over and confirmed that she'd inhaled chloroform and sustained a blow to the head. Two things Blake already knew.

Fury had taken hold of his insides, growing and spiraling by the second.

Chloroform was like a poison, goddammit! He just had to hope she hadn't inhaled much. The harm it might cause, particularly to internal organs, was something that doctors couldn't immediately tell.

His hand tightened around hers.

It wasn't just the drug or the head injury that had him feeling like murdering the person who did this. It was the possibility of what *could* have happened. People used chloroform to knock out their victims so they could be taken easily. If Willow hadn't fought the guy off—which was obvious from the blood that wasn't her own, and the fact she'd made it into her bedroom—she might not be here right now.

His breath hissed through his lips as he thanked every damn

god out there that she was so strong. Strong enough to fight. To lock herself away from her attacker.

Aidan re-entered the room. "Tyler and Liam are at Willow's house getting a blood sample. They'll send it off to see if it matches anyone in the system."

Blake gave a short nod. He didn't have any words right now. Or at least none that would help the situation.

"Flynn picked up Mila from school and took her to Courtney and Jason's for the night," Aidan continued. "They set up a spare bed, told her that Willow wasn't feeling well and that they're having a movie night."

A deep swallow. He needed to call his daughter and talk to her. But right now, he couldn't. The words would come out rough and jumbled. He trusted his team to keep her safe, and he knew Mila was comfortable with Courtney and Jason. The conversation needed to wait.

At the small movement of Willow's hand in his, Blake's breath halted in his chest. For a moment, she remained still. Then there was a slight scrunching of her eyes. A small swallow at her throat.

A second later, her eyes fluttered open.

The air whooshed out of his chest. He'd never been so glad to see those green eyes.

Her breaths were deep as she looked at the ceiling. When her gaze met his, there was confusion on her face. Then her skin paled, and she was leaning to the side.

He quickly grabbed the bowl the nurse had left, helping her lean over as she was sick. They'd warned him this could happen. An after-effect of the drug. Blake just bit off his curse, stroking her hair gently.

When she lay back down, her eyes shuttered. "I don't...feel good."

He quickly jabbed the button for the doctor before touching her forehead, hating how pale her skin was. "The doctor will be here in a second, honey."

Her brows tugged together. "Someone...was in...my house."

In each pause was a deep breath. Like she was struggling to talk. To breathe.

Blake's jaw ticked. "Did you recognize him?"

A small shake of her head, then her frown deepened, like the motion brought pain to her skull.

God, he couldn't wait to kill the guy.

"I heard something. Thought Mila left one of her toys on. When I got to her room, the window was open. Then I turned..." The heart rate machine sped up. "There was a tall man standing there. Wearing some sort of white bag over his head. Like a pillowcase or something. He had a cloth in his hand..."

She paused to breathe and swallow. Then she turned to look at him.

"I threw my tea at him and tried to run, but he grabbed me. I remembered what you taught me years ago. How to get out of a hold. To do whatever I could to hurt him. I used that to get away."

He forced himself to internalize the rage. To smooth his features. "You did good, honey."

So damn good.

He made a mental note to do a refresher with her on self-defense. The lessons he'd given her had been before Mila was born. Too long ago.

"I made it to my bedroom and locked him out. Pretended to call you. I couldn't actually call because I couldn't see my phone or work my fingers..."

Her voice started to drift off. He was losing her.

"I'm sorry I couldn't see enough to know who it was."

He stroked her hair again. "Is there anything you can tell me about him?"

Another small frown. "He was a few inches shorter than you, with broad shoulders, dark brown eyes. That's all." Her breaths started to deepen.

He leaned forward, pressing a kiss to the side of her head. "Sleep."

He remained where he was, watching and listening as her breaths evened out. Then he stood, walked over to Aidan, and looked his friend dead in the eye.

"Stay with her. Don't leave her side or take your eyes off her for a second. Protect her like she's your own."

Aidan's eyes were questioning. "Of course. But where are you going?"

"I'm going to question the fucker who fits that description and has motive."

# CHAPTER 19

*T*he second Blake dropped into the car, he called Callum. The guy was still at Blue Halo Security and would be able to find the information he needed.

Callum answered on the first ring. "Blake."

"I need an address for a guy called Rob. I don't have a last name or a car registration or anything else. I just know that he lives in Ketchum, and is completing an online Bachelor of Education degree through Strayer University."

The clicking of a keyboard sounded over the line. "Give me five. I'll call you back."

Blake nodded, already driving toward Ketchum. Three minutes later, his phone rang.

"Rob Clark. I found him through Willow's Facebook page, then dug deep into places I'm not supposed to for an address. He lives at five Batter Road, Ketchum."

Blake quickly typed the address into his GPS, pressing his foot harder on the gas. "Thanks."

"And he works at a local pizza shop, Smoky Mountain Pizzeria Grill."

He committed the name to memory. "Got it."

"You need me to come with you?"

"No. I'm almost there. But I'll call if I need backup."

It didn't take Blake long to get to the house. When he did, he parked out front before moving to the door and pounding his fist against the wood. His muscles were vibrating with fury. It was only his years of training that kept his anger under wraps.

When the door didn't open, he took a moment to listen, detecting the single heartbeat inside.

Another pulse of anger shot through him. He banged harder. "I can hear you, and if you don't open the door right the fuck now, I'm going to smash it down."

He wasn't even joking. He'd go to the end of the goddamn world to make sure his family was safe. A wooden door was hardly a barrier.

A beat of silence. Blake lifted his hand, seconds from breaking the lock, when slow footsteps sounded from the other side. The door opened and a man wearing jeans and a baggy black hoodie stood in front of him.

Blake recognized him immediately. The other guy from Willow's study group, Toby.

"Where's Rob?" The words hissed through his teeth.

Toby opened and closed his mouth before speaking. "I-I don't know."

The guy's heart kicked at the words, his pupils dilating.

Lie.

Blake took a threatening step forward, but the guy quickly held up a hand, retreating. "Okay, fine, I do! He's at Lefty's Bar and Grill, grabbing lunch with Janet."

This time, the guy spoke the truth. His lucky fucking day, because Blake wouldn't have hesitated to get his answer another way. "Good. Don't even think about texting or calling anyone. If you do, I'll be back—and you'll be fucking sorry."

Yeah, that was a threat. He knew he was being an asshole, but when it came to Willow's life, he couldn't afford to be anything else.

At the guy's frantic nod, Blake turned, storming back toward his car. It took two minutes to reach the bar. Two minutes too long.

Pulling the car to a stop in the parking lot, he climbed out, slamming the door after him. The moment he stepped inside the small bar, he scanned the tables, spotting the guy immediately.

Janet was the first to look up, fry pausing midway to her mouth, lips separating.

Fear. That's what he saw on her face. Blake was sure he looked as murderous as he felt.

He was beside Rob in a second, tugging him from the seat by the collar of his sweatshirt and shoving him against the wall. The guy's eyes widened, mouth dropping open.

"Was it you?" Blake's loud words boomed through the bar.

He fit the description to a T. Just a few inches shorter than Blake. Dark brown eyes. Wide shoulders. And he had motive. Hell, being rejected, only to have the woman choose a guy you thought wasn't even human, was all the motive Rob needed.

The bar silenced around them, even the music turned off. A few sharp gasps penetrated the quiet.

The guy's face lost all color, terror filling his eyes. "W-what?"

Blake inched closer so that he could just about smell the guy's fear. "Don't fucking mess with me. Did you go to Willow's house today, put a cloth soaked in chloroform over her mouth, and try to kidnap her?"

If he actually said yes, Blake wasn't sure what he'd do—or whether he had the strength to rein in his anger.

The sound of the door opening barely pierced Blake's focus.

"No! I...it wasn't me."

Blake studied his face. His eyes. Listened to his heartbeat. Looking for something, any sign of deceit.

There was none. He was telling the truth.

Blake's next breath was more of a hiss.

*No.* That couldn't be right. It *had* to be him. There were no other suspects. No one else who had expressed an interest in Willow and a dislike for him.

A shaky female voice spoke quietly behind him. "He's telling the truth."

Blake looked over at Janet.

"We've been here all day." Even though she looked nervous, there was also something else in her eyes. Hate. "Studying and eating."

Blake clenched his jaw, fingers refusing to release Rob.

"She's right, they have." This time it was the bartender who spoke up, the same woman who'd been serving last weekend.

A strong hand grabbed Blake's arm.

Callum. He didn't say anything. Not out loud.

The guy must have tracked him down using the GPS on his phone. Not surprising. He'd probably sounded crazed. Hell, he felt like his hold on sanity was barely there right now.

Blake turned back to Rob, dipping his head. "Stay away from her."

There was a small flash of anger across the guy's face. The first emotion other than fear. Then it was gone.

Blake released him, stepping back. Then he moved across the bar, shoving the door open and stepping into the late afternoon. He scrubbed two hands over his face, wanting to yell. To kick something. Punch his fist through a brick wall.

"It may not have been him," Callum said quietly, "but we'll find whoever did this."

Blake shook his head. "Who else could it be? She works and studies from home. After the other night at the bar, I was so sure it was him." Or maybe he'd just wanted it to be Rob. Because he'd be able to eliminate the threat quickly. "If it's not him…"

Callum stepped closer. "Then it's someone else. Someone else we'll hunt down and bury."

Yeah, that was the only way this was going to end. With her attacker deep in the ground.

~

Willow woke slowly to the sound of soft voices in another room.

She peeled her eyes open, and for the first time in days, her head actually felt clear. Nausea didn't well in her stomach and confusion didn't muddy her mind.

She had no idea what day it was, or what time, but she did know that she was at Blake's house. *Had* been at Blake's house since being discharged from the hospital.

She drew back the sheets and cautiously sat up. No dizziness. She almost sighed in relief.

Easing her feet to the floor, she tested her legs with a little bit of weight. When that seemed okay, she stood slowly, keeping a firm hold on the bed. Her knees didn't wobble, her ankles didn't threaten to collapse.

Carefully, she let go of the bed.

Thank God. She could stand and think clearly. She really was on the mend this time. She'd woken at various times, always feeling sick.

Moving gingerly across the room, she used the bathroom, brushed her teeth, and tugged her hair into a quick ponytail. She could use a shower but didn't want to test her legs for that long. Not yet. Plus, she wanted to see Mila.

How was her daughter doing? Was she worried? Sad?

Throwing one of Blake's baggy sweaters over her head, she moved out of the bedroom and into the kitchen.

An immediate smile stretched her dry lips. The smile felt unfamiliar and rusty after days in bed. But it also felt good.

Blake was holding Mila in one arm, an open bag of chocolate chips in his other hand. Mila was grabbing the chocolate chips and sprinkling them onto pancakes. Every time her hand dipped into the bag, she snuck one into her mouth, and Blake tickled her tummy with his mouth.

Her little laugh echoed through the room.

Willow's heart swelled.

When Mila came up from another bout of laughter, Blake turned around. Mila's eyes widened seconds before she was wriggling out of his hold and running toward her.

"Careful, Mila."

Blake's words came seconds before the collision of Mila hurtling into her arms, almost sending them backward. Willow only just saved herself. Then she was holding her daughter closely, shutting her eyes and breathing her in.

Any time she'd been semi-conscious over the last few days, there had been one thing on her mind. One thing she'd been so unbelievably grateful for.

That Mila hadn't been with her.

If she'd been home during the attack…

No. Willow couldn't think about that. It was too hard. Too terrifying.

She opened her eyes at Blake's kiss against her temple. His gaze was soft as he gave her a look before he walked back to the frying pan.

"Are you feeling better, Mama? Daddy said you were sick again."

Sick…so they hadn't told her the truth. Good. Mila deserved to feel safe. "So much better, baby. But I've missed you."

"I've missed you too. Daddy and I made you some chocolate chip pancakes to make you feel better."

"Mm. That does sound like something that could make me feel better. Although I think I saw someone stealing some of those chocolate chips."

Mila giggled. The sound was medicine. "I won't admit to anything! Daddy taught me that."

Willow chuckled. Good Lord, the kid was going to grow up to be a mini-Blake.

When she glanced up, the man in question cleared his throat, focusing way too intently on the pancakes.

Willow took a seat at the island, lifting Mila into her arms and holding her on her lap. To be honest, she wasn't sure she'd ever be letting the kid go. "What have you and Daddy been up to?"

Mila tilted her head. "We did some painting. And Daddy helped me with my homework. We made my favorite pasta for dinner last night. Oh, and I made you a card!"

All too soon, she was wriggling out of Willow's arms and running down the hall.

Immediately, Blake was in front of her, like he'd been waiting to get her alone. "How are you feeling?" There was a new intensity to the way he looked at her. Like he was scared she'd disappear before his eyes.

She reached up, holding his cheek. "Better. Have you, uh, found the guy?"

The second the question left her lips, she knew the answer. The air of anger and disappointment fused his features. "Not yet. But we will." He looked like he wanted to say something else, but hesitated.

Her heart sped up, her gut telling her it was nothing good. "What is it?"

"The day it happened, I paid your friend Rob a visit. I shoved him against a wall at the bar. I thought it was him."

"But it wasn't." She wasn't sure if it was a question or a statement.

She actually didn't know the guy well enough to say that it was or wasn't. And this incident had knocked her faith in people. She'd like to think she would have recognized his eyes, but the truth was, fear had made it difficult to even think. All she'd been able to concentrate on was escape.

"No. It wasn't." He sighed. Was he disappointed?

She gave a small nod. "Has Mila been back to school?"

"No. But I've spoken to the principal and we're going to station some of the guys there so she can go back, just so her life isn't too disrupted. She'll be protected, I promise."

"I believe you. And I trust your team." Suddenly she straightened, remembering something. "Wait—you're supposed to be away on your mission!"

A small frowned tugged his brows together. "You think I'd leave you when you need me?"

"But you've spent so long planning and preparing. And one of the other guys could have protected me while you were gone."

Something fierce and primal flashed over his features. "I'll be here to protect you until we find the asshole who hurt you. I *will* take him down. You and Mila are my priority."

Something ticked in her chest. A little flutter. A little more of her heart being taken back by the man she loved.

# CHAPTER 20

*W*illow said goodbye to her last tutoring student for the day and clicked out of the session.

She was working in Flynn's office at Blue Halo, while Blake worked in his office next door. Flynn was still away with his other team members on their current job. The job that Blake was supposed to be on.

He'd said he wasn't sure when they'd be back. If the tightness around Blake's eyes whenever it came up was anything to go by, the job wasn't going well, so it probably wouldn't be anytime soon.

She knew that after the kidnapping attempt, he would have preferred to have the entire team here. He'd told her as much. But she also knew it was important they completed their mission. Not to mention the amount of work they'd put into preparing for it.

Even though it wasn't her fault that Blake hadn't gone, she still felt guilty. He'd put as much time into preparing for it as anyone else. And being one man down would put more pressure on the guys who'd gone.

Sighing, she rose to her feet just as Grace stopped in the doorway of the office. "Hey!"

Willow smiled. "Hi. Are you here to see Logan?"

"Yep, grabbing a ride home. Still haven't bought a car. Truth be told, I kind of like having to share one. More time together." Grace scanned the room. "Is this your new office?"

She lifted a shoulder. "Until Flynn returns, or until the person who tried to kidnap me is found."

The smile slipped from Grace's features, concern flickering over her face. "How are you doing?"

Courtney and Grace had both visited numerous times over the last few days. With casseroles. Cake. Friendly smiles. The women were godsends.

"I'm doing okay. Feeling extremely lucky to have Blake. To have *everyone*. If I have any complaint, it's that I feel bad that everyone is doing so much for me."

It had been a week since the attack, and she'd basically been holed up in Blake's home for most of that time. She'd only started coming to Blue Halo these last couple days, so Blake could get some work done.

She wasn't complaining. She'd rather be safe and sheltered than vulnerable. But she did feel like a bit of a burden for everyone.

"Oh, don't feel bad, everyone just wants you to be safe and happy. Courtney and I could come over one night this week after Mila goes to bed, and have some girl time." She lifted a shoulder. "You haven't been out much, which can take a toll on mental health."

The woman was literally an angel. Courtney too. "I would absolutely love that."

"Perfect. Just send us a text when you're ready for some company."

"Oh, I will. Thank you." Willow smiled.

Grace returned the smile, before disappearing down the hall. Willow closed the lid on the laptop. If she was glad for anything at the moment, it was the distraction that work offered. When tutoring kids, that was all she could think about. They deserved a hundred percent of her attention, so that was exactly what she gave.

She was just reaching for her bag on the edge of the desk when she accidentally nudged the thing right off, sending everything spilling out. All the million and one items that she kept in there and rarely touched, going everywhere.

*Great.* Maybe the head injury was still affecting her.

Crouching down, she grabbed handfuls of stuff, chucking everything back into her purse. The second she got home, she needed to do a big cleanup of the bag. She didn't even use half the stuff.

She'd reached the last couple of items when her hands closed around a small box of tampons.

She paused, a frown marring her brows. How long had it been since she'd had to use them?

A small sliver of unease trickled down her spine. Reaching back into the bag, she grabbed her phone, flicking into the app she used to religiously track when she was due.

She swallowed hard. She was late. Three days late.

That never happened. Not to Willow. It actually shouldn't be possible. She was on the pill. Had been on the pill since having Mila, never missing a dose.

Willow sat there for a solid thirty seconds, brain working overtime to figure out how she could be late.

She'd almost convinced herself the app was wrong, that she'd somehow keyed in the wrong dates, when something flickered through her mind. A memory of *that* morning. The one after she'd had sex with Blake for the first time. She'd just taken the pill before getting sick.

Oh, sweet Jesus. Was that it?

Her breath shortened. Why had she not taken another one straight away?

But she already knew the answer. She'd been distracted. By Blake. By the shift in their relationship. And with wondering and worrying about what Mila would think and ask.

Her skin felt cold and clammy.

Pregnancy was not something she wanted or felt ready for right now. Heck, she didn't know if she'd ever feel ready again. Mila hadn't been planned. And before Mila, she'd convinced herself that kids weren't for her.

She loved her daughter with everything in her. But there was fear. So much fear. Were people more likely to experience post-partum depression with consecutive pregnancies? Could she spiral into that same hopelessness again? That state of sheer survival?

She had no idea. She'd always assumed Mila was it, and she didn't need to research any of those questions.

Her heart pounded in her chest, fear shortening her breaths.

When strong arms snaked around her waist, a loud yelp fell from her lips and she shot to her feet, tampons falling from her fingers.

Blake's face immediately flickered to concern as he studied her. "Hey. Are you okay?"

No. She wasn't. She opened her mouth to tell him, but the words never made it to air. She could barely think it, let alone say it out loud.

Her lips snapped shut. It might not be true. She might just be late. She could wake up tomorrow and everything would be okay.

Forcing a smile she didn't feel, Willow nodded, leaning into his chest and hiding her face from eyes that saw too much.

BLAKE'S FINGERS tightened around Willow's hand. She wasn't okay. Not even close. But she wouldn't tell him what was wrong.

Why?

As they stepped outside and headed toward his car, he made sure to scan the area. Looking for any possible threats. The street was quiet.

Was she worried about another kidnapping attempt? Worried that he couldn't protect her?

Even if that was it, why had it suddenly come to the forefront now? She'd been fine all day.

Unlocking the car, he held her door open as she climbed in, before moving around to the driver's side. He shot a quick look her way. Whether she knew she was doing it or not, her brows were tugged together in a deep frown, her fingers pulling at a thread on her jeans like she was nervous.

Now that he thought about it, it kind of reminded him of... before. The days when she'd go deep into her own head. When, he now knew, anxiety had gotten the best of her.

Reaching out, he wrapped his fingers around her thigh as he pulled onto the road and started heading toward Mila's school. There was a quick intake of breath before her eyes fell on him. As if she realized she was giving herself away, she smiled.

The smile was all wrong.

"Is it that we haven't identified the attacker yet?" he asked quietly. That would be understandable. Heck, he was pissed as hell about it himself.

There was a small pause. "I know you'll protect Mila and me."

His fingers tightened. "Of course we will." They had to. Because the alternative was something he couldn't consider.

Willow blew out a long breath, gaze shifting to her lap. "Do you ever feel angry about how I was after having Mila? You were a new Navy SEAL. You needed support. And I didn't give that to you. I was a weight."

He frowned. What had caused her to bring that up? "No, you

weren't. You were everything to me. You *and* Mila. I never felt angry at you. And even now, all I feel is regret and guilt, because I didn't realize what was going on. Because I didn't do more to help you at a time when you needed me most."

She sighed. "Do you think those years would have been easier if I'd gotten help sooner?"

"I think getting help would have required us to pause our lives to really see what was going on. But we were both in too deep, you in postpartum depression, while I was navigating my way through being a first-time dad and a SEAL. We didn't stop to question that maybe it wasn't supposed to be so hard."

One silent nod.

Worry crawled up his spine. "Things are different now, Willow. But if we ever get to that point again where you find yourself feeling like you're not okay, you tell me."

Even if she didn't, Blake would see. Like he could see right now. And he wouldn't stop trying to make things better.

When he pulled up outside the school, he turned to watch her. Waiting for her confirmation. Needing it.

She looked at him and opened her mouth to say something, then a knock came at the window.

He almost cursed, just stopping himself when he saw Jason there, Mila in his arms.

Willow quickly climbed out of the car, like she couldn't wait to get away from him, her face transforming into a genuine smile as she took their daughter from Jason.

Anyone looking at her would think she was fine.

Blake knew better. He'd find out what was wrong—and he'd find out soon.

# CHAPTER 21

*W*illow fiddled with her glass of water. She could feel Blake's eyes on her, intense and demanding from the kitchen. Blake, Logan, and Jason were getting beers, then they were supposed to be disappearing into Blake's study.

Usually, she loved his presence. Right now, she needed him gone. How long did it take to grab some beers? Not this long.

She didn't look over. She couldn't. Because ever since he'd found her in Flynn's office earlier that day, he'd been asking too many questions. Studied her face too closely.

Grace and Courtney's voices fluttered through her thoughts. She was pretty sure they were asking "would you rather" questions, but she was struggling to follow.

*Come on, Willow, concentrate on them,* she scolded herself. *Not the big looming man in the kitchen.*

The second they'd gotten home, Willow had texted the women and asked them to come over for girls' night *tonight*. Because otherwise, Blake would get the words out of her. And then he'd make her take a test and possibly turn this "maybe" into a reality.

No. Not tonight. Tonight, she was hanging on to hope that

she'd wake up tomorrow with her period, and all her worry would be for nothing.

"What do you think, Willow? How long would you survive?"

She blinked at Courtney's words, forcing herself out of her head. "I'm sorry, what?"

"A zombie apocalypse comes, you're on your own—so no relying on any super-fast, super-strong boyfriend to save you—how long do you survive?"

Grace smiled. "I've already admitted I wouldn't last long. A few days, maybe a week, tops. Depends how quickly they find me in whichever nook I've curled myself into."

Courtney leaned forward, hand on her chest. "Whereas I think I'd do quite well. As long as I had a dagger to slice and dice those dead scumbags." She turned to Grace. "And I think you'd do better than you think."

A look passed between them. Something that left Willow yet again wondering about the details of Grace's past.

When both of them looked at Willow again, she sighed. "I've never considered a zombie apocalypse. Would Mila be with me?"

Courtney lifted a shoulder. "It's possible."

"Well, if Mila was with me, I'd be there for the long haul because I'd do anything and everything to survive and protect that kid." Alien invasion. Ice Age. She'd do whatever it took, fight whatever other-earthly creature she had to.

Courtney's and Grace's expressions softened.

"But if it was just me," Willow continued, "I'd probably be more like Grace. Find a nook and hide." Because really, who had the energy to fight off zombies for the rest of their life without external motivators?

Grace tapped her chin. "Okay, so, I need to have a child in order to have the will to fight zombies."

They all chuckled. Willow nodded. "Exactly."

A smile tugged at Courtney's lips as she took a sip of her

wine. "Better get on that, never know when one's around the corner."

Willow had taken a glass of wine too, mostly because she'd already said yes when she remembered she might be pregnant. It sat on the coffee table, untouched.

The guys stepped into the room. Willow shot a look up at Blake. It was the first time she'd looked directly at him since getting home. He was wearing a dark gray shirt that matched the gray of his eyes. It pulled snugly across his biceps and chest, making him look huge, as per usual.

When their gazes clashed, she sucked in a quick, deep breath. Yep. Just as intense and questioning as they'd been all afternoon.

She quickly looked away.

"We'll disappear into the office," he said quietly, beer in hand. "But trust me, none of you are going into a zombie apocalypse without us."

"Damn straight," Jason said. "I'll be right there with you to dice those zombies, Courtney."

She scoffed. "You say that now, but then you get turned into a super-zombie, and where does that leave me?"

"Yeah, then you'd have to become a zombie with me. You're the first one I'd come after."

Courtney's eyes closed. "I'm doomed."

Willow snuck a peek up at Blake. Mm-hmm, still watching her. He bent down, pressing a small kiss on her cheek, lips lingering like they always did, before leaving the room with the guys.

Willow gave a little involuntary shiver, still feeling his lips right there, even after he'd left.

"So, if the guys don't make it, none of us will," Courtney grumbled.

Grace lifted a shoulder. "Eh, might be fun to be a zombie. We've been human long enough."

Willow laughed, and it felt good. "Interesting way to look at it." She rose from the couch. "Anyone want candy? We have Red Vines, M&M's, Reese's Peanut Butter Cups...we might even have some Twinkies."

Courtney had brought some pastries from The Grind but they'd been devoured within minutes of everyone arriving, mostly by the guys.

"Holy Moses, woman, you have all that in your kitchen?" Courtney sounded shocked.

"We're like a candy store over here." She opened the pantry door, hearing footsteps behind her as Courtney and Grace took seats at the island.

"I'd love some peanut butter cups," Grace said.

"Twinkie for me, please," Courtney added.

She eyed the candy shelf. Yes, Blake had an entire shelf dedicated to candy. He called it his "Willow and Mila Emergency Shelf". He'd stocked the same things in their previous home, before Mila was born, claiming most arguments originated because she was hungry and needed a hit of sugar. Before Mila had been born, that was probably true.

She grabbed a bit of everything and dropped the stash onto the island. "Blake says that every man needs a sugar shelf for when his woman is hangry."

"Smart man," Grace said, taking a peanut butter cup and tearing the paper. She frowned. "I doubt there'd be any candy in a post-apocalyptic world. Not for long at least."

Courtney grabbed a Twinkie. "You'll just need to raid all the shelves at the stores and take candy to your hiding spot. Unless you choose to dagger them with me."

Grace smiled. "Guess it depends on how brave I'm feeling."

Courtney rolled her eyes. "Grace, don't even make me start. We all know you're the bravest woman around."

Willow remained quiet, studying both women.

Grace caught her gaze, tossing the wrapper on the table. "Sorry. We keep referencing things that I haven't shared."

Willow opened her mouth to promise she didn't need to share anything unless she wanted to, but Grace was already talking.

"When I was in my early twenties, I was kidnapped by a man who worked for a sex trafficking ring."

Willow's jaw dropped open. She'd heard about Courtney's brush with the Italian Mafia, but Blake had never mentioned a sex trafficking ring. "Oh my gosh, I'm so sorry."

She gave a small smile. "Thank you. The guy who did it had me in his basement for a week before I escaped. For a long time, I was scared he'd find me, and then, eventually, he did."

Willow's heart crashed against her ribs.

"It was…traumatic. And incredibly hard to recover from. But by the time he found me again, I'd met Logan," Grace continued. "And long story short, Logan killed him."

"I'm glad you're okay. But, God, I really am sorry." She couldn't even imagine the hell that must have been Grace's life.

"I'm very grateful to be where I am right now. Logan is…" Grace closed her eyes before opening them again. "He's every-thing. As well as protecting me physically, he's really helped me heal."

Willow's heart went out to the woman.

The three of them carried the candy into the living room. Courtney paused at a picture on top of the fireplace. "This is cute."

It was a picture of Willow holding Mila when she was a newborn. Blake had his arm around them.

Willow remembered that day well. It had been her first outing after getting out of the hospital. They'd gone to a park for some fresh air. Willow had been so hopeful that getting outside would help her feel more like herself. "Mila was only a few weeks old there."

Courtney smiled, placing the picture back down. "You all look happy."

Willow could have laughed. That's how deceptive photos

were. They could show you anything, even rewriting history with a beautiful lie. "Behind the smile was a lot of grief."

Not just grief. Sadness. Anxiety. Emotions she'd had no idea how to handle.

Courtney's brows pulled together as she took her seat again. "I'm sorry."

Willow's eyes went back to the picture. It was almost strange, knowing that no one looking at her that day had seen the internal struggle she'd been going through. Not even Blake, the man who'd always seen everything.

"No one prepares you for the emotional side of mother-hood," she said quietly. "From the second I gave birth, I didn't feel like myself. I thought it would pass but it just…didn't. Blake wasn't able to take much time off work, and I just remember feeling so alone and isolated. My hormones were all over the place."

"PPD is so much more common than people think," Grace offered.

Willow knew that now. "I wish people would talk about its prevalence more. About the grieving that women go through for the body they once had. The changes in the relationship with their partner. The loss of the life they'd led up to that point." She gave a little shake of her head. "I remember feeling guilty about grieving for those things when I had the most precious gift of all. I mean, I had a beautiful child, who I loved and felt so grateful for, but I was still so sad."

It was Grace's turn to shake her head. "You should *not* feel guilty. The hormonal changes after having a baby, not to mention the lack of sleep, all affect our emotions. Postpartum depression doesn't discriminate, but it does look different on every woman." She paused. "The struggles of becoming a mom—whether that's a first-time mom or a fourth-time mom—need to be de-stigma-tized and normalized."

"I agree. The therapist I went to was wonderful. I saw her for a year. She prescribed some medication, and I took it for almost as long."

Willow wet her lips, debating over whether to admit the next part, but needing to talk about it.

"I'm scared that I could fall back into that dark place again." The words tumbled out. And they were more true today than they'd ever been. Tackling that illness was one of the hardest things she'd ever had to do. It scared the heck out of her.

"You know the signs now," Grace assured her. "Blake knows the signs. You've got people here who love and will look out for you. If you ever feel yourself going there again, you'd have help immediately."

She was right. Of course she was. But the fear was still there.

Courtney nodded. "I know I've said it before, but I think it warrants repeating. She's a kick-ass therapist."

Willow chuckled, lifting her glass of water. "Thank you. You've both been such great friends to me."

Grace smiled. "Of course."

"And we're so happy you and Blake made it work." Courtney sighed. "That man looked at you with those sad, lovesick eyes for too long."

Willow was sure it was exactly how she'd looked at him, too.

# CHAPTER 22

*T*hree Years Ago

Willow wrapped her arms around her waist, nails digging into the soft flesh of her skin. She watched Blake closely as he did up the laces on his boots.

He was leaving. Again. Another mission with his SEAL team. A dangerous mission to God knows where, fighting God knows who.

While she remained here on her own with Mila.

She swallowed, trying to calm the bile churning in her gut.

Her gaze flicked to the baby monitor. Mila was now two, but Willow still used the monitor for every nap and sleep. It was close to nine o'clock at night, but that didn't mean her daughter wouldn't wake. In fact, she'd probably wake multiple times before morning.

Mila had never been a good sleeper. She'd gotten better over the last two years, but Willow herself couldn't remember the last time she'd had eight straight hours of rest.

Her gaze swung back to Blake. He was checking the bag at his feet.

He'd been a SEAL for just over two years now. A part of her had thought—hoped and prayed—that his deployments would be easier by now.

They weren't. And she was starting to think they never would. That

161

*watching him walk away, knowing he might not return, would always cause her insides to knot and her skin to ice.*

*Anxiety tried to crawl up her throat, an emotion she'd grown intimately familiar with over the last two years.*

*It wasn't just anxiety about Blake leaving. It was also a byproduct of parenting that no one had warned her about. She was beginning to think of the anxiety, of the pit in her stomach, as an unwelcome guest she couldn't get rid of in her own body.*

*And every time Blake left, the anxiety grew. The hole in her gut widened to the point she was sure she'd fall apart.*

*It wasn't normal. And she couldn't believe it had taken her so long to acknowledge the fact.*

*Blake stood, and suddenly her hands grew clammy. Blood roared between her ears.*

*He waited until the last second to look at her. He sucked in a deep breath. It was the first time he'd looked at her in hours. He always avoided eye contact the nights he left. Probably because he knew what he'd find. A panic she couldn't hide. An anxiety she couldn't push down.*

*He turned to lift his bag, but before he could, her voice penetrated the silence. The first words either of them had spoken since putting Mila to bed.*

*"I'm struggling."*

*She watched the thick muscles in his back tighten through the shirt. She hadn't admitted that out loud before. Not in the entire two years they'd been parenting together. She'd just kept pushing through. Kept swimming, even when she felt like she was drowning.*

*But tonight, something inside her screamed at her to speak up. To put voice to the battle raging in her mind. The overdue acknowledgment that this couldn't continue. "I can't do this by myself."*

*God, she felt weak admitting that. She was Mila's mother. Other than studying part-time, taking care of her daughter was all she had to do. It shouldn't be so hard, should it?*

*"I need more from you," she whispered.*

*At the back of her mind, she knew this wasn't the right time to tell* him. His job wasn't like most. He couldn't just call in sick to be with her. He had a mission to complete. But now that she'd started, she couldn't stop. Each word tore from some dark place inside her.

"Some days I can barely breathe." Most days... "I don't ever feel... good anymore."

She couldn't remember the last time she'd smiled. Not the fake smile she gave for show, the one that took all her strength to muster and left her heavy and exhausted after.

No. A real smile that had little parts of her soul rising with her lips. Was she even capable of those anymore?

"I need you."

There it was. Two years after birthing her daughter. Two years of crippling anxiety, brain fog, low self-worth, and a rocky relationship. This was her cry for help.

She wasn't coping. Hadn't been coping. With any of it.

And even though the words had been hard, were way overdue, and said at the complete wrong time, she felt...lighter. Because Blake knew. Her pain wasn't only her own anymore. And Blake would help her navigate this, like he'd helped her with most other things in her life.

When he turned, his brows tugged together, and his mouth opened.

Her breath caught as she waited for his words. Words of reassurance that things would change. That she'd be okay. That this crippling pain in her chest was temporary and wouldn't last forever. Because she needed those words like she needed oxygen to breathe. She'd told herself it would get better. Easier. But it never did. And now she was desperate.

When his lips sealed shut, she was confused. Was he trying to think of the right words? The right actions?

Then he lifted his bag, stepped forward, pressed a lingering kiss to her head—and left. The door clicked behind him.

For a moment, Willow stood there, the suffocating silence seeping into her bones, pressing down on her heart. It kind of felt like a dream. Like she was looking in on someone else's life from above. Like her body wasn't her own.

*Then reality started to trickle back, and suddenly, the hollowness that she knew so well flooded her.*

*She felt empty. Lost. Like her best friend had just left her in the middle of a hurricane without a backward glance.*

*Maybe by kissing her, he'd been trying to reassure her. But she didn't need his kiss. She needed words. Solutions. Someone to tell her, promise her, that the day would come when it didn't feel like surviving was all she could do.*

*Somehow, she landed on the couch. Then she was lying down.*

*She couldn't even cry. All she could do was stare at the oak door, feeling the emptiness spider through her limbs while letting the silence of the house drown her.*

～

"I NEED YOU."

*Blake paused at Willow's words. For a second, he couldn't move. He could barely breathe.*

*She was struggling.*

*Hadn't he known that, though? Even without her words, hadn't he suspected as much for a long time?*

*And yet he'd barely done a damn thing—because the truth was, between the responsibilities of being a first-time dad, a husband, and a SEAL, he was barely keeping his head above water himself.*

*The constant war that raged in his chest between his love for his family and the country he swore to protect tore at him.*

*He turned slowly and looked down at the woman he loved. The woman he'd always loved.*

*He opened his mouth to say something.*

*His head felt jumbled. He had no words to make this better. He hadn't had words for two damn years. Anything he could say just felt...inadequate.*

*His stomach twisted with unease. And not just unease about what was happening here and now. The unease had been sitting in his gut like a brick all day. Hell, all week. The feeling of foreboding, like some-thing big and soul-destroying was right around the corner, was one he couldn't shake.*

*Every part of him wished he could stay. Hold her. Be with her. But the fact was, he couldn't. It wasn't just that he'd be court-martialed if he didn't show up. People expected him. Needed him. His country. His team. Being even one man down meant every other man shouldered that loss, possibly paying for it with their life. They needed him to be there. To be his best.*

*His mouth closed. Words between them had been hard since Mila. Stilted. But the one thing that had always remained unbroken was their love...their physical connection.*

*So instead of giving her fragmented words that would probably be empty because he couldn't abandon his mission, he pressed a long, slow kiss to her head. A kiss that he hoped conveyed everything he couldn't say any other way.*

# CHAPTER 23

*B*lake watched Willow's brows tug together. She was dreaming.

Dreaming probably wasn't the right word, actually. The woman had been tossing and turning all night. Something was pressing on her mind. *Had been* pressing on her mind since yesterday afternoon.

After everyone left last night, Willow continued to avoid him like the plague, all but running to the bedroom, brushing her teeth, and slipping between the sheets before he'd even made it into the room.

He should be thinking about his team. They were returning today. He'd received notification overnight that they'd captured Ahmad's brothers, but not the man himself. *That* should be plaguing him. But right now, Willow was all he could think about.

He traced a finger over the lines between her eyes, wishing they would smooth out.

*What's on your mind, honey?*

Blake watched her for a while, almost temped to wake her. Then he saw a twitch in one of her fingers. And another.

When she looked up, her gaze caught his. And something akin to pain flashed through her green eyes before she blinked it away.

A thick dread slammed into his gut. He pushed it down, plastering a smile he didn't feel to his face. "Good morning, baby." He'd greeted her with those exact same words just yesterday. She'd smiled and her eyes had softened, muscles relaxed.

Today it was the opposite. There were no smiles. Her eyes were clouds of anxiety, her muscles tense.

"Good morning."

He waited a moment for words that would make sense of what was going on. They never came.

"Tell me," he said quietly.

She swallowed, pushing the sheets back.

The second she tried to sit up, he looped an arm around her, holding her close, not able to let her leave. He needed to know. "Willow—"

"I just need to use the bathroom. I'll be right back."

Slowly, he lifted his arm, watching her cross the room and disappear into the connected bathroom. Reaching toward the nightstand, he checked the time on his phone. Mila would be up soon. He just prayed he got to the bottom of this first. He wasn't a patient man any longer. Not after finally getting his family back. He couldn't wait.

When Willow walked out, she looked even more dejected than when she'd gone in.

His blood pressure rose, unease prickling his skin. What the hell was going on?

She perched on the edge of the mattress beside him. He sat up.

"Before I tell you, can I ask you something?"

He was careful to keep his features neutral. "Anything."

"That last night before you were taken, just before you stepped out the door for your mission..."

He swallowed. God, he hated thinking about that night. About the mistakes he'd made and everything he should have done differently. About the words he couldn't muster.

"I know it wasn't fair of me to dump that on you seconds before you walked out the door, but...why didn't you say something? *Anything* would have been better than nothing."

There was something akin to desperation in Willow's voice. She'd been wondering a long time.

He blew out a long breath before reaching over, wrapping his fingers around her thigh. "You have no idea how many times I've replayed that night in my head." Every damn day while he'd been away from her. "The regret that I didn't say anything has been like a physical pain tormenting me."

His fingers tightened. How could he explain this to her when he could barely explain it to himself?

"When you and I were in the thick of things, I remember thinking it was just a rough patch in our lives. A rough patch in our relationship. That we were both tired and stressed and it was normal for you to not want me to leave you on your own with Mila. I thought it was a temporary season of our lives, and it would end."

He met her gaze, needing her to hear it all.

"I was in my head that night, thinking about the mission. About my team. I had this bad feeling in my gut, like I already knew something was going to happen. Something big and life-changing. So when you were talking to me, I didn't hear what you needed me to hear. The desperation. The cry for help. I wanted to tell you that it would be okay, but I didn't have the words, so I went for a kiss...because even when our relationship was hard, the physical always remained good."

She gave a slow nod.

"But that wasn't enough," he continued. "You needed me to say something, even if it was just to acknowledge what you were feeling. I know that now. And I'm sorry. So damn sorry."

A glimmer of tears washed over her eyes. "You knew."

She wasn't talking about her depression or their relationship. She was talking about Project Arma.

"I knew *something*." And he would never ignore his gut again. He leaned forward. "Please, Willow…say you forgive me."

Her eyes shuttered. "I forgive you." When they opened again, the tears were still there.

"Now, please tell me."

A shuffle sounded in the other room. Small feet hitting the floor. Sounds only Blake could hear.

"I'm late."

The whispered words had barely left Willow's lips before Mila was bounding into the room, jumping into her mother's arms.

Blake didn't move. He barely breathed.

Late. As in her period…

She might be pregnant.

He watched as Willow's face transformed into a smile. But it wasn't the kind of smile that reached her eyes. And under the smile, he finally saw what had been there since yesterday.

Fear of having another baby with him. Fear of history repeating itself.

# CHAPTER 24

*W*illow tried not to squirm at Blake's constant and intense stare. He sat across the table from her at The Grind. Mila was talking about something her teacher had taught the class that week. Surprisingly, Willow was participating in the conversation more than Blake.

Pretending everything was fine was somehow easier while in public. And definitely easier with Mila there to distract everyone.

"What about on my sixth birthday?"

Willow blinked. "What was that, baby?"

"I know you said my fifth birthday wasn't the right time for a puppy like Jessie's, but what about on my sixth birthday? Now that we're living at Dad's, there'll be two parents to look after a puppy."

Willow wet her lips. "We can think about it. Remember though, if you get a puppy, *you'll* need to take responsibility for it. That means walking and feeding and cleaning up after it."

She gave a vigorous nod. "I know. Jessie said it isn't too hard. You guys would just be my backup."

Backup...hm. Willow would believe that if the time came. "Like when we got Goldie the fish?"

A cheeky smile curved Mila's lips. "Yeah." She turned to Blake. "I promised Mama I'd take care of Goldie, but she ended up feeding him. Then he went to fish heaven."

He smiled down at their daughter. "I've never been able to keep a fish alive, either."

Mila giggled.

Courtney stopped beside their table. "Hey guys, how're we doing today?"

"Good!" Mila rose to her knees. "Mama said she'd think about getting me a puppy next year."

Courtney chuckled, giving Willow a pointed look. "Is that right?"

"It wasn't a yes, but it wasn't a no." She frowned. "You're working again?"

The woman was on every day. Yes, she was the owner, but surely she got some days off.

She sighed. "Yeah, replacing the multitude of hours that Joey worked has been…hard."

There was a hint of pain in the woman's voice. Joey hadn't just been Courtney's second in charge at the shop, he'd also been her friend. She'd had to let him go after he'd gotten Courtney injured and almost killed.

"I'm sorry," Willow said softly.

Courtney lifted a shoulder. "It is what it is. Am I getting the usuals? One latte, one long black, and a chocolate milkshake with sprinkles?"

Mila nodded vigorously.

Blake leaned forward in the booth. "Hey, any chance Mila could help with the sprinkles?"

Willow's brows rose.

"Sure." Courtney offered her hand to Mila. "Let's not stop at the sprinkles though, she can help with the whole milkshake shebang."

"Really?" Mila's eyes were so wide they almost looked like

they were going to pop out of her head. She grabbed Courtney's hand, scrambling out of the booth.

*Oh no...*Willow immediately wanted to tug her daughter back. That kid had been her big distraction. The only thing stopping Blake from questioning her. Making her talk about...*it.*

As soon as Mila was gone, his voice lowered. "Have you taken a test?"

And just like that, the suffocating anxiety returned. "No."

He frowned. When he opened his mouth, she almost thought he was going to ask why not, but instead, he reached across the table, lacing his fingers through hers. "Tonight."

Some of the edge tapered off the anxiety at his touch, and at the delayed deadline. At least she had a few more hours of ignorance. Which was a small reprieve.

After a minute of silence, his eyes softened. "I hate when your smile doesn't reach your eyes."

His words skittered through her insides, warming some of the places that had been chilled since yesterday. "You can see that?" she asked quietly.

"I see it, and it makes my chest ache. It makes me desperate to help you, but also frustrated because I don't know how."

She swallowed, not sure how to respond.

His thumb rubbed over her hand. "It will be okay."

For a moment, she wanted to close her eyes. Replay those words in her head and let them calm some of the storm inside. Because he said them with so much confidence, so much conviction, that she wanted to believe, desperately needed them to be true. "How do you know?" she asked quietly.

Another swipe. "Because I have faith."

Courtney and Mila returned to the table. Willow tried to take her hand back, but Blake's grip firmed. Holding her. Continuing to cherish her skin.

Willow looked up slowly. Courtney held Mila with one hand, the milkshake with the other.

"Mila...do you want to tell Mom and Dad what you just told me?"

Willow studied her friend's face. Something was wrong. Neither Courtney nor her daughter were smiling. In fact, both looked worried.

Mila pointed through the glass. "There was a man out there watching me."

Willow swung her head around, and Blake immediately straightened.

"It was the man I saw outside my school. He's wearing a blue jacket and jeans today."

Oh God. Willow had forgotten all about that. Christ, how had she forgotten to tell Blake?

He pushed out of the booth, pulling his phone from his pocket and placing it to his ear. He met Willow's eyes for a second. "Stay inside. Don't leave."

Then he was gone.

Worry darted over Mila's face. "Is everything okay, Mama?"

Even though smiling was the last thing she felt like doing, she forced her face to cooperate in an attempt to put her daughter at ease. "Of course. Daddy's just checking to see if the guy's still there. He'll be back in a sec."

Her daughter gave a small nod.

Courtney slid into the booth, pulling Mila in beside her. "I'll wait with you guys."

Willow opened her mouth to tell her friend she didn't need to do that, but the words stuck in her throat, because the truth was, having Courtney stay with them made her feel just a bit calmer.

Courtney pushed the milkshake in front of Mila. "What do you think? Is this one better than the others?"

Immediately, Mila's attention diverted to the milkshake as she wrapped her fingers around the glass. Willow could have kissed her friend for distracting her daughter.

Mila took a sip, her eyes lighting up. "It is!"

Courtney chuckled. "Well, there is quite a lot of chocolate syrup in there, so I'm not surprised."

Willow's gaze flicked toward the window. Blake stood by the front door, scanning the street. It was probably killing him that he had to remain by the shop. She'd known he would though, because leaving to search for the guy would leave her and Mila unprotected.

She turned back to the table just in time to see Mila reaching for a napkin, knocking over the milkshake with her elbow in the process. About a third of the drink spilled everywhere before Courtney could straighten the glass. She tried to get up, but Willow shook her head.

"You're blocked in. I'll get a cloth."

"Thanks. There's one that I just rinsed behind the counter."

Rising from the booth, she went to the counter, scanning the other side before reaching across. She was just turning when a hand touched her shoulder.

Willow jolted, her entire body on edge, but she immediately calmed when she saw who it was. "Grace, hey!"

The other woman frowned, her gaze shooting to Blake outside the shop. Willow noticed that Logan now stood with him. "Is everything okay?"

"I'm not sure. Mila saw a guy watching her from outside. Apparently, he was outside her school as well." Willow rubbed her temple, still in disbelief that she'd forgotten to mention that to Blake.

"Oh, gosh. That's not good. But you're well protected with the two of them guarding the place." The other woman took a small step closer. "Is there anything I can do?"

"No. I'm fine." Okay, she'd said that far too quickly.

Grace's brows tugged together, head tilting. "Are you sure?"

"I might be pregnant."

The words just tumbled from her lips. She definitely hadn't meant to say that.

To Grace's credit, her features didn't change.

"I'm going to take a test tonight," she added quietly.

Grace gave a small nod. "And the possibility of being pregnant scares you. That's why you were talking about it last night? About being scared of returning to that dark place."

"I'm terrified, Grace. I just...I don't think I can do it all again."

At the back of her mind, she knew it would be different a second time around. She knew what to look for if she were to develop PPD again. She knew the help she needed. But still, her mind feared it all.

"Do the test," Grace said softly. "And remember that you have support. That all of us love you. And everything will be okay." She paused. "Also, Jason's sister Sage is in town, visiting her brother and Courtney. She arrived this morning. She's a doctor, and she's very easy to talk to. She cared for the women in Marble Falls who got pregnant."

There was a sharp gasp from behind them.

Willow turned, mouth dropping open at the sight of Janet. "What are you doing here?"

The woman's face was white. "You're *pregnant?*"

Willow's gaze shot to the booth by the window. She almost sagged in relief when she saw Mila wasn't looking their way. Janet had said that entirely too loudly. "That's none of your business."

Janet took a small step back, shaking her head at Willow like she was diseased or something. Her eyes were wide...in fear?

"A woman already birthed one of those *things* in Marble Falls. The child isn't human!"

Willow's spine straightened, and Grace stiffened as well. "Excuse me?"

She leaned forward, whispering loudly, "They're not natural, Willow! They're not the way God intended!"

Anger spiked in Willow's chest, hard and fast. She'd had enough of this woman's ignorance. "I've told you this before, but obviously you weren't listening. The men didn't choose what happened to them. And they're not less human than anyone else. Just like their babies wouldn't be."

"I think you should leave," Grace said, her normal calm gone, a vicious anger Willow hadn't heard before coating her words.

Janet shot her gaze between them, head continuing to shake. Then she turned and left quickly.

Willow dragged in a shuddering breath before blowing it out slowly.

Grace touched her shoulder. "Are you okay?"

She nodded quickly. "Yeah. Just angry."

"Me too," Grace said quietly.

# CHAPTER 25

The test was heavy in Willow's hand as she stepped into the living room. Her insides roiled.

Blake was on the couch. His face was so clear, she had no idea what he was feeling or thinking. But then, he'd been like that most of the day.

How he was able to hide his emotions so well, she had no idea. It was probably better that way, though, wasn't it? If she knew he was anxious, it would definitely make her more anxious.

He patted the spot beside him on the couch. "Come here, honey."

She hadn't even realized she'd stopped walking. Giving herself a small shake, she closed the distance between them, lowering beside him. He immediately shuffled closer, arm going around her shoulders.

Swallowing, she looked up at him. "I can't look at it."

His arm tightened around her. "How long will it take?"

"Maybe another minute."

One small nod. "Whatever it says, whatever happens, we'll deal with it together. It'll all be okay."

She tried for a smile, but she was too nervous to muster it.

Blake opened his mouth, but then he frowned, gaze shooting across the room to the hall. Suddenly, the test slipped from her fingers, disappearing behind a cushion. A second later, Mila walked into the room.

Willow jumped to her feet and moved over to her daughter. She lifted her into her arms. "Baby, what are you doing up?"

Mila scrubbed her hands over her eyes. "I'm scared."

Willow's heart gave a thud.

"What are you scared of?" she asked, even though she already knew. She felt Blake at her back, hand smoothing along her spine.

"That man I saw today. Do you think he'll be back?"

Willow's heart broke.

"He's not coming near you, Mila." Blake's voice was hard, edged with a darkness Mila probably wouldn't recognize for what it was. Willow did.

Mila leaned her head on Willow's shoulder, curling into her body. "Can you both come sleep with me?"

She pressed a kiss to the top of her head. "Of course, darling." She carried Mila to the bedroom, tucking her beneath the blanket before crawling between her daughter and the wall. Blake lay on Mila's other side.

Immediately, Mila closed her eyes, snuggling into the blankets. "I like it when you're both here." Mila's voice was a whisper into the pillow.

Willow looked up at Blake. The teddy bear nightlight cast a red haze over his face, the glow and the shadows making him appear even more dangerous than usual.

He reached behind the pillow, grabbing her hand. Immediately, she laced her fingers through his. Touching him was like holding his strength in her hand, feeling it pulse up her arm.

How many times had Willow lain in bed, waiting for her daughter to fall asleep, wishing Blake was right there with them? Not just over the last three years, but even before that. There'd been so many nights she'd sat beside the crib, sleep-deprived. Empty. Lonely.

She felt none of that now.

Blake's gaze heated. And there was something else. An unspoken promise. That he would continue to be there. Watching out for his family. Present both physically and emotionally.

The anxiety that had been eating away at her all day suddenly fizzled, and in its place, a calm. A whisper that she would be okay. A gentle reassurance that even if the stick turned pink, Blake would be there, more present than last time.

A small smile touched her lips, the first one in a while that wasn't forced. Slowly, she leaned her head back into the pillow, eyes shuttering, allowing the comfort that her family gave her to relax the muscles that had been tense for so long.

She didn't know how long her eyes had been shut, but when Blake's hand tightened, her eyes snapped open. She realized Mila's breaths had evened out. Their daughter was asleep.

It was time to look at the test.

Shuffling down the bed, she took Blake's hand again as they reentered the living room. Willow stopped. "Can you look first and tell me?"

He moved forward without hesitation and lifted the test from behind the cushion. He scanned the screen, and again, nothing changed on his face. The man was completely unreadable.

When he looked up, he studied her carefully. "Not pregnant."

A small frown marred her brows. She stepped forward, taking the test and looking at the screen. He was right. Not pregnant.

Blake's arms wrapped around her waist. "We can test again tomorrow."

She gave a small nod. She was never late. She'd been so certain that it meant she was pregnant. Was it possible the chloroform had messed with her hormones? Could it do that?

She peered up again, wishing the man would show her some sort of emotion. "How do you feel about a negative?"

"If you're not pregnant, then we're not meant to have a baby right now."

She gave a small tilt of her head. "Right now?"

There was a short pause. It was heavy. Thoughtful. "I *would* like to have another baby. But only if and when you're ready. And if that day never comes, that's okay too. Because I already have you and Mila, which makes me the luckiest guy around."

Willow ran her hand over his shoulder, smoothing the material of his shirt. She'd never even considered having another. Not after how tough it was with Mila. But she loved Mila so much that her chest ached. And just now, in the bedroom, she'd felt a level of peace in whatever this outcome would be.

She quieted her voice. "I think, maybe, there might be a time I'll feel ready to have another. I'm slowly learning to trust that things won't be the same as they were before."

His hands went to her cheeks. "I guarantee you they won't be the same. I won't let them. I'll protect your mind as strongly and fiercely as I protect your body."

That final little barrier around her heart, the one she hadn't been aware still existed, crashed down. He had all of her.

"I love you," she whispered.

He pressed his head to hers. "I love you so much it physically hurts."

Leaning up, Willow kissed him. And in that kiss, she tried to give him everything. Every little part of herself that he already owned.

Immediately, she was lifted from her feet. Her eyes remained shuttered, but she felt him moving, a door closing behind them. Then he held her against the door, her core pressing against his hard stomach.

The kiss was primal, and it was hungry, causing tiny flickers of heat to ignite deep in her belly.

Willow curled her fingers against his shoulder, digging them into his skin as deep moans attempted to escape her lips. He swallowed all of them, his tongue swirling in her mouth, dueling with hers.

The way the man kissed her was everything. It was her comfort. Her salvation. Her refuge.

Warm hands brushed across her lower stomach seconds before her shirt was torn over her head.

Then his lips were grazing down her neck and her chest. He sucked a nipple through the bra and her back arched, a whimper escaping her lips.

A second later, the bra fell, and his tongue slid over her tip, thrumming it.

A shudder slithered up her spin, the heat in her abdomen spidering through her system. The man played with and licked her nipple for endless minutes, knowing exactly what tormented her most.

When he switched to the other, his tongue swirled that peak in exactly the same way. Sucking and nipping.

"Blake, please."

His mouth remained for another second. Then he stepped to the side, lowering her gently on top of the low dresser.

His finger slid into the waistband of her jeans and underwear. She didn't even need to be told to lift her hips, they did of their own accord, the need for there to be no barriers between them too strong.

Two muscled hands wrapped around her thighs, tugging her right to the edge of the dresser. He bent, head hovering over her. For a moment, her breath caught, the ache between her legs throbbing in anticipation.

Then his lips closed around her clit and he sucked, using his tongue in the most intimate, drive-her-crazy kind of way.

Willow's teeth sank into her bottom lip to silence the cry.

Blood soared between her ears as the most intense pressure built in her core.

Every swipe of his tongue, every vibration from his lips, pushed her closer to the edge. The small thread that was her sanity was moments from snapping.

Her breaths became choppy, back arching.

Then suddenly, she felt Blake's finger at her entrance. Her body jolted, but he held her firmly with his other hand around her thigh.

Slowly, he entered her, the warm invasion a gentle torture. His mouth continued to swipe and play as his finger slid in and out.

"Blake..." She writhed and ground her hips, the flames in her body so close to catching and lighting up the entire room.

Suddenly, he crooked his finger, pushing against a place inside her that he knew drove her crazy. That's when the thread broke. Her muscles bunched, the orgasm ripping through her with an intensity that exploded through her entire body.

She opened her mouth, but suddenly, Blake was there again, mouth taking hers, silencing her cry.

BLAKE STRAIGHTENED. Willow's beautiful breasts rose and fell, pressing against his chest with each deep breath. His hands went to his shirt, then his jeans, removing every scrap of clothing while only briefly losing her lips.

She was fucking magnificent. Every inch of her.

Taking hold of her hips, he was about to lift her and carry her to the bed when she grabbed his wrists, halting him. "I want you here. Like this."

It was like gas on a fire. Blood roared so loudly between his ears that it was deafening.

Reaching across, he opened the top drawer for a condom.

With the pregnancy scare, it felt best. And she didn't question him. In fact, just as he was about to cover himself, Willow took it from his fingers.

Slowly, so slowly it almost killed him, she slid the latex over his length. Her fingers applied more pressure than they needed to. And she grazed and played with his hardness as she went.

The thing had barely made it all the way on when he was tearing her hands off him, growling deep in his throat. Then he was there, right between her heated thighs.

The woman robbed him of his sanity. Of every scrap of self-restraint and patience he had.

"Forever," he said quietly, lowering his temple to touch hers. "You and me, we're forever."

He'd known she belonged to him since the first day they'd met. And that knowledge had never waned. Never shaken. Not even on their darkest days had he questioned whether they should be together.

"Forever," she whispered.

He sank deep inside her, reveling in the soft sigh that fell from her lips and bathing in it. It was the same for him. An ache that would never subside.

He didn't move right away. Instead he paused, leaned down, and pressed a kiss to her neck. Feeling that deep connection to the woman he loved, and thanking God that they'd found their way back to each other.

His lips trailed up, taking hers, tongue pressing between her lips. Slowly, he rocked his hips back, then thrust forward. He swallowed her quiet moan.

Then he did it again. And again.

Every thrust annihilated him. Every touch burned.

Her hands wrapped around his neck, threading through his hair. Immediately, he lifted her, stepping to the side and pressing her back against the door.

He pushed deeper. Thrust harder. Faster.

It wasn't enough. None of it was. Lowering his head, he latched on to her throat, sucking and licking, never slowing his pace.

Her hands lowered to his chest, scratching down his skin. She hummed and whimpered, every sound pushing him to move faster, inching him closer to breaking.

One of his hands closed over her breast. Pressed and massaged. He could feel her walls tightening around him.

He was so damn close, he almost hurt. It was pleasure and agony meshed into one.

A low growl rumbled from his chest.

Her nails scraped down his heated skin again. With his thumb, he grazed across her nipple, and her eyes shuttered, back arching. Finally, she shattered around him.

Blake kept thrusting, his pace never slowing. He watched her, needing to see the depths of her desire. But too soon, at the twitching of her walls around his length, his own climax tore through him, so powerful it almost sent him to his knees.

His mouth crashed back onto hers. Giving. Taking.

He thrust until he physically couldn't move anymore. Until every part of him had been given to her.

When the waves stopped crashing, and his heart slowed, his temple returned to hers, and they took a moment to be still. To hold each other. To feel and absorb the intimacy of what had just taken place.

# CHAPTER 26

*B*lake's eyes shot open and every muscle in his body tensed. The room was pitch black, as it should be in the middle of the night, and Willow slept soundlessly beside him, but something had woken him.

He sat up slowly. Concentrating. Listening.

There it was again. The noise that had pierced his sleep—the crunching of grass beneath shoes. And heartbeats. Maybe five or six. Not only at the front of the house, but at the sides too.

They had visitors.

Leaning over, he touched Willow's shoulder, giving it a small shake.

A low groan fell from her lips. "Blake?"

"There are people outside. We need to get up."

Her eyes flew open, and she jackhammered into a seated position. "Mila—"

"We'll go to her now."

He grabbed his phone from the bedside table, sending a quick message to his team. Then, reaching behind his headboard, he grabbed the gun strapped to the wood.

Willow was already on her feet, wearing one of his shirts that

185

reached her knees. He tugged on a pair of pants and took her hand, tugging her behind him as they moved out into the hall. Even though she'd be almost blind in the darkness, he could see everything.

When they stepped into Mila's room, the soft haze of her nightlight cast dim redness throughout the room. Willow ran to her side, lifting her from the bed. Mila only stirred slightly before snuggling into Willow's chest.

Blake turned off the nightlight, wanting the advantage of darkness, before leading Willow into the hall and instinctively toward the back of the house.

They'd almost reached the end of the hallway when the deafening sound of glass shattering exploded throughout the house. The master bedroom window. The living room window. Even Mila's bedroom window where they'd just exited.

Blake tugged Willow behind him, close to the wall, using his body to shield her and Mila as four people, all with guns drawn, stepped into the hall from the three rooms. One man carried a camping lantern, which cast a dim glow over the hall.

His muscles tensed, finger itching to pull the trigger of his own gun. He barely stopped himself. He couldn't shoot all four of them at once, and he couldn't risk receiving return fire, getting himself killed, and leaving his family unprotected—or dead.

He inched back and tuned his hearing toward the backyard. Nothing. Whereas he could see the outline of a couple more people outside. Were they waiting for him?

Behind him was the study. The last room in the hallway. They couldn't hole up in there, not with the French doors. Too much glass they could easily shatter. But he could use those doors to access the backyard.

His yard was huge. He could try to hide them, while forcing the attention onto himself—at least until his team arrived.

His alarm would have gone off the second they crashed through the windows. A silent alarm that went straight to his team. Not that it mattered. He'd already notified them. They'd be here soon.

He heard the small gasp from Willow behind him.

Janet stepped forward. Rob and Toby were two of the three men gathered behind her.

"Hello, Blake. Willow."

Blake's grip on the gun tightened, his stance widening, making sure Willow was covered. He shuffled back a step, hearing Willow do the same. "What the fuck are you doing here?"

Janet's features hardened. "We're doing God's work, Blake. We need you to hand over Mila now."

Willow's heartbeat sped up. Another shuffle toward the end of the hall.

"You really think we'd hand our child over to you?"

The woman was batshit crazy.

She tilted her head. "What I *think* is that the child is innocent and needs protection." Janet cast her eyes over him like he was the devil reincarnated. Then her gaze slid over his shoulder. "We can't let any more abominations be created. You'll all just multiply if we don't do something. Soon the country will be crawling with you."

There was a slight tremble in Janet's arm. And the way she held the gun was all wrong. Both hands grasping the weapon, fingers interlaced around the handle, index fingers pointed. She wasn't familiar with the weapon. But she still had it aimed at his family.

He tightened his own grip, taking another step back.

"We didn't want it to come to this." It was Rob who spoke next. Blake studied him, noticing discomfort with his weapon. In fact, they all looked unpracticed and nervous with the firearms. "We wanted a different outcome for both Willow and Mila."

But not him. So they always planned to attack him or his brothers? Then what? "Save" his wife and child?

Hell no.

He shuffled back another step. Another step closer to the study.

"What's your plan here?" Willow asked, a slight tremble in her voice. "To kill us? Take Mila? You know, the second you shoot your gun, she'll wake. It's a miracle she's not awake already. Can you imagine what it will do to her, seeing her parents murdered in front of her?"

Smart. Willow was pleading to their compassionate side.

And right on cue, a flicker of remorse flashed over Janet's face. She sucked in a quick breath. "Then hand her over. I'll take her outside, and the guys will take care of you quickly."

They were all fucking deluded.

"Come on, you don't really have any other choice here," Toby said, almost pleading.

That's where the asshole was wrong.

Suddenly, Blake saw Rob's trigger finger twitch.

Nope. He wasn't doing this any longer.

Before anyone could anticipate his move, Blake swung his arm faster than the human eye could track—shooting the lantern and plunging them into darkness. He swept both Willow and Mila into his arms and raced into the study. Gunfire peppered the silence as he slammed the door closed. Pain radiated at his shoulder and side. Two bullets. Neither of them kill shots.

He ignored his injuries, breaking the lock on the French door and sprinting outside.

He moved to a back corner of the yard, depositing Willow and Mila behind the toolshed. The fence was too tall to climb with both of them, so hiding was their only choice until his team arrived.

Blake ran to the other side of the yard. He estimated his team would be here in two minutes, tops. That's how long he had to keep the attention away from his family.

He'd just made it to the other corner of the yard when he saw them. Coming out of the house and from around the front.

∽

WILLOW DUCKED down behind the toolshed. She could hear Blake across the lawn, making noise and taking the attention off them.

Fear tried to shake her limbs, but she kept them still.

Mila's beautiful brown eyes looked up at her, confused and sleep-glazed. "Mama?"

Willow forced a small smile to her face. She felt like she was smiling in the middle of a war zone. So much danger surrounded them. But the need to put her daughter at ease was so strong it almost choked her.

"Hey, baby." She kept her voice low. Blake's yard was large, but there was always the chance they might hear her.

Mila rubbed her eyes. "Where are we?"

Willow pushed a lock of hair from her daughter's face, every part of her demanding she protect this child. "We're in the backyard. Daddy's backyard." Her mind scrambled to come up with something to say. Something that she could use to protect her daughter emotionally while Blake protected them physically.

"Where's Daddy?" She scanned the toolshed, the fence, looking more awake by the second.

"You know how he protects people for his job?" Mila gave a small nod. "Right now, he's protecting us."

There was a small tugging together of her brows. "From bad people?"

"Yeah, baby. From bad people. Now, I need you to be really quiet for me. Can you do that?"

Mila swallowed, studying Willow's eyes. Then she gave a small nod, tucking her head into Willow's chest. Willow tightened her arms around her daughter.

Gunshots sounded around them. Loud shots that blasted through the otherwise quiet night. But the bullets were only firing for seconds when suddenly, she heard fighting. Hand-to-hand combat.

Then Willow's stomach curled in dread when she heard something else…the shuffling of footsteps. Close footsteps.

Willow tensed, immediately regretting it when Mila noticed and straightened in her lap.

Janet stepped around the toolshed. The second her gaze fell on Mila, the gun disappeared behind her back.

Willow drew to her feet, pushing Mila behind her.

"Janet?" Mila's voice was quiet and confused.

Janet's eyes turned steely as they looked at Willow. "Do the right thing, Willow."

"The right thing would be for you to leave. Get the hell away from my family."

Janet gave a slow shake of her head. "I'm doing what needs to be done. That child needs safety. Something she will never have if she's living with one of *them*. With multiple of them." Her gaze went to Willow's stomach in disgust.

"She's safer with us than she is with anyone else." Her voice was firm, her hand tight on her daughter's arm.

Janet's gaze skittered to the yard behind her then back. "I'm sorry for what you're about to see, Mila, but they're already here."

Willow's eyes widened even as Janet pulled her hand from behind her back.

She didn't think, she just leaped, tackling Janet to the grass before she could aim the gun.

Willow wrenched the woman's hands over her head, gun pressed to the ground. Tightening her hold on Janet's wrists, she lifted them up and crashed them down as hard as she could. Then she did it again. Over and over, until the gun released, falling just beyond Janet's reach.

The second it was gone, Willow freed a hand, punching the woman in the face. She swung back to do it again, but Janet's fist slammed into her side. The woman raised a leg and kicked her away. Immediately, Janet rolled onto her stomach, stretching out, reaching for the weapon.

Willow jumped on top of her, hands once again going to her wrists.

"Janet, *stop!*"

Janet rolled, elbowing Willow in the process. "This is what needs to happen! Humanity needs to remain pure!"

Willow was only on her back for a second before tackling her again. "The only thing that needs to happen is for crazy people like you to be locked up!"

They both reached for the gun at the same time. Before either of them could grab hold, Janet head-butted Willow hard, sending her backward. Her brain fogged, pain shooting through her skull.

She blinked once. Twice.

The third time, she saw the gun being drawn—

Suddenly, Janet was yanked off her feet.

Willow couldn't quite make out who held the flailing woman. Aidan? Flynn?

Then Mila was on Willow's stomach, small hands on her cheeks. "Mama! Are you okay?"

Immediately, she wrapped her arms around her daughter, holding her close. When she sat up, she saw men standing around the yard. Not the men who had come with Janet.

Blake's team.

From across the lawn, she saw someone striding toward them. Even though she could only see his outline through the darkness, she'd recognize him anywhere.

Blake.

The second he reached them, he dropped to his knees, tugging them both into his arms. He didn't speak any words. None of them did. They just breathed each other in. Held each other. And let the quiet moment calm some of the terror inside them.

# CHAPTER 27

*W*illow stroked Mila's hair. Her daughter had fallen asleep in her arms the second they'd reached the hospital. Which was a good thing, because Willow didn't want to leave Blake's side, but she also didn't want her daughter to watch bullet wounds being stitched up.

"Okay, I think that should do it."

Willow lifted her gaze at Sage's words.

She hadn't met the doctor before but was beyond grateful the woman was here because, unlike the doctors in Cradle Mountain, she was familiar with the team's altered DNA and healing abilities.

"No getting it wet for a few days," she continued, "and in about a week, it should be almost completely healed."

Willow's muscles relaxed. Blake reached over, wrapping his fingers around her thigh. He sat on the hospital bed wearing nothing but blood-stained jeans, while she sat on a chair beside him.

He dipped his head. "Thank you."

Sage gave him a small smile before turning to Willow. "I'll just step out to see if your blood test results are in."

Nerves skittered up Willow's spine. While Blake had been stitched up, she'd asked for a blood test to double check that she wasn't pregnant. Even though her at-home test had been negative, she needed confirmation.

When Sage left the room, Blake turned to her, his gray eyes so dark they were almost charcoal. "Are you sure you're okay?"

Was the man serious? "Blake, *you're* the one who got shot." Twice. Shot *twice*. Those words didn't sound right in her head. "You're also the one who fought off a group of deranged psychopaths with guns who were trying to kill us and take our daughter."

Her arms tightened around Mila. Everything about tonight left her feeling so sick that she was afraid her stomach would never settle.

Blake lowered his voice, anger sharpening his words. "They were never going to take her. And I would never have allowed them to kill you."

The hand on her thigh moved to her cheek, caressing her skin. For the first time all night, his eyes softened. "I'm sorry they got so close."

She closed her eyes, leaning into his touch, needing the warmth and connection more than ever before. "Please don't say sorry. It's because of you we're all okay. I'm just so glad it's over. That we can go back to living our lives. That Mila will be safe again." She took a small, shuddering breath. "I can't believe it was them. I mean, I hadn't exactly known them for very long, but for the most part, they just seemed so...normal."

Heck, before all the Blake stuff had come up, she'd considered them friends.

Had there been signs that the three of them were extremists? Signs that she'd missed because she hadn't been looking close enough?

"They're either dead or with the police now," Blake said

quietly. "I'm going to ask Steve to pull some strings so I can question Rob and Janet myself."

Rob and Janet were the only two who had survived the night.

She frowned. "Why do you need to question them?" Even though Blake was beyond capable of protecting himself, she didn't want him anywhere near them. She didn't want *anyone* she loved near them ever again.

His eyes narrowed, that dangerous glint returning. Had he been a stranger to her, she was sure the look would have sent her running.

"Because I need to make sure that they're it. That the plan to kill my team, to take my daughter, started and ended with them. The only reason those two are even alive is because we intended to question them right there in the yard. But when the police arrived, we ran out of time."

That was the neighbors' doing. They'd heard the gun shots and called the police, who had arrived shortly after Blake's team.

His thumb stroked across the skin of her neck gently, in complete contrast to his words. "Unlike the police, I'll be able to tell if they're lying. And I won't rest until I know that everyone I love is safe."

She swallowed, giving a small nod. Knowing that she could trust Blake to take care of the situation.

The door opened, and Sage stepped back inside. Blake's hand lowered back to her thigh. The doctor stopped in front of Willow, face completely clear. "You're not pregnant."

For a moment, Willow was silent, turning the words over in her head, unsure exactly how she felt about them. It wasn't quite relief, but it wasn't disappointment either. She caught Blake's gaze. His expression was as clear as the doctor's.

She looked back to Sage, wetting her lips. "And that's definite?"

"Yes."

"Do you know why I might be late?" She *still* hadn't had her period.

Sage offered a small smile. "We can run some more tests, but it sounds like you've been under significant stress these last couple weeks, and stress can affect hormones and delay ovulation, therefore affecting your period."

She gave a nod. That made sense. "Okay. Thank you for doing the bloodwork."

Sage nodded. "You're welcome. Is there anything else I can do for either of you while I'm here?"

Willow massaged her temple, suddenly feeling the lack of sleep and events of the night. "Maybe if there are any painkillers available for my headache?"

"Of course."

Sage left the room again, and immediately, Blake climbed off the bed, lowering to his haunches in front of her.

She gasped. "Blake, you should stay in bed! Your bullet wounds—"

"I barely feel them. Are you sure you're okay?"

Her eyes softened. "My family is safe. I have everything I need right here in this room. I'm more than okay."

His eyes remained on hers for a beat, hot and intense. Studying. Then, almost simultaneously, they both looked down at their child, sleeping so peacefully in her arms.

And a part of Willow knew that one day, she may just feel ready to have another. But right now, she needed to hold and love and appreciate exactly what she had.

# CHAPTER 28

Two days had passed since the attack. Blake had finally been allowed into the station to question the psychopaths who'd tried to take his child and kill his wife.

He was mad. Murderous-level mad. Had been mad since that night.

He shoved it down, at least for the moment, following the police officer down the hall to the interrogation room.

Flynn was with Willow and Mila this morning. Blake didn't want them left alone until he knew for sure everyone was safe from this group of zealots. He needed confirmation that they were working independently and the rest of the church wasn't involved.

The police had already done their own investigation, claiming the group had been working alone. And his team had been watching the church ever since, just in case.

But he still needed to see and hear the truth from the source.

The officer pulled the door open and Blake's jaw immediately tightened at the sight of Rob sitting at the table, hands cuffed, eyes narrowed.

The officer stepped back into the hall. "You have ten minutes."

The door was pulled shut, then it was just him and Rob.

Blake stalked forward a step. "You don't look nearly scared enough for what's about to happen."

There was a small flaring of his eyes, a slight shift in his breathing, but other than that, nothing. "Why would I be afraid? The path I've chosen is the right one."

Fuck, but the guy was deranged. "The right path involves kidnapping a child and murdering her parents?"

"The right path involves protecting the purity of the life God created here on Earth. It involves ridding the planet of atrocities like you and ensuring your kind doesn't spread."

Another step forward. "I don't think it's people like me society should worry about." In fact, every second he stood in this guy's company, he was hit with more regret for not putting a bullet into his skull.

Rob's eyes narrowed. "Why are you here?"

"I need you to tell me something. And if you lie, it's not going to work out well for you."

He scoffed. "I doubt you can do much when people are watching." Rob shot a pointed look toward the glass on one side of the room.

Blake almost laughed. "No one's watching, Rob. No one's going to run in here and save you. This is you and me. So don't fuck with me, because I'm not in the mood." He was right on the edge. Saying the guy wasn't safe with him was an understatement.

Rob almost looked bored. Like he didn't believe him. "What do you want to know?"

Blake took a final step forward, planting his hands on the table, spanning his fingers, and lowering his head. "Are there more of you?"

One brow lifted haughtily. "More?"

And that was the tipping point.

Blake yanked the guy from his seat, smashing him back onto

the table, and leaning in close. "I *said*, don't fuck with me. You know exactly what I'm asking, so answer the goddamn question. Are there more people from your church wanting to hurt my family?"

The calm facade finally slipped from the guy's face, fear and panic dropping his jaw, chilling his skin. His gaze shot to the mirror again.

Blake moved even closer. "I told you. No one's going to save you. Now, answer my question before I slam my fist into your face."

He swallowed. "No! I—it was just the six of us. No one else knew what we were planning."

Blake watched the guy's eyes, listened to his heart...he was telling the truth.

"Whose idea was it? Who was the ringleader?"

A moment of hesitation.

Blake lifted him up before slamming him back down. One hand moved to the guy's throat.

Rob's teeth rattled as his head bounced off the wooden table. "Okay! I'll tell you! When we found out about you, we made a group decision to try to lead Willow toward the church. Then she got back together with you and...and we didn't know what to do."

The guy gave a small cry when Blake's fingers tightened.

"Then Janet heard her say she was pregnant!" He swallowed. "It tipped her over the edge. She wanted Mila. She has a calling to save vulnerable kids. She convinced us all that you and Willow had to die."

A calling to save vulnerable kids? Was the guy fucking with him? "No. She doesn't. If she did, she would have stayed the hell away from my daughter." Not to mention, she wouldn't have tried to murder a woman who she thought was pregnant.

"Why did you try to take Willow from her home? And why were you watching Mila's school?"

Rob frowned. "What? I told you that wasn't us who attacked Willow."

Something must have flashed through Blake's eyes, because the man flinched, cuffed hands flying up to protect his head.

"I'm telling the truth! I swear, we wouldn't even know where to get chloroform. And none of us have ever been to Mila's school. We would never do that! It would scare her."

For a moment, Blake watched him, desperately searching for signs of a lie. He *had* to be lying, because the alternative was worse.

The alternative meant there was someone else out there. Someone watching his family. His daughter.

Blake only saw truth.

He stepped back, releasing Rob as unease stabbed at his heart.

Motherfucker. There *was* someone else.

Rushing to the door, he banged three times. He'd barely stepped into the hall when his phone rang. He grabbed it from his pocket. "Steve?"

"Blake, Ahmad's here, in the US. He's been here for weeks. He used a disguise and a fake ID to get into the country and has been staying under the radar ever since. We only found him because he showed up on CCTV footage."

Blake was already running, his unease shifting to terror. Rushing outside, he hung up on Steve and called Flynn. The phone rang out to voicemail.

A fear like he'd never known consumed Blake.

His friend would never let it go to voicemail. Not while protecting his family.

WILLOW STRAPPED Mila into the back seat, leaning down and pressing a kiss to her cheek. Before she closed the door, she gave her little belly a tickle.

Mila giggled, her hands pushing at Willow's shoulder. "Mama, stop!"

Pulling back, Willow sighed. "I can't help it. I just want to smoosh and tickle you all day."

Mila's eyes softened. "I love you too, Mama."

She pressed another kiss to Mila's head before closing the door. It was barely nine o'clock in the morning and she'd probably kissed her kid a dozen times already. In fact, she hadn't stopped kissing her since the incident. Or touching her. Holding her every chance she got. Last night, she'd actually fallen asleep by Mila's side. She'd only woken in the master bedroom because Blake had carried her there.

Flynn opened the passenger door for her.

"Such a gentleman. Thank you," she said, stepping forward and sliding inside.

He chuckled. "I know, someone should hurry up and wife me, right?"

He closed the door, moving around the car and climbing behind the wheel.

She fastened her seat belt. "I have a feeling none of you guys will be single for long."

How could they be? They were all gazillion-feet-tall, beautiful men who spent their days protecting people. If there was a "perfect man" ad, they'd all fit the bill.

He pulled the car onto the road. "Well, I have kind of been seeing someone. It's not serious though. Just casual dating."

Willow straightened. "Ooh, that's exciting? You never know where casual dating could lead, so I wouldn't be too quick to say that it's nothing serious. Do I know her?"

There was a small pause. "She's a doctor at Cradle Mountain Hospital. I met her when I took my mom in for an appointment." He cleared his throat. "Doctor Astor."

Willow's mouth turned down all on its own. Okay, now she kind of hoped he was right and it *was* only casual.

"I don't like Doctor Astor," Mila said from the back seat.

Willow gasped. "Mila!"

Flynn chuckled. "It's okay. I know Victoria can come off a bit cold."

A bit? Willow had only met the woman once. It was their first week in Cradle Mountain, and she'd taken Mila in for a routine checkup. She'd mostly just wanted to assess some of the doctors here.

Doctor Astor hadn't smiled once. Not when she'd stepped into the room and introduced herself, and not while looking over Mila. There'd been no stickers or suckers or getting down on her haunches to talk to Mila at eye level.

Willow scrambled for something nice to say. "I'm sure she's great. We only met her the one time." And who knew, maybe the doctor had been having a bad day.

Flynn's gaze shot her way. She almost cringed. She'd never been good at hiding her feelings.

"How's your mom?" She needed a change of subject. But more than that, she genuinely wanted to know how his mom was doing. The poor lady had dementia and was the reason the entire team had relocated to Cradle Mountain. From the little Blake had mentioned, she was deteriorating fast.

His gaze checked on Mila in the rearview mirror before landing back on the road ahead. "She's okay."

Willow could read between the lines. She wasn't okay, but he didn't want to say more in front of Mila. "If she needs anything, even if it's just a casserole or some company, please let me know. I'd love to help in whatever way I can."

He gave a small nod.

"Mama, will Daddy meet us at The Grind?"

She looked over her shoulder. "Probably not. He's…working." She hated lying, but she couldn't tell Mila the truth, that he was interrogating the people who had tried to kill her and Blake and take Mila.

"I doubt he'll be long," Flynn said quietly, hands tightening on the wheel.

Willow gave a small nod. Turning back around, she gazed out the passenger window. She knew that was true. Rob and Janet wouldn't stand a chance, not against a guy like Blake, who was trained to interrogate the meanest, deadliest criminals out there.

They were just passing a side street when Willow's heart stopped.

Her mouth dropped open to scream.

Flynn saw it the same time she did—immediately engaging the hand brake and sharply swinging the car around milliseconds before the speeding vehicle collided with the driver's side.

Willow's head hit the passenger window hard, the seat belt scoring into her chest. There was a ringing in her ears, almost like white noise, washing out every other sound.

She blinked, trying to get her bearings, forcing her cloudy mind to work. She was vaguely aware of the pressure of the air bag against her stomach and chest. Of the warm trickle of liquid dripping down her temple.

She ignored it all, turning her head to search for Mila.

What she saw made her lungs seize in icy terror—a man wearing a black ski mask opening the back door, quickly unbuckling her daughter.

Then she was gone.

*No!*

Willow wasn't sure if she said the word out loud or in her head. Her hands went to her seat belt, fumbling with the buckle. She shot a desperate glance at Flynn, but the man was unconscious. He'd swung the car to take the brunt of the hit. The wheel was pressed into his chest, blood trickling down his face.

Oh God!

She pressed the latch to the seat belt harder, but the thing wasn't giving.

Suddenly, her door opened. Then there was a knife slashing at her belt and rough hands pulling her from the car.

Willow fought against the hold. She hit and kicked, but her limbs were sluggish and slower than they should be, and the arms around her were too strong.

When she eventually landed a hit, the guy behind her grunted. Then pain blasted through her head from behind. It had her body going limp, the buzzing in her ears growing louder.

She was thrown onto a hard, carpeted surface...a trunk? A small body landed against her side.

*Mila.*

That was her last thought before the darkness took her.

# CHAPTER 29

Willow faded in and out of consciousness. Every time her eyes opened, darkness surrounded her, tugging her back in. Her head pounded, hard and painful. Her skin was clammy and cold.

She was vaguely aware of the light vibration of a car. Of the small, warm body nestled beside her own.

At one point, there were voices. Faint voices that barely reached her ears. And the little she heard didn't make sense. It took her muddled brain a while to realize that it wasn't just because her head felt cloudy...they were speaking another language.

The fogginess tried to pull her back under again, but she resisted, tugging the voices back, something inside her knowing it was important that she listened.

What language was that?

Suddenly, Omar came to mind.

Then it hit her.

Arabic. The men were speaking Arabic.

She started allowing the darkness to pull her back under,

doubting the handful of words he'd taught her would help her understand. Her mind had almost retreated fully, back into the safety of oblivion, when something penetrated the fog.

Seattle.

Were they taking her and Mila to Seattle?

Then there was another word. A word that nudged her mind in an oddly familiar way.

*Albisbul.*

She knew that word. Omar had used it. Taught it to her recently. There was the slightest tugging together of her brows. What did it mean?

The heaviness returned, only this time it was too strong to resist. Her mind shut down, the fog drowning her, sending her back under.

WILLOW SCRUNCHED HER EYES SHUT. She wanted to keep them closed. There was a familiar aching in her head that she knew to be the beginnings of a migraine. The only way to help it was to rest. To distance herself from the world and lose herself in oblivion.

But there were also other pains. Unfamiliar ones that had worry spiraling through her chest, nausea swelling in her gut.

Her chest hurt. Her ribs. Her wrists.

Why?

She couldn't let the darkness win this time. Her gut told her it was important that she wake up. Slowly, she forced her eyes open.

Darkness. That was all she saw. It made her feel disorientated and lost. There was one light though. A small green one to her right.

"Mama?"

*Mila...*

She tugged her brows together, begging herself to remember. To pull back the memories that were so important. One by one, small fragments of what happened before the fog returned to her.

The crash. Flynn unconscious. The men in hoods dragging Mila out of the car, dragging her out of the car, throwing her into the trunk of another one.

Fear engulfed her. Choked her. "Mila, are you okay?"

She tried to reach for her daughter, but something stopped her. Something tight that dug into the flesh of her wrists, holding her arms behind her back.

A zip-tie, maybe?

"I'm okay, Mama."

Mila's voice was steady, but the need to see her daughter, touch her, ensure she was okay...it drowned Willow.

Like Mila had heard her thoughts, her daughter scooted closer, her body heat thawing a tiny bit of the cold that had taken root in Willow's skin.

"Are *you* okay, Mama?"

She sucked in a deep breath. She couldn't fall apart. Her daughter needed her to be strong. To figure out a way to escape. "I'm okay."

"I couldn't wake you up. You've been asleep for a long time."

Willow's heart broke at the first sound of fear in Mila's voice. "I'm awake now, baby. And I'm not closing my eyes again."

No matter how painfully her brain beat against her skull, she refused to give in. She could rest once her daughter was safe.

There were still voices in the car. Dull voices from the front that had Willow's breath catching. Small snippets of the conversations she'd heard came back to her. Seattle. And something else...

Her mouth opened when she remembered. *Albisbul...baseball.*

Were they taking her and Mila to a baseball game in Seattle? Why?

"Mama...?"

Willow dragged her attention back to Mila. This time when she spoke, her words were barely a whisper. "Baby, we've got to be really quiet when we talk, okay? Like when we play that animal game, and I say mouse and we both whisper really softly."

Mila's voice lowered. "Okay."

Willow shot her gaze to the light in the corner. It was the emergency release lever at the top of the trunk. All cars had to have them, legally, which was no doubt why she'd been zip-tied with her hands behind her back.

"Are your hands tied behind your back, Mila?" Willow asked quietly.

"I got my feet through, so they're in front now." There was a small pause. "I can get out of them though."

Mila's words had Willow pausing. "You can?"

"Yeah. Daddy taught me how. But I didn't want to try until you woke up and said it was okay." Smart kid. "He showed me how to put my shoelaces through the zip-tie, tie the laces, then saw it off."

The first hint of hope fluttered inside Willow's chest.

"Yes, honey. Release your zip-ties."

Mila moved beside her. Then she heard the small, muffled sounds of her daughter sawing at the zip-ties with her laces.

Willow swallowed her angst, praying the guys in the front of the car didn't hear anything. They shouldn't, the movement was nearly silent. But it didn't stop the fear from crawling up her throat.

"Okay, I'm free!"

Mila's small hand touched Willow's cheek. Her eyes shuttered, tears pressing at her eyelids. She pushed the emotion down.

"Can you get your hands to the front, Mama?"

"No, baby. I can't."

Not only was there not enough space in the trunk for her to move, there was no way her arms were that flexible.

But Mila was free. That's what she needed to focus on.

"Mila, when the car stops, I want you to reach up and push the green lever. When the trunk opens, I need you to jump out and run. Find someone and ask them to call Daddy. Tell Daddy I think we're going to a baseball game in Seattle."

A tremble of panic shot through her limbs at the idea of separating from her daughter. At sending her out into the middle of God knows where on her own. But what was the alternative? Let her remain here with people she knew meant her harm?

"But what about you?" Mila asked.

"I won't be able to get out, baby."

And even if she tried, it would take too long and draw too much attention. Mila was the priority.

There was a short pause. Then Mila sucked in a deep breath. A breath of courage.

God, the kid was brave.

"Okay." Mila reached out a hand, touching her. "You don't have to worry about me, Mama. I'll get Daddy to save you."

The car slowed. Willow's breath caught at the *click* of the lever unlocking.

Her heart catapulted into her throat.

Mila's little arms pushed the trunk open. The lid only lifted a short distance. Willow realized they'd tied something to the trunk to restrict how far it opened.

Her stomach cramped. Would Mila fit?

Mila leaned down, wrapping her little arms around Willow. Her heart squeezed, emotion clogging her throat.

All she wanted to do was keep her daughter close and never let go. But she couldn't. Not here, not now.

Mila's hand dropped, and she turned, squeezing through the small opening, only just closing the trunk quietly before the car started to move again.

An odd combination of pain and relief fizzled in her chest.

Letting her five-year-old daughter out of her sight made her heart physically hurt. But she was smart. And Willow had to believe that she'd find safety. She was her father's daughter. If any kid could do it, it was Mila.

# CHAPTER 30

*M*ila slipped out of the trunk. Her feet had barely hit the ground when the car started moving. She quickly ran toward a bus stop, hiding in case the bad men inside the car looked back.

When the car disappeared, she glanced around. She didn't see any people. But there were buildings on either side of the road, kind of like in Cradle Mountain. And the streets on Cradle Mountain were sometimes empty, but if you walked around, you found people eventually.

Spotting an alley, she turned and started moving. She ran as fast as her legs would take her. She'd always been quick. Mama said she got her speed from Daddy. But then, Mama said she got a lot from Daddy.

Her eyes watered at the thought of Mama in that trunk. She hadn't wanted to leave her alone with the bad men, but if she'd let Mama see how scared she was, it would upset her. Mama always got upset when she was sad or scared.

She sucked in a deep breath. She had to be strong. Strong and brave, at least until Daddy came. He'd get Mama back. Daddy was a superhero, like the ones she saw on TV. He was fast, and strong, and he saved people. She'd even heard kids at school talking about him and his friends and how cool everything he could do was.

She moved her legs faster, scrunching her nose at the smell of garbage. Gross. It reminded her of when Daddy didn't take the trash out for a few days, something that never happened with Mama. She took the trash out every day at five o'clock on the dot. Mama liked things clean.

A scuffling noise sounded in the alley. Mila almost tripped over her own feet. The fear tried to rise in her chest again, but she clenched her fists, refusing to let it.

Daddy always said that fear was a logical reaction, but it didn't help you in bad situations. Courage did.

Up ahead, she saw people walk past the alley. She heard some voices, too. Footsteps.

Her legs started to hurt with how fast she was moving. And her chest hurt a little too. But she didn't slow down. She couldn't. Mama needed her.

When she reached the street, she looked around, sucking in deep breaths.

*Find someone and ask them to call Daddy.*

Mama's instructions replayed in her head. She scanned the street. Mrs. McCauliff had taught a lesson on safe strangers last month. Safe strangers were people in uniforms. Like police officers and fire fighters. Those were the people you should ask for help.

She scanned the street. There were two women holding bags and laughing as they walked down the sidewalk. There was a man on a phone, leaning against a car door. And there was a building with some men sitting around a table outside, drinking from cups.

She scrunched her dress with her hands. It was a nervous habit. Something she didn't do a lot, only when no one was watching and she needed to keep her fingers busy.

Panic welled in her chest. There were no safe strangers.

She closed her eyes for a moment. Daddy always said when a decision is tough to trust your gut. Your gut was your tummy and when it felt bad about someone, you felt sick, but when someone made you feel good, it meant you could probably trust them.

When she opened her eyes again, she started walking down the street, scanning the few people again. Her steps were slow and careful.

When she drew closer to the men at the table, her feet stopped. One of the men was looking straight at her.

They were all big, just like Daddy and his friends. Big shoulders. Big arms. Long legs. The one who was looking at her had eyes a bit like Daddy's. Not the same color, they weren't gray. But there was something about them that reminded her of Daddy and his friends.

She pressed a hand to her tummy. Nope, no sick feeling.

For the first time since being taken from her car seat, Mila didn't feel so panicked.

JACKSON LEANED back in his chair. The afternoon sun was shining, and he was back in his hometown with friends—brothers—who he hadn't seen in over a year. He should feel good. Hell, he should be over the fucking moon.

He wasn't. Because only two of his three brothers were here, and they would never see the third again. It felt like living in a nightmare he couldn't wake up from.

There was no talk around the table. Had barely been any talk between them since they'd all arrived in town. Because none of them knew what to goddamn say.

What did you say when a teammate died? What *could* you say?

Only a year ago, they'd been Delta Force Operators. Together, they'd made up a quadrant. A quadrant that would never be whole again.

"So this is where you and Ryker grew up," Declan said, finally breaking the heavy silence that had been their constant companion all morning.

Not a surprise, it was Dec. He always was the bravest one of the group.

Jackson nodded, scanning the street outside the cafe. "Yep. Lindeman, Washington." He had a memory in just about every damn corner of this town. Some good. Some downright shit. Almost all involving Ryker. "There was once a time I couldn't wait to get out of here. Now I'd give my right fucking kidney to go back and have one more day here with him."

Cole nodded. "I'd give up a kidney just to hear his voice."

Jackson sucked in a deep breath. It was as painful as every other breath since getting that call. He went to take a sip of his coffee, but when he lifted the mug, the smell made his stomach churn, so he put it back down. He couldn't seem to stomach anything right now.

Instead, his attention went back to the street. Looking. Watching. Like he was waiting for his friend to walk around the corner. Give him that big smile of his.

The street wasn't busy, but then, it rarely was in this small town. The few people he'd seen continued where they were going with purpose.

What was it about being in pain that made you just expect the world to stop? For everyone to feel the same grief and gut-wrenching agony as you? He remembered looking out the window of his apartment after the call and being so angry that everyone was still going on with their lives, no one stopping or pausing, when his entire world was crashing down around him.

He gritted his teeth when two women laughed across the road. People whose lives hadn't been altered forever.

Suddenly, his gaze stopped on a girl. She looked young...

maybe four? Five? Her brows were tugged together and her face seemed a stone's throw away from breaking.

He scanned the area around her, frowning. Where were her parents? Or a caregiver of any form? Was she alone?

His gaze shot back to her, and little details started to straighten his spine and tug at his instincts. The way her hair was disheveled. The way her hands scrunched the material of her dress, something he knew to be a nervous habit.

And then there was the way she scanned people, like she was searching for something. Or someone. And with every passing second, her expression became more anxious. More desperate.

When her gaze caught his, she paused, studying him in much the same way she had the few others on the street. Only this time, he didn't see elevating anxiety. No, he saw…

Hope?

Dec and Cole were talking about something, but Jackson's entire focus remained on the girl. Something was wrong. He didn't need his fifteen years in the military to tell him that. And it wasn't as simple as losing her mom in a crowd, not when the street was nearly empty.

The second she approached the table, his friends went silent.

Slowly, Jackson got off his seat, lowering to his haunches in front of her, making sure he was eye level. He knew he was intimidating at six-five, and the last thing he wanted was to scare the kid off when she so clearly needed help.

"Hi." He tried to gentle his deep voice.

The girl's gaze darted to his. "Hi. I'm Mila."

Even though she looked nervous, her voice was clear and strong. Brave kid.

"I'm Jackson." He smiled, tilted his head toward the guys. "These are my friends, Declan and Cole."

She looked up, giving them both the same tiny smile she'd given him.

"Is your mom or dad around?" he asked, drawing her attention back to him.

For a second, her little face looked like it was going to crumple. The corners of her mouth wobbled and her brows lifted a fraction. But then she swallowed, shoulders going back. "My mama's in trouble and I need to call Daddy to save her."

Jackson's jaw clenched, but he was careful to make sure he remained completely still. "I can call your dad. First, can you tell me what kind of trouble your mama's in?"

Again, that same heartbroken expression crossed her face, but only for a second. "Bad men hit our car and put Mama and me in the trunk."

Every muscle in Jackson's body tensed.

"I think Flynn got hurt. He was driving us. And I think they did something to Mama, because she slept for a long time. When she woke up, I broke my zip-ties. Daddy taught me how. Mama told me to open the trunk but that she couldn't get out. She told me to find someone to call Daddy. Mama thinks they're taking her to a baseball game in Seattle."

Rage heated his insides. Rage that this young girl actually may have been kidnapped. That her mother could still be in the hands of whatever scumbags had taken her. He felt the same rage bouncing off Dec and Cole, although they remained silent.

This is exactly why he'd joined the military all those years ago. To fight pure fucking evil.

He locked down the anger. "Can I see your wrists, sweetheart?"

She held up her arms. Gently, he pushed her sleeves back.

Sure enough, the skin was red and raw. She was telling the truth. She'd been bound.

Another flurry of anger crashed through his system. "You said your dad taught you how to break zip-ties?"

She nodded, locks of brown hair falling onto her face. "With a shoelace. He protects good people and fights bad people."

He sounded military. "We've done a lot of that too, sweetheart. Do you have his number?"

Another nod. "I know the car color, and the numbers and letters on the back," she added.

God. Such a smart kid.

"Let's call your dad."

# CHAPTER 31

*B*lake couldn't breathe. Air literally wasn't making it from his throat to his lungs.

Where were they? What did that asshole plan to do to them? And how the hell could he get them back?

Aidan reentered the Blue Halo conference room, phone in hand. "Flynn's stable. A lot of blood loss, but Jason and Callum are there now, donating."

Good. One small reprieve. While the three of them were at the hospital, Logan, Tyler, Aidan, and Liam were with him at Blue Halo, trying to find his family. Steve was also on the screen, his team working from their end.

"It's been too long," Blake growled to everyone in the room. "Eight and a half damn hours have passed!"

The police had been called to the crash and witnesses had reported the car plate, but that same car had been found on the side of a road two towns away. The assholes had switched vehicles. Who knew what they were driving now or where they were heading?

Hell, the guy could have boarded a private jet and flown them out of the goddamn country by now.

Blake scrubbed his hands over his face. His heart was racing at that possibility.

So many years he'd been taught how to handle his emotions in this kind of situation. How to switch off the fear and tune into his training. But this was different. It was too close to home. He'd never felt terror like this before.

It was debilitating and all-consuming, spiraling through every inch of his body, suffocating him.

The Blue Halo phone rang. Tyler lifted it. "Tyler speaking."

"Put Blake Cross on."

Everyone in the room stilled, a murderous rage thickening the air. Blake's body turned to stone, fear and fury warring at the sound of Ahmad's thick accent.

Tyler's jaw clenched as he put the phone on speaker.

"Ahmad." Blake growled the man's name just loud enough for it to reach the phone.

"Hello, Blake."

"Where are they?"

"Did you really think there would be no retribution for what you did?"

Blake's hands slammed against the table. "Where the fuck are they?"

Ahmad's voice lowered. "You came into my home. You took my wife and child. The fate of your family was sealed the second I saw you on that roof."

Blake only just controlled the breaths hissing from his chest. "What do you want from me?"

"I want you to feel the loss of your family, and to know that it was at *my* hands. I want you to mourn them, knowing you did this. I want it to tear you to fucking shreds!"

The line went dead.

Blake straightened, turning, and punching his fist through the wall. Pain exploded in his hand. His arm. It wasn't enough. Not to take away the internal pain. Nothing would be.

His chest heaved. The room was silent bar his anguished breaths.

They needed something, *anything*. But right now, they had nothing.

He was just turning back around to face his team when his cell started to vibrate in his pocket. He pulled it out, noticing it was an unknown number. He put the phone on speaker.

"What?" Another growl he couldn't control.

"Daddy!"

For a moment, the world around him fell away. Everything blurred and darkened except that voice.

"Mila! Where are you, baby? Is Mama with you?"

"No, Mama isn't here." Thick emotion clogged his daughter's voice. "She's still with the bad men. I got my zip-ties off the way you taught me, but her hands were behind her back and the trunk wouldn't open far enough for her to fit."

His eyes shuttered as his daughter spoke too fast, a part of his chest cracking wide open. Mila had gotten away. But Willow hadn't. She was still with them. Still with *him*. "Where are you, honey?"

"Um…" Mila paused as a male voice sounded in the background. "Lindeman, Washington, near Ellensburg."

His team started moving around him, opening cupboards and taking out weapons and supplies.

"Who's that with you?" Blake asked.

"Jackson. He let me use his phone and said he might be able to help Mama."

"Can you put him on, baby?" It killed him to ask. His daughter's voice was the only connection to his family. Hell, it was just about the only thing keeping him sane right now.

"Okay."

There was a slight shuffling sound. "Hello."

"Who are you?" Blake didn't have the time or energy for niceties.

"My name's Jackson Ford. Your daughter approached me and my two friends at a cafe here in Lindeman."

"Is Mila safe with you?"

"Yes."

God, he wished he could see the man in person to ensure that single word was true. "Why did she say you might be able to help?"

"My friends and I are former Delta Force." Blake immediately lifted a chin to Steve to look the guy up. "Your daughter thinks her mother is being taken to Seattle. She's only been with us for about ten minutes. We can start driving now and be there within a couple of hours."

Steve nodded once, confirming the guy was a former Delta. Almost immediately, Steve turned to one of his guys, no doubt organizing transport for Blake and his team to Seattle.

"Why would they take her to Seattle?" Blake asked.

"Mila's mother heard them mention baseball and Seattle. My guess would be the game tonight between the Mariners and the New York Yankees. It starts in about an hour. The game's supposed to be a big one, with a full house. That means over fifty thousand spectators. Although why anyone would take her there, I have no idea."

Blake's chest seized. He could only think of one reason a man like Ahmad—a man who was wanted by the FBI for terrorism and suicide bombings—would be headed to a place with such a dense crowd.

*Fuck.*

Now people were moving even faster around Blake. Packing equipment. Finalizing details with Steve. He gave Jackson his full attention, knowing the team had everything else covered. "Her kidnapper's a terrorist."

Jackson cursed. "We're trained in bomb disposal. Dec and I can head to T-Mobile Park now. Cole's great with kids, so he can stay with Mila."

"I need your friend to protect Mila with his life."

"Already planning on it." It was another man who spoke. Presumably Cole.

"Can you put her back on for a sec? Then we'll organize details."

As the phone was passed over, Blake heard snippets of his team talking about a military aircraft and communication with T-Mobile Park.

"Daddy?"

His team started moving out of the room, and Blake moved with them, his focus on the voice on the phone. "Baby, I need you to wait with Jackson's friend Cole for a bit. You'll be safe with him. Can you do that?"

"Are you going to save Mama?"

"Yes."

~

WILLOW'S EYES were closed when the car came to a stop. The vehicle had stopped a few times since Mila had gotten out, but this time was different. The engine turned off. Then the sound of movement from the men inside.

She opened her eyes slowly, swallowing against the beginnings of her migraine.

Noises sounded around the car. Doors opened and closed. Footsteps. Willow sucked in a sharp breath, fear attempting to crawl into her throat.

The lid opened, and she scrunched her eyes against the sudden light. It blasted her skull, shocking her system after being in darkness for so long.

The voices above her turned loud and angry. She scrunched her eyes tighter, this time in a weak attempt to ward off the noise.

Rough hands latched onto her upper arms, dragging her from

the trunk. Every movement had fresh pain shooting into her head. If the hands hadn't been holding her, she was sure she would have tumbled to the ground.

She blinked three times before her vision was clear enough to see. She scanned the large space slowly. A garage. A huge one, with cars and tools scattered around the place, the smell of oil and gas permeating the air.

When her eyes finally focused on the men in front of her, her skin prickled and chilled. There were six of them, all watching her, plus the two guys holding her arms, one on each side.

She squinted at one of the men. He had a bandage over half his face, but that wasn't what had her looking twice. It was his eyes.

Eyes she recognized.

Her insides jolted. He was the man who'd been in Mila's room. The one who'd drugged her with chloroform and tried to take her.

Sucking in a quick breath, she looked at the other men. It was easy to see who was in charge. He was a bit older, maybe mid-fifties. And even though he was shorter and less muscular, there was a hardness about him. An authority that had the air around him thickening.

He stepped forward, and she was struck by an overwhelming urge to move back. To run.

"Where is she?" His accented voice was quiet and deadly, sending shards of ice up her spine.

Willow swallowed. "Not here."

His fists clenched and the veins on his neck popped out. That probably should have sent her fear spiraling. It didn't—because all she could feel was an overwhelming relief that they didn't have her daughter. That whatever these men had planned for Mila would never transpire.

She'd take whatever punishment they shelled out again and again if it meant Mila was safe.

The man stopped in front of her. Rough fingers grabbed her jaw, bruising her. "How did you get her out? Your hands are tied behind your back!"

Willow met his furious gaze calmly. "I didn't get her out. *She* did. She broke her zip-ties with her shoelace. Then escaped through a crack in the trunk." She hoped the men felt the weight of embarrassment, knowing that a five-year-old girl had bested them.

The man's fingers tightened, the pain rivaling the throb in her head. But she forced the last words out, needing him to hear.

"She's gone. And you won't be getting your hands on her. Ever."

The strike came fast, snapping her head to the side and blasting a fresh wave of pain through her head.

His hand returned to her chin, forcing her face up again. His head lowered. "I wanted you both! I wanted him to feel the loss of his wife and child, like I felt the loss of mine!"

Willow gave a small frown. Even that hurt. "He took your wife and child?"

"*Yes.*" His eyes flashed black. "He came into my home, killed my men, and took my family. That day, I committed his face to memory. Vowed to find him. To take from him like he took from me."

She was glad Blake took the man's family. She couldn't see a scrap of humanity in him. There was no softness. No kindness. Anyone forced to live with him wasn't safe. She'd only just met him, yet she knew it as well as she knew anything.

He took a small step closer. "At seven thirty tonight, you will die. And not just you. Tens of thousands of people will die with you. Then tomorrow, I will hunt your daughter. And I will not stop until she dies, too."

Rage swept like a tidal wave through her body, washing out the pain. The fear. "If you think Blake will ever let you touch our daughter again, then you know *nothing* about him. You won't so much as see her face, let alone touch a hair on her head." She paused for a moment. "And if you kill me, he will dedicate every second of the rest of his life to tracking you down and destroying you."

The man stepped forward again, so close that she could feel his breath on her face. "You're wrong. About all of it. You will die. Your daughter will die. And Blake will have no doubt who took his family from him—and why."

The next hit was harder than the first, the metal of his ring cutting into her cheek and sending her world back into familiar darkness.

# CHAPTER 32

The van careened through the Seattle streets. Blake had spent the last two hours in a military aircraft with his team, and in about fifteen minutes, they would pull up outside T-Mobile Park.

"You still haven't been able to make contact with the security office?" Aidan asked Steve, frustration heating his words.

Steve was on Aidan's phone via video call.

"No." The agent's frustration rivaled everyone else's. His lips were tight and his shirt rumpled where he'd been tugging at it repeatedly. "I'm almost certain they've taken over the security booth and the control room."

*Goddamn it.* That essentially gave them control over the entire stadium—without drawing attention to themselves. It could give Ahmad just enough control to pull off an attack.

Steve, as well as everyone else on his end at the FBI, wanted Blake and his team to go in quietly to avoid mass hysteria and a panicked stampede of tens of thousands of people trying to get out. Worked for Blake. It would keep Ahmad from being tipped off that they knew exactly where he was. It gave them some much-needed time to find Willow.

"We're inside."

Jackson's voice came from Blake's earpiece. He hoped to God there weren't any bombs involved today, but if there were, Jackson and Declan's advanced training on bomb deactivation and demolition were Willow's best shot. They'd done a comprehensive check on all three guys from the plane. Their backgrounds checked out.

Both men had been sent a picture of Willow and Ahmad. They knew who they were looking for.

"The place is packed," Declan said quietly.

Blake's teeth ground as he checked his weapons.

Steve straightened, looking at someone else in the room. "You got it?" He looked back at the screen. "We just hacked into security footage at the park."

A second later, the screen flicked to the field at the ballpark. It was only on the screen for a second before the view changed to an interior hallway, then another. Steve's men didn't stop until they reached the security office.

Blake's fists clenched. Dead security guards lay on the floor of the room while two men sat in front of the cameras. Ahmad's men, no doubt.

"Ahmad's men have breached the security office," Callum said to Jackson and Declan.

"How many?" Jackson asked.

"Two," Blake replied.

"I'll go there now," Declan said quietly.

"I'll search for Willow," Jackson added.

Blake's team huddled over the phone, knowing there would be more men elsewhere. The footage flicked from camera to camera in the stadium.

"Stop!" Blake said, leaning forward. "Go back to the last screen with the staff entrance."

The screen flicked back.

Blake's fists clenched. "More of Ahmad's men."

They were both wearing the same security uniforms as staff at the other entrance points. Both were Middle Eastern, one with a scar across his right temple, the other with a scar on his right hand. But what set them apart from others was the way they held their guns. The way their eyes searched the area, as if waiting for something.

A second later, a group of men approached the two guards.

A thick dread seized his lungs. And not just because one of the guys was Ahmad.

But because of what two of his men were holding.

A long black bag. He was betting anything Willow was inside.

The air hissed from his chest in dark rage and every muscle in his body vibrated with the need to get to her.

"Ahmad and four of his men are entering the park via the north side staff entrance," Logan said to Jackson.

The man cursed. "I'm on the other side of the park. It'll take me a while to get there, especially with the crowds, but I'll head there now."

They continued watching Ahmad and his men, Steve's guys flicking through the security cameras as they went.

Blake's rage continued to bloom. "What's his plan?"

They watched them enter the Mariners' locker room. A security guard tried to stop them. One of Ahmad's guys quickly shot him with a silent bullet to the skull before pulling him into the room.

Blake's heart pounded in his chest. The locker room was the perfect place to detonate a bomb. Ahmad and his men would never be able to get on the field. Not with all the security. But the locker room was close.

If the bomb was big enough, not only would the explosion be heard, but the stands sitting directly above the locker room could collapse, injuring, even killing, thousands of spectators.

~

THE LOUD SOUND of a zipper tugged at Willow's consciousness. Then there were heavy footsteps, walking away from her.

She scrunched her eyes at the throbbing pain in her skull. The migraine was in full force now, pounding in her head like a drum. Blinding her. Making it hard for her to think.

Something in her brain told her she needed to open her eyes. There was danger. Something she needed to be awake for.

Forcing her eyes open, she frowned, the room a blur of bright light.

Slowly, she pushed to her feet. Everything around her spun, and she almost fell back down. She barely stopped herself by grabbing onto a wall.

She felt heavy. So unbelievably heavy. She wasn't sure her legs would hold her.

She took a step forward, only to have bile rise in her throat. Pausing, she sucked in deep breaths, doing everything she could to push down the nausea. Then, she took slow steps toward what looked to be a door. Her legs still felt wobbly, her body heavy, each step taking all her effort. It was all she could do to remain on her feet and keep moving. To not collapse.

But there was still something in her head, a whisper that demanded she go. Get out.

Reaching for the handle, she pushed it down. A small whimper escaped her lips when it didn't open. She tried again, this time pressing harder.

Oh God. Locked. She was locked in this room.

When muffled shouting permeated the air, a soft moan fell from Willow's lips. She had no idea where the noise was coming from, but it was loud, stabbing at her skull like a knife.

She forced herself to breathe. Deep breaths, in and out of her chest. Then she scrunched her eyes, trying to force the shapes in the room to clear. It took several blinks, but she began to make things out.

Was she in a...locker room?

Something to the side caught her vision. A scream tore from Willow's chest when she realized what it was. She pressed a hand to her mouth to stop herself from being sick.

The body of a security guard. He had a bullet wound between his eyes. Eyes that were open and lifeless.

Turning away, she bent over, pressing her hands to her thighs, and breathing deeply.

That's when she finally noticed something else. Her jaw slipped open, trembling fingers going to her chest before quickly pulling away.

A bomb. Strapped to her chest.

Her entire body seized. Raw terror bolted through her heart, and fear paralyzed her limbs.

That was the heaviness. That's why her entire body felt weighed down.

Her vision hazed, and this time she wasn't sure if it was because of the migraine or fear.

"Breathe, Willow! Breathe."

She sucked in more gulps of air, but they were barely reaching her lungs. Turning back to the door, she banged her fists against the metal, screaming as loud as she could.

"Help me! Please!"

Every bang caused a fresh wave of pain to skitter through her head. Every scream pierced her ears. But she gritted her teeth and continued. Needing someone to hear her.

She'd barely been banging for a few seconds when a voice responded. An angry voice that she had no way of understanding, speaking Arabic.

She pulled her fists away quickly. Oh God! They were guarding the door. Were they intending to stay out there even as the thing blew up?

Suddenly, something else penetrated her muddled mind. The guy said she'd die at seven thirty.

What was the time? She had no watch or phone.

Her gaze shot to the security guard. It looked like they'd taken any weapons he might have had, but the watch on his wrist remained.

She took a reluctant step forward, and a wave of nausea caused her legs to buckle. Her head pounded so hard she could feel the vibrations through her entire body now.

She took another slow step forward. And another. When she reached the dead body, she lowered to her knees, and with trembling fingers, lifted his wrist.

Seven twenty-two. She had eight minutes.

Willow's eyes shuttered, and a tear she couldn't stop trickled down her face. A tear for her daughter who would lose her mother. A tear for all the kids and parents in the ballpark about to lose their lives and their family and friends about to lose loved ones.

She sucked in a breath. Mila was strong. She'd be okay. Eventually. Blake would make sure of it.

And Blake…

At the thought of him, another part of her heart cracked. She and Blake had only just found each other again. And now they would be separated…this time forever.

A sudden bang from outside the door pulled Willow's attention. Then another.

She forced herself to her feet. Could that be help? Blake?

Icy fear rolled over her skin. She didn't want him anywhere near this bomb!

Then the door flew open, and a man stepped into the room. A man she'd never seen before, tall and broad, with a gun in his hand and a bag strapped to his back. He was wearing casual clothing but there was something about him, something that had her thinking of Blake. Of his team.

Military. He had to be.

"My name's Jackson Ford," the guy said, shoving the bag off his shoulders as he approached. He rummaged through it from the ground. "I'm working with the FBI and the US military." He studied the vest before meeting her gaze. His eyes softened, voice gentling. "I'm going to deactivate this bomb."

Behind him, she noticed two men lay by the door, blood pooling around their heads. Then she noticed another man... someone who looked a bit like this Jackson guy. His gun was drawn and he scanned his surroundings.

"That other guy is Declan. He's with me. If there was anyone in this world I'd want watching my back or yours, it would be him." Without looking up, he said softly, "I met your daughter."

Hot tears she couldn't stop or slow flooded her eyes. Her vision blurred as he rose and started working on her vest. "You did?"

"I did. She found me at a little cafe in Lindeman. We called her dad. She's safe with one of my guys. They're probably eating hot dogs and watching Netflix."

Suddenly, the pain in her skull dulled just a little. The tremble in her limbs lessened.

Mila was safe. Would be safe forever, regardless of whether Willow lived.

"The bomb's going to explode at seven thirty," Willow said quietly, watching the man's face rather than what he was doing. "You and your friend should go. Save yourselves."

He gave a quick head shake. "I can't do that, Willow. I've never left a woman behind before, and I don't intend to start now. Plus, I already promised your daughter and Blake that I would get you out of here alive. And I never break a promise."

She caught a glimpse of his watch. Seven twenty-five. Five minutes.

Blowing out a slow, shuddering breath, she shut her eyes, allowing thoughts of Mila and Blake to flood her. Calm her. All her best memories were with them. Every single one.

As Jackson worked, she prayed that Blake and Mila would keep making memories together. That they'd fill every moment with joy and laugher and love so thick that it consumed the heart.

"Stay with me, Willow. I've almost got it."

She opened her eyes, watching the guy's face. He was concentrating fully on his task, his hands steady. He didn't look fazed at all that the bomb could explode at any second.

She tried to stop herself, but she couldn't. She shot a look at his watch. Seven twenty-seven.

Her heart felt raw, her limbs barely holding her up. This time, she didn't draw her eyes away from the time. She watched, waiting for the last three minutes to tick down.

*You have my heart, now and forever, Mila and Blake.*

She whispered the words in her head, praying that the words floated through the ether and touched them.

"Got it."

Her legs caved—strong arms just catching her before she hit the ground.

# CHAPTER 33

*T*he ballpark came into view up ahead, and it had every cell in Blake's body vibrating. Ready to maim. Capture. Kill.

Steve had remained in contact with them the entire trip. Blake watched everything through the security cameras. He watched the footage of Willow being dumped in the locker room. He saw the bomb strapped to her torso.

His muscles tried to seize up on him, but he pushed down the fear. The fear that Jackson may not be able to deactivate the bomb in time. That everyone was going to be too late.

He couldn't think about that right now. All he could do was trust in a man he'd never met. A stranger. To save the woman who was the center of his world.

The van slowed at the front of the ballpark and Logan, Callum, Liam, and Jason got out. Steve had mustered help in the way of three local soldiers and an officer to take down Ahmad's team. The four guys were joining his teammates.

Steve's men had raked through the security footage and found at least a dozen of Ahmad's known associates inside, some masquerading as security, others as spectators. That wasn't including the guys they'd already seen with Ahmad himself.

Declan had taken out the two men in the security room, and Jackson was currently on his way to take out the two guys Ahmad had stationed in front of the Mariners' locker room.

Blake and Aidan remained in the back of the van, Tyler behind the wheel as he drove them to the north exit. Ahmad was their target. And Blake wouldn't be stopping until the man breathed his last breath. Because as long as he was alive, his family wasn't safe. Would never be safe.

"Jackson made it inside the locker room. He's with Willow," Steve said through the earpiece.

Blake struggled to keep his breathing steady at Steve's words.

When the man cursed, Blake frowned. "What is it?"

"Ahmad just left the north exit with half a dozen guys."

Tyler pushed the van to move faster. Blake's hand tightened on his gun, refusing to believe even for a second that Ahmad might get away.

When Tyler whipped the van around a corner, Blake saw them. Seven men climbing into a white van. A second later, the van was moving.

Tyler didn't slow.

Ahmad's driver spotted them and figured out what was going on pretty damn quickly, because almost immediately their vehicle sped up.

Blake cursed under his breath as they gave chase. Opening his window, he aimed and shot at the van. Aidan did the same on the other side.

A traffic light in the distance turned red, but Ahmad's van didn't slow.

Blake saw it seconds before the collision—a bus moving through the intersection. Ahmad's vehicle hit it at high speed.

There was the loud crash of metal hitting metal. And not just from the van and the bus. The busy road around them ground to a halt, half a dozen other collisions taking place as car after car rear-ended each other.

Tyler stopped the van at an angle, and they jumped out, using it as protection.

They'd barely stepped onto the road when bullets started to pepper the air, hitting the other side of the vehicle. Blake cursed. The assholes were probably out of the van, realizing they were sitting ducks if they remained where they were.

Blake turned to the van, using his enhanced strength to wrench the door clean off the side of the vehicle. He turned to his teammates. "Cover me while I move forward."

Tyler and Aidan nodded. The second they started shooting, the return fire ceased and Blake ran, holding the metal door up as a shield in front of him.

As bystanders ran from the scene, their screams echoed off the buildings. He reached the van in under two seconds to find only one guy remaining. The man was just straightening, poking his gun out the open driver's window, when Blake fired, shooting the guy in the side of the head.

A bullet hit the metal door in Blake's hand. He turned, shooting a man twice in the heart and once in the head.

Moving away from the van, he kept the metal door up like a shield. When he spotted a guy hiding between two cars, Blake moved closer. He kicked his leg out, giving one of the vehicles a big shove. A grunt sounded from between the cars. Blake moved to the side, gun trained on the man who was now stuck and coughing up blood, shooting him in the temple.

Ducking, he moved along the cars again. He knew his friends would watch his back, shooting anyone they spotted. But they could only shoot who they could see. Blake needed to find the men they couldn't. Including Ahmad.

From his peripheral vision, he caught a glimpse of a guy's head inching forward as he used the backed-up cars as protection.

Blake ditched the metal door and remained low as he weaved between the cars. Then he stopped, crouching and lifting his gun. The second the guy popped his head up again, Blake shot him dead.

At the sound of fast steps from behind, Blake spun, unsheathing a knife as he went, and slashing a man's throat as he lunged forward.

Another one dead. Not the man Blake was looking for. The man who really *needed* to die.

*Where are you, Ahmad?*

Blake circled the area, all the while remaining low and quiet. His gaze paused on the bus. He hadn't boarded it because of the civilians he could still see inside.

But that didn't mean Ahmad hadn't.

Moving cautiously up the steps, Blake paused. Passengers sat to either side, some shaking and staring. Some too scared to look up. Blake barely glanced their way.

His entire focus remained on Ahmad—standing in the aisle at the back of the bus, holding the driver in a death grip, gun held at the driver's temple.

Blake's fingers tightened on his pointed gun. "Let him go."

"No." Ahmad's eyes were full of rage and hatred. He knew he'd lost. The fight. The war. He'd lost everything.

Steve's voice sounded through Blake's earpiece. "Jackson deactivated the bomb. Willow's safe."

Outwardly, Blake didn't react to the words at all. Internally, the shards of ice and fear thawed in his chest.

"The bomb's deactivated," Blake said quietly. "My family will live."

Ahmad growled his fury.

"You failed," he continued, gun never wavering from his target. "And I hope that torments your soul while you rot in hell."

Ahmad's eyes widened even as Blake pulled the trigger, expertly missing the bus driver and hitting Ahmad in the skull.

# CHAPTER 34

*W*illow stroked Blake's arm. His head rested on the hospital bed beside her hip, his back rising and falling as he slept in the chair.

Her heart ached for the man and how tired he must be. Usually, all it took was a tiny movement from her, the smallest sound, and his eyes would shoot open. The fact that she'd roused in her hospital bed, that she could stroke his arm, his hair, and he didn't so much as stir, meant that he was beyond exhausted.

It was probably more emotional exhaustion than physical. The man had almost lost his family. That would have torn him in two.

Willow's heart gave a little thump at how close she'd come to death. At how close Mila came to losing her mother, and Blake to becoming a single parent.

The "could haves" of it all tormented her.

She ran a finger down his arm, trailing a thick cord of muscle.

His fist clenched. Then he shot up into a sitting position, gray eyes wide and alert, as if he'd never been asleep. When he looked at her, he scanned her face, her body.

"Willow," he whispered.

Her eyes shuttered, replaying his voice in her head. A voice she thought she'd never hear again. When she opened her eyes, her gaze moved to his. "Are we really here right now? Alive and together?"

He reached out, taking her hand, and holding it tightly between both of his. "Yes." He pulled her hand closer, touching it to his lips. For a second, she thought she saw a glimmer of tears in his eyes, but when he looked at her again, the glimmer was gone.

"And Mila's safe?" She could barely get the words out.

"She's safe, honey. She's with Courtney right now. She'll be here soon."

Relief flooded her.

"How's the migraine?" he asked quietly.

"I don't even feel it." She knew even if there were still remnants, the doctor would have given her pain meds to dull most of the ache.

Blake nodded, so much emotion on his face. "That was too close, Willow. Never again will anything like that happen."

"Never again," she whispered, knowing those words were a promise more than reassurance.

Slowly, she lifted her other hand, grazing his cheek before holding the side of his face.

One of his hands lifted, covering hers. "Thank you for getting our daughter out of there. We think they planned to use her to force you to walk into the ballpark alone and blow everyone up at seven thirty."

Anger and fear of what could have been welled in her chest. Not only would Willow have killed thousands of people, she had no doubt the terrorists would have killed Mila the second they stopped needing her.

Willow shoved that thought away, not able to properly deal with it right now. "I didn't get her away. *She* did. With your help." She swallowed as emotion tried to clog her voice. "You taught her how to call you. How to release zip-ties. You ensured our daughter's safety. Thank you."

He dipped his head.

"Lay with me," she whispered.

The words had barely left her lips when he was toeing off his shoes, climbing onto the bed, and crawling beneath the covers. The second his arms wrapped around her, Willow's eyes closed again. She listened to the beating of Blake's heart beneath her cheek, its quiet drum matching her own.

They lay there for a while like that. She was pretty sure she dozed off at some point, because when she opened her eyes again, the room was slightly brighter and a small, familiar voice came from the other side of the closed door.

Her breath caught.

"Mila." Her voice was barely a whisper.

Blake's arms tightened around her. "Courtney flew here to stay with her overnight at a hotel."

She looked up at Blake. "Who did she find to call you?"

He smiled. "She found three former military guys."

Willow's mouth dropped open. "Jackson?"

Blake nodded. "And Declan and Cole."

Willow blew out a long breath. "Jackson saved me."

"He did." Blake's voice was deeper this time, with a rough edge to it. "And I'll be indebted to the man until the day I die."

She gave a small shake of her head. Trust Mila to find a group of military men who knew how to deactivate a bomb. "Our kid is amazing." There were so many other words she could use. Stronger words. But for now, amazing would do.

"She is. But self-defense lessons start tomorrow. Then I'm gonna teach her how to shoot."

Willow laughed softly, even though she wasn't entirely sure if he was joking or not. Regardless, it felt good to laugh.

A second later, there was a small knock on the door.

Willow's heart sped up. She ached to see her daughter. Touch her. Hold her. And she was pretty sure that once she had Mila in her arms, she would never be able to let go.

"Come in," Blake called.

The door flew open, and Mila ran into the room.

Willow's eyes flooded with tears at the sight of her. And when Mila climbed onto the bed and crawled into her arms, every part of her cracked soul realigned. She held her daughter tightly, Blake's arm still around her.

Never in her life had she felt more grateful to have both her husband and her daughter here. Safe. Together.

BLAKE WATCHED Willow hold their daughter. The final lines of strain left her face as happy tears streamed down her face.

He kept one arm around Willow's waist, the other around Mila's back as he thanked every god there was that his family had come out of this unscathed. That everyone he loved was still alive.

He looked across to the door, seeing Courtney standing inside the room, tears in her eyes, Jason beside her. Past them, in the hallway, Blake saw Jackson, Declan, and Cole talking to Aidan and Callum.

Jackson's gaze caught his.

Blake needed to have a long conversation with the man. Thank him properly. Make him understand exactly how indebted he was to the guy for risking his life to save his woman. The difference between them both living and dying had been mere minutes.

The man had risked everything for a stranger.

And he wasn't just thankful to him for defusing the bomb, but also for finding his daughter. Listening to her. Making sure she was safe until his team could get there.

Blake dipped his head. A silent thank you. And a promise that, should Jackson ever need him, Blake would be there in seconds.

Jackson dipped his head in return.

Returning his gaze to his family, he tightened his arm around Willow.

"Daddy, Mama said we can get that dog now."

One side of Blake's mouth lifted. "Is that right?"

Willow lifted a shoulder. "Well, Mila said she'll be in charge of feeding and you'll be in charge of cleaning the yard."

Blake grinned. "Which yard would that be? Yours or mine?"

"Ours." Willow wet her lips. "I thought we could sell the house Mila and I have been living in and move into yours…together."

Blake swallowed the emotion crawling up his throat. That was all he wanted. All he'd ever wanted since returning to his family. For them to be together again, all in one place. "I can't think of a better idea."

Willow's gaze softened. He pressed a kiss to her cheek, lips lingering a moment too long, like always. Then Mila was leaning into them both. "I love you, Mama and Daddy."

Blake wrapped his arm tighter around his daughter. He loved his family too. So damn much his chest ached.

# CHAPTER 35

"*A*re we still doing dinner tonight at Paulie's?"

Flynn put on his indicator before turning onto his mom's street. Victoria was on speaker, having just finished her shift at the hospital.

"I'm not sure, Vic. Depends on how my mom's doing. I might just stay with her."

He almost thought he heard a small huff, but when she spoke, her voice was smooth and sympathetic. "That's okay. I'll call and cancel again. I'm sure they'll understand. Want me to come over and keep you and your mom company?"

Flynn cringed at the thought. Not because he didn't like Victoria's company, but because he knew his incredibly honest mother didn't. And how'd he figure that out? Because she'd told him, of course. She may be old with quickly advancing Alzheimer's, but she still knew what she liked and what she didn't. And Victoria was definitely one of the latter.

"You've probably had a long day at the hospital. You go home and rest. I'll text you tonight when I get home."

"If you're sure, babe?"

He pulled into the driveway of his mother's old home,

glancing up at the small cottage. It was the home he'd grown up in. The home that held so many memories. Of his mother baking and gardening. His father using his tools to construct whatever piece of furniture he had in his head that week...before his stroke, that was.

"I'm sure. Chat later, Vic."

He hung up the phone. He hadn't been dating Victoria for long, and if he was honest with himself, he didn't see it going anywhere long-term. But he also didn't have the same dislike for her that others did. He knew she could be somewhat stand-offish, but that's just who she was. She wasn't intentionally cruel.

Climbing out of the car, he grabbed the casserole from the passenger seat before making his way up the three steps to the front door.

When he'd gotten to town, the house had been falling apart. Guilt had suffocated him at the sight of what his parents' home had become. Because he should have been here, helping his mother keep the place together. Not locked away in a goddamn compound. Not living in Lockhart for a year after his rescue.

Bit by bit, and with the help of his team, he'd been returning it to the home of his youth. So far, with a fresh coat of paint and a heck of a lot of gardening, the cottage was only just starting to resemble the place Flynn remembered. The garden had been his mother's pride and joy, and seeing it so neglected...it had torn at Flynn's chest.

It had been a week since the car crash with Willow and Mila. A week since he'd seen his mother. She had a good nurse who lived just down the street, so he knew she was well cared for.

After a short stay in the hospital himself, physically, Flynn was healed and feeling fine. Mentally, he was pissed. Pissed that Blake's wife and child had been taken while under his protection. Pissed that he hadn't seen that car coming.

He was just grateful that he'd been able to turn the car in time to avoid a collision on Willow's side, and both Willow and Mila had come out of everything alive and unscathed.

Using his key, he unlocked the door and stepped inside. Quietly, he moved through the living area and into the kitchen. He was just placing the casserole in the fridge when he heard voices from the other room.

His muscles immediately tensed, body stilling.

That wasn't the voice of the usual nurse, Mrs. Anderson, talking to his mother. It was someone else. Someone he'd never heard before.

"You get some rest, Mrs. Talbot. Call me if you need anything before I go."

"Thank you, dear. I'll be okay. You go home, settle in."

Flynn listened to the gentle closing of a door, then the quiet footsteps of this mystery woman.

He waited by the kitchen counter, anger brimming in his chest. He was his mother's primary caregiver, her only son and only living relative. If there was a need for a new nurse, he should have been notified, and *he* should have been the one to choose the replacement.

He didn't make a noise as the woman stepped into the adjacent dining room and up to the table. She didn't notice him right away, instead grabbing her handbag on the table and rummaging inside.

Her brows drew together as she muttered curse words under her breath. There was something familiar about the woman. Something that tugged at the back of his mind, but he couldn't quite put his finger on what it was.

Slowly, he moved across the kitchen, surprised when the woman didn't so much as look up. He wasn't trying to be quiet. But he wasn't loud, either.

"Who are you?"

The woman shrieked, spinning around, hand pressing to her chest.

For a moment, Flynn stilled. The woman's pale blue eyes were huge, seemingly taking up half her face. Her lips were full and her hair was golden. Her ample chest rose and fell rapidly under her hand.

"Oh my God! You scared me to death." Her chin dipped to the chest he'd just been trying hard not to stare at, before she quickly looked up again. "Where…Were you hiding in the kitchen?" The woman didn't seem scared that a man had just snuck up on her. More inquisitive than anything.

"I wasn't hiding. This is my mother's house. I have a key."

Her lips transformed into a smile. And fuck, but his gut gave a sharp kick. "You're Flynn? Okay, yes, that makes sense. Your mother hasn't stopped talking about you since I got here."

He lifted a brow. The woman was one up on him then. "And how long have you been here, exactly?"

"Since Saturday. Mrs. Anderson had a family emergency. No one could get through to you. I just moved to town, so the agency sent me in."

"Your car isn't out front."

Her smile remained, despite his frosty attitude. "Yeah, I live really close. Closer than Mrs. Anderson, actually. I guess the job was kind of fate."

He tilted his head slightly. "And you're a nurse?"

The laugh that followed had her eyes crinkling at the corners. The sound was light and lyrical and every damn thing about it had his body tightening. "Did I not say that? Good grief, I'm a bit of a mess, aren't I? Yes, I'm with the nursing agency. I had a small break between my last job and this one…"

She trailed off, and something flickered over her face. Anxiety, maybe? It came and went so quickly, he could almost convince himself he'd made it up in his head. Almost.

And that's when he realized. The woman was hiding something. He was good at reading people, but even if he hadn't been, the lady's quick expression made that fact abundantly clear.

Even though her smile made him feel something confusing, he couldn't let his mother be around a nurse with secrets. He needed a background check on her, and he needed it now.

Her brows drew together, the smile never leaving her face. "You're kind of intense, aren't you, Mr. Tall, Dark, and Handsome?"

His brow lifted again. "You call every man you just met that?"

"Nope. Only the ones who are." She nibbled her plump bottom lip before letting her gaze roam around the room. "Anyway. My shift is over, so I'll be back tomorrow."

Not until he'd looked into her, she wouldn't.

She lifted her purse and took a step toward the door.

"Can you tell me your name before you leave?"

She paused, and that same laugh sounded again. God, why did it have his gut clenching? Why did the sound bubble up in his chest and hit some part of him he didn't even know existed?

"Sorry, I'm Carina Murphy."

She reached a hand out, and he took it in his larger one—and suddenly he knew why she looked familiar.

Despite living in a different town, she'd applied for this job a few months ago when Mrs. Anderson had requested some leave. And in his more extensive background check, the one that went beyond the information given to him by the home-care company, he'd found that she'd been suspended from a previous job after an accusation of stealing drugs.

No. Hell no.

Order FLYNN or JACKSON today!

# ALSO BY NYSSA KATHRYN

JOIN my newsletter and be the first to find out about sales and new releases!

https://www.nyssakathryn.com/vip-newsletter

# ABOUT THE AUTHOR

Nyssa Kathryn is a romantic suspense author. She lives in South Australia with her daughter and hubby and takes every chance she can to be plotting and writing. Always an avid reader of romance novels, she considers alpha males and happily-ever-afters to be her jam.

Don't forget to follow Nyssa and never miss another release.

Facebook | Instagram | Amazon | Goodreads